Dragontide's Son

Connie S. Myres

The Book:

Seventeen-year-old Pryce Harper-Green dreams of becoming more than just another struggling fisherman in Crystal Shores. When he discovers a rare talent for dragon training, the mysterious Dragonkin offer him power, status, and the heart of their princess. But as secrets emerge and loyalties are tested, Pryce finds himself caught between two worlds with the fate of his village hanging in the balance. With the help of his storm dragon Stormwing, a mischievous cat named Ash, and a messenger bird called Skye, he must navigate increasingly dangerous waters where one wrong choice could destroy everything he loves.

The Author:

CONNIE S. MYRES writes books and short stories in the horror, mystery, suspense, and science fiction genres. She is an author, developer, and registered nurse. Sometime in the future—whether by choice or by arm-twisting—she will join the digital nomad movement.

Born and raised in Michigan, she has been creating stories since childhood. Children she had babysat as a teenager loved to hear her mystery stories, especially since she carefully included all the children listening into the storyline, causing suspense for everyone.

Connie's website is ConnieMyres.com

.

Dragontide's Son

The Second Book of Dragontide

by

Connie S. Myres

Feather and Fermion Publishing - Michigan

Feather and Fermion Publishing
Connie S. Myres
Michigan, USA
ConnieMyres.com

ISBN-13: 978-1-957819-21-1 (eBook)
ISBN-13: 978-1-957819-26-6 (hardcover)
ISBN-13: 978-1-957819-25-9 (paperback)

Dedication

Dedicated to my family and friends, especially my sons Lucas and Charles Kraus for their loyal support and encouragement of all my projects. I appreciate you.

And to my dear grandson-to-be: May you always find magic in the pages of a book. This is a small gift from your grandmother, penned with love before you were born.

Table of Contents

1. Dreams Beyond the Dock

Pryce Harper-Green squinted at the murky waters of Lake Dragontide. The lake, usually serene, looked almost foreboding under the approaching storm clouds. With blistered hands, he hauled the last net onto the trawler's deck. Empty. Or close enough. A few scrawny fish flapped listlessly, barely worth the effort.

"Another wasted morning," he said, tossing the net to the side with more force than necessary.

Crystal Shores mirrored his mood. The once-vibrant village seemed to droop under the weight of its own struggles. The cottages with their peeling paint and sagging roofs huddled together against the chilly breeze blowing in from the lake. Pryce's eyes traveled over to the docks where Old Man Finnegan stood, leaning heavily on his gnarled walking stick.

The old man shuffled over as Pryce tied up his boat. "Rough day?"

Pryce nodded. "Nothing worth keeping," he said, kicking at an empty barrel on the dock.

Finnegan chuckled. "Lake's been stingy lately," he said. "But that's how it goes sometimes."

"Yeah, well, I'm tired of it," Pryce snapped before catching himself. He glanced at Finnegan. "Sorry, it's just . . . this isn't what I want."

"Got bigger dreams than this old dock, do ya?"

Pryce looked out over the lake again. "I want more than just scraping by."

"Ah," Finnegan nodded, tapping his stick on the wooden planks. "That wanderlust in your veins, boy?"

"It's not just that," Pryce said. "I want to be a dragon trainer."

Finnegan studied him for a long moment before speaking again. "It's good to have dreams, lad. But don't forget where you come from."

Pryce frowned at that. He knew Finnegan meant well, but Crystal Shores felt like a cage to him—one that grew smaller each day.

As Pryce helped Finnegan untangle a particularly stubborn net, a small, leather-bound book slipped from his back pocket and landed on the dock with a soft thud. The cover was worn from frequent handling, and the title, "Legends of Dragontide," was barely legible.

Finnegan bent down with a grunt, picking up the book. He turned it over in his hands. "Still got your nose in dragon tales, eh?"

"It's just a story," he said, reaching to take the book back.

Finnegan held it out of reach for a moment longer, peering at the faded cover. "This one about that old legend? The Dragonkin Marauders and their promise of power?"

"Yeah," Pryce said. "It's about how they tamed dragons and became the most feared group in all of Dragontide."

Finnegan handed the book back to him. "Dragons ain't pets, lad. They're dangerous beasts. Takes someone special to tame 'em."

"And you think I'm not special enough?" Irritated, Pryce stuffed the book back into his pocket.

The old man shook his head. "Didn't say that. Just saying it's not all glory and gold like those stories make it out to be. Back in my day, I tangled with more than a few dragons. Lost good friends to those encounters."

Pryce's eyes widened. "You fought dragons?"

"Some say hunted. But there were times when we had no choice but to kill 'em." He glanced at Pryce, his expression serious now. "If you really want to be a dragon trainer, you need to understand what you're getting into."

Pryce nodded slowly, digesting Finnegan's words as they worked in silence for a while longer.

"Ever seen one up close?" Finnegan asked suddenly.

Pryce shook his head. "Only in pictures."

"They're more than just pictures," Finnegan said softly. "They're living, breathing forces of nature."

The wind picked up, carrying the scent of rain and stirring the dark clouds overhead. The first fat droplets began to fall as they finished with the nets.

"Storm's coming," Finnegan remarked, looking up at the sky.

"Better get inside," Pryce said, gathering their tools.

They hurried toward the shelter of Finnegan's cottage as the rain began to pour in earnest. The storm washed over Crystal Shores like an uninvited guest, drenching everything in its path.

Finnegan shuffled around his cottage, lighting an oil lamp and stoking the smoldering fire in the fireplace. The warm glow chased away the dimness that had settled in with the storm. Pryce watched as the old man reached for a battered kettle.

"How about some seaweed brew?" Finnegan asked, filling the kettle with water.

Pryce nodded. He'd heard of the Shorlings' peculiar tea but had never tried it himself.

As Finnegan busied himself with the kettle, and the storm raged outside, Pryce's eyes wandered around the cottage. He'd never been inside before, and what he saw left him awestruck. The walls were adorned with paintings—dragons, serpents, and ships locked in fierce battles on stormy seas. Each piece was vivid, capturing moments of chaos and beauty.

Thunder rumbled outside, and a flash of lightning illuminated a particularly striking painting of a storm dragon, its electric blue eyes seeming to glow.

"These are incredible," Pryce said, stepping closer to one of the paintings. It depicted a massive dragon with scales that shimmered like molten gold, its wings outstretched as it soared above a burning ship.

Finnegan glanced over his shoulder. "Collected those over the years. Each one tells a story."

Pryce pointed to a painting showing two dragons locked in combat, their bodies coiled around each other in a deadly embrace. "What's this one about?"

"Ah, that's the tale of Aurathorn and Nightclaw," Finnegan explained as he adjusted the kettle over the fire. "Aurathorn was a guardian dragon, protector of an ancient elixir. Nightclaw sought to steal it for his own gain. Their battle lasted for days, shaking mountains and boiling rivers."

Pryce's eyes moved to another painting showing a ship being attacked by sea serpents. The crew fought valiantly but seemed hopelessly outmatched. "And this?"

"That's 'The Last Voyage of Captain Draven.' He was one of the finest sailors to ever navigate Lake Dragontide," Finnegan said. "But even he couldn't escape the wrath of the seadrakes."

Pryce marveled at each piece, feeling as if he were stepping into another world with every glance. The storm outside raged on, lightning flashing through the windows and illuminating the paintings in brief bursts of light.

"You've seen all this?" Pryce asked quietly.

"More than I care to remember," Finnegan replied, turning back to face him. "These are just glimpses of what lies out there."

As the kettle began to whistle, Pryce found himself drawn to a smaller, more subdued painting. It depicted a rider atop a dragon, soaring over what looked like Crystal Shores.

"I didn't know we had dragon riders here," Pryce said, excitement creeping into his voice.

Finnegan poured the hot water into two chipped mugs. "We don't, not anymore. In my youth I was a dragon hunter, but that there's the last Dragontide rider. Disappeared years ago."

Pryce opened his mouth to ask more, but Finnegan handed him a steaming mug of seaweed brew, effectively ending the conversation.

Pryce sipped the tea, its briny taste oddly comforting. Suddenly, a deafening boom shook the cottage, rattling the windows and sending tremors through the floorboards. Pryce nearly dropped his mug.

"What in the name of—" Finnegan said, already hobbling towards the window.

Pryce joined him, peering out into the tempest. The sky had turned an eerie, sickly green, crackling with energy that made his skin prickle. Lightning forked across the heavens, illuminating the village below in stark, terrifying flashes. It was unlike anything he had ever seen.

"By the gods . . ." Finnegan's voice trailed off as he stared at the spectacle.

Crystal Shores was in chaos. People ran through the streets, their screams barely audible over the howling wind. Doors slammed, and shutters banged against walls as villagers scrambled for shelter.

Without thinking, Pryce bolted for the door. "I have to help! he shouted over his shoulder, ignoring Finnegan's protests.

The moment he stepped outside, the wind nearly knocked him off his feet. Rain lashed at his face, stinging his eyes as he stumbled down the path. Panicked villagers rushed past him.

"Get inside!

Finnegan yelled, but Pryce pressed on.

He saw Old Man Doyle's prized goats running loose, bleating in terror as they darted between houses. Chickens flapped wildly in the wind, their feathers scattering across the muddy ground. Even the usually placid village dogs were howling, adding to the clamor of panic.

Pryce pushed through the throng, searching for any sign of what might have caused this disturbance. His mind raced with possibilities—had one of those seadrakes come ashore? Or was it something even more sinister?

Suddenly, a sound cut through the chaos—a roar so powerful it seemed to shake the very air around them. Pryce's gaze shot up to the sky, searching for the source of the sound.

And that's when he saw it.

A monstrous shadow descended from the swirling green clouds, blotting out the light of the storm. It was a shape too large, too powerful to be anything else. A wave of terror washed over him. This wasn't a painting. This was real.

Dragon.

2. The Storm Dragon's Fall

Pryce watched as the storm dragon plummeted from the sky, its massive wings struggling against the violent winds. Each flap sent arcs of electric blue energy crackling through the storm, illuminating its dark scales that shimmered like the clouds above. Rain lashed at Pryce's face, the wind whipping his hair into his eyes. He could barely see through the downpour, but he couldn't tear his gaze away.

The dragon's descent was far from graceful, a stark contrast to the creatures Pryce had read about in his books. It twisted and turned in midair, desperately trying to right itself against the storm. Pryce could see that the beast was gravely injured; one of its enormous wings hung at an awkward angle, and its roars were laced with agony.

"Look out!" Finnegan shouted, pulling Pryce back just as the dragon crashed into the village square. The old man swore under his breath.

The impact sent a shockwave through Crystal Shores, toppling carts and shattering windows. Pryce felt the ground tremble beneath his feet, the force nearly knocking him over. Debris flew through the air, and a cloud of dust rose, mingling with the rain. The air reeked of ozone, and somewhere nearby a child screamed.

Pryce grabbed Finnegan's arm and pulled him toward the crash site. The storm had begun to subside, rain lessening to a drizzle, and the wind dying down to a whisper. The village square lay in ruins, splintered wood and shattered cobblestones strewn across the ground, but amidst the wreckage lay a sight that stole Pryce's breath away.

The young storm dragon sprawled on the ground, its scales glistening in shades of deep blue and silver. It panted heavily, each breath sending small sparks flickering around its nostrils like miniature lightning strikes. Its eyes were a piercing electric blue, filled with a mixture of fear and defiance.

"Stormwing," Pryce whispered, the name surfacing in his mind as if it had always been there.

Finnegan moved beside him. "Careful now," he warned, gripping his walking stick tightly. "A cornered dragon is dangerous, even a young one."

But Pryce felt no fear—only a strange connection to the creature before him, a pull in his chest like an invisible tether. He took a cautious step forward, his eyes never leaving Stormwing's, his hand outstretched in a gesture of peace.

Around them, fearful Shorlings began to creep out of their homes. Armed with whatever they could grab—pitchforks, fishing spears, axes—they moved slowly toward the fallen dragon.

"Stay back!" Finnegan shouted at them, his voice carrying the weight of authority. "It's hurt and scared; don't provoke it!"

Pryce knelt down slowly, extending a hand toward Stormwing. "Hey there," he said softly. "We're not going to hurt you. You're safe now."

Stormwing's eyes flickered toward him, and for a moment, they locked gazes. Pryce felt a jolt run through him—not of fear but of recognition, a deep sense of familiarity.

The villagers kept their distance, their whispers a low hum in the background as they watched Pryce inch closer to the dragon. He could feel their eyes on him. The rain had almost stopped now; only a light drizzle remained. Droplets clung to Stormwing's scales, making them shimmer in the light of the thinning clouds. Pryce marveled at the creature's beauty even in its weakened state.

Pryce could feel Stormwing's fear, the dragon's emotions pulsing through their newfound connection like a living current. This was his moment—a chance to prove his worth not through power or conquest but through compassion and understanding.

"Easy now," he whispered again, reaching out until his hand hovered just above Stormwing's injured wing. "We'll help you."

Pryce held his breath as Stormwing flinched at his touch, a low growl rumbling in its chest. The air around them crackled with energy, making the hair on Pryce's arms stand on end. He didn't dare move, didn't dare breathe, waiting for the dragon to accept his presence or unleash its fury.

"It's just a juvenile," Finnegan said beside him, his voice low so as not to startle the beast. "Inexperience got it caught in the storm."

Pryce nodded, his gaze fixed on Stormwing. He felt an odd sense of kinship with the creature, as if they were both struggling to find their place in a world that often seemed too harsh.

Pryce tore his gaze away from Stormwing to glance at the gathering crowd. Fear painted their faces—fear and something else. Anger? Resentment? He couldn't be sure, but a wave of hostility seemed to emanate from them, directed at him and his dragon.

Whispers rippled through the crowd, growing louder, more frantic. "What do we do?" "It's a monster!" "We should kill it!"

Pryce wanted to make them understand that the dragon wasn't a threat.

"We should kill it before it causes more trouble," a Shorling shouted from the back of the crowd. The man's voice was tinged with panic, and he brandished a fishing spear. His eyes were wild, darting between Stormwing and the villagers as if looking for an excuse to act.

"He's right," another villager echoed, her voice trembling. She clutched a child close. "What if it brings more dragons? We can't risk it."

Pryce always known his fellow Shorlings feared dragons, but he'd never imagined they could be so quick to violence. He glanced at Finnegan for guidance, hoping the old man had a plan because he sure didn't.

Before either could react, some villagers began tossing fishing nets over the dragon to immobilize it. The
coarse ropes entangled Stormwing's wings and legs, causing the dragon to thrash in pain. Sparks flew from its
scales, and a low growl rumbled from its throat. Pryce
felt every jerk and twitch as if it were his own body being
bound.

"Stop!" Pryce yelled, stepping forward with his
hands raised. "You're hurting him!"

"Stand back, boy!" the first man yelled, advancing
with his spear. "This beast is dangerous!"

Pryce placed himself between Stormwing and the
villagers. He spread his arms wide, trying to shield as
much of the dragon as possible with his own body. "He's
just scared! Look at him—he's not attacking us. Please,
just give him a chance."

Finnegan stepped forward too. "Listen to the lad.
Killing this dragon won't solve anything." As Finnegan
spoke, Pryce noticed some of the villagers lowering their
weapons.

The villagers hesitated. Pryce seized the moment of
uncertainty to kneel beside Stormwing again. Once
more, placing a hand on one of the dragon's tangled
wings. Beneath the thick scales, he sensed a tremor run
through the creature, a wave of fear and pain.

"We need to help him," Pryce said, looking up at the
gathered Shorlings. "If we show him kindness, maybe
he'll do the same for us. Isn't that what we've always
believed in Crystal Shores? Helping those in need?"

For a moment, silence hung in the air as everyone
waited for what would come next. Pryce could hear the

lapping of waves against the shore and the distant cry of a gull, sounds that seemed oddly out of place in this tense standoff.

Then the villagers closed in on Stormwing. Without hesitation, he stepped forward again.

"Please," Pryce's voice cracked with urgency. "No! Don't kill it. It's just a baby. Can't you see?" He gestured towards Stormwing. "Look at him. He's scared, just like we are. We can't condemn him for simply existing. Please, give him a chance."

A burly fisherman scowled at Pryce. "Wounded dragons are dangerous, boy. We've seen what they can do. We'll use long spears to puncture its heart, it'll die quickly. It's the only way to be sure it won't turn on us when we least expect it, especially once it has grown."

Pryce locked eyes with Stormwing, seeing not a monster, but a frightened, injured being. "I can nurse it back to health. I can train dragons. I know what to do."

Finnegan hobbled closer, his eyes narrowed as he examined the dragon. With a heavy sigh, he shook his head. "Its wing is broken, lad. That's hard to heal—like a horse with a broken leg. It might never fly again, even if it survives."

The villagers muttered among themselves. "It can't be healed," one man said, hefting a makeshift spear. "We need to end this now, before it becomes a threat to us all."

Ignoring the warning, Pryce reached out and gently petted Stormwing's snout. The dragon's scales felt cool and smooth under his fingers, like polished stone.

Stormwing let out a low, rumbling purr as it calmed under Pryce's touch.

"Careful now, Pryce," Finnegan warned.

The crowd gasped in amazement at how Pryce managed to soothe the dragon. The dragon, once thrashing in pain and fear, now lay relatively still, responding to Pryce's gentle touch.

"See? I can calm it," Pryce said, turning to face the villagers. "Let me try to heal it."

Despite Pryce's efforts, the villagers continued to secure the dragon with nets, causing the dragon to whimper in pain.

Several men approached with long spears, their faces set in grim determination as they prepared to end Stormwing's life.

"You're not a dragon trainer, Pryce," one of the Shorlings called out. "You're just a fisherman's son. Know your place and step aside."

Pryce drew himself up to his full height, trying to project a confidence he didn't entirely feel. "I've been studying dragon training. I know how to do it. I've read every book I could find. Give me a chance to prove it! I'll train it to protect Crystal Shores and all of us."

Old Man Finnegan spoke up. "The boy has the touch. You all saw it. There's no denying it." He paused, then said, "A sapling denied sunlight will never grow into a mighty oak. We ought to give the boy his opportunity."

The men stood still, their spears wavering. For a moment, Pryce dared to hope. But then they began to move forward again. This was it. He had failed.

3. Into the Depths

Spears hovered menacingly; their tips poised to strike Stormwing's heart. Pryce positioned himself between the dragon and the villagers, his arms spread wide, serving as a shield. Sweat beaded on his brow, trickling down his face as his legs trembled. He shut his eyes tightly, bracing himself for the inevitable.

"STOP!"

Pryce's eyes opened at the sound of his mother's voice. Relieved, he saw his parents pushing their way through the agitated crowd, with Faye and Kai following closely behind. His sister's eyes were wide with fear, while Kai maneuvered through the crowd, his hands raised to ease people aside.

"What in the Dragon's Sea do you think you're doing?" Ellie said. "Have you all gone mad?"

His father, Tyler, stood beside her, a hand resting on the hilt of his fishing knife.

"He's dangerous, Ellie!" said the elderly mayor, Helen Wright. "We have to put it down before it hurts someone!"

Pryce glanced between his parents and the hostile villagers, reluctant to believe his mother's intervention would be enough to save Stormwing's life.

"It's wounded, not rabid," Tyler said. "Look at it."

"Aye, wounded and liable to lash out," another villager said. "We can't risk it."

Ellie turned her eyes to Pryce. "What's going on? Why are you guarding this dragon?"

Pryce took a deep breath. "It's a young storm dragon. It fell during the storm, and its wing is broken. But I can nurse it back to health. I can train it to protect Crystal Shores."

He gestured to the agitated crowd. "They want to kill it, but it doesn't deserve that. It's just scared. It's not lashing out, not trying to hurt anyone."

The murmurs of dissent grew louder. "We should kill it before it kills us!"

"Please, just look at it." Pryce stepped closer to Stormwing. "Watch."

Slowly, Pryce ran his hand down Stormwing's snout, feeling the dragon's fear vibrate through its scales. "Easy, Stormwing." The dragon tensed for a moment. Then, gradually, it relaxed. A low rumble, almost a purr, emanated from Stormwing.

He looked back at his mom. "See? It trusts me."

Ellie's expression shifted from fear to amazement. She turned to Mayor Wright. "Helen, look at this. It . . . it seems Pryce can actually tame it. He's doing it right now, in front of all of us."

"The boy has a way with dragons," Finnegan said to the mayor.

"A dragon's a dragon! Can't be trusted!" a woman shouted from the back. "You two should know better! You faced Aurathorn yourself!"

The mayor stood before Ellie. "I agree with the woman; the dragon cannot be trusted. My job is to keep Crystal Shores free of threats, and this dragon is a threat."

The argument grew louder with conflicting opinions. Pryce fought the urge to shout back. How could they not see?

Amidst the turmoil, Kai and Faye appeared at his side. Faye's hand slipped into his. With a soft voice, his little sister said, "I believe you."

On his other side, Kai kept his distance from the dragon. His best friend said, "Are you sure you know what you're doing?"

"I've never been more sure, Frostborne."

Just when it seemed the shouting would never end, his mother spoke up. "I have a proposition." The crowd fell silent, all eyes turning to her.

"Let Pryce heal and train the dragon on the nearby Islad of Emberfall. The dragon is injured and poses no immediate threat. If it dies, the problem solves itself. If it lives, we gain a protector."

Murmurs rippled through the crowd. Mayor Wright's face twisted with concern. "And if it turns on us?"

"Then I'll deal with it. I'll kill it myself," Tyler said, his voice leaving no room for argument.

"We'll use my boat and a barge to take the dragon to the Island of Emberfall," Tyler said, pointing toward the distant, uninhabited island. "It's a few hours' sail from here and there's an abandoned Oceanrider base there. It's sturdy enough to hold the creature until we know what to do with it." He paused, looking around the crowd once more. "Who here is willing to help with the transport?"

A few hands tentatively went up, and Tyler nodded in appreciation. The villagers worked quickly, reinforcing the nets already around the dragon.

Nearby, they pushed a large hoist, usually reserved for lifting heavy logs, up to Stormwing.

Tyler turned to the crowd. "Alright, everyone, on three. One, two, three!" With a mix of grunts and groans, they hoisted Stormwing off the ground.

"Watch the tail, it could knock someone off their feet," Kai called out, his voice strained with effort as he helped support a wing.

Old Man Finnegan, leaning heavily on his walking stick, said from the side. "Mind the left wheel, it's looking wobbly. Someone get over there and steady it."

Grunting with effort, Pryce adjusted his grip on the netting. "Stormwing's heavier than I thought. Are we sure the cart can take this weight?"

"That cart's seen better days, lad. But if the ropes hold and the wheels don't betray us, it should be able to carry the lizard's weight. Just keep an eye on that left wheel, it's more temperamental than a dragon with a toothache."

As they finally managed to lift Stormwing onto the cart, the wheels creaked, but held steady. Tyler wiped his hands on his pants. "Good job, everyone. Let's move quickly."

With the dragon securely on the cart, the group began their journey towards the docks, where Tyler's boat awaited to take them to Emberfall. Pryce helped push the cart, assisting the struggling horses.

"I can't wait to get him to Emberfall," Pryce said.

Finnegan nodded as he walked toward his cottage. "Aye, lad. The sooner we reach the island, the better."

Pryce kept pushing the cart towards the pier, where a barge waited. It was the best option they had for transporting something so large. They carefully hoisted the dragon onboard and strapped it down securely, folding its wings tightly against its body.

Tyler would tow the barge, which is usually used to haul lumber, behind his fishing vessel, the Blue Horizon.

They fastened the dragon with additional ropes and chains once it was onboard the barge, ensuring complete immobilization.

Just as they were preparing to depart, the clatter of hooves and wheels announced Old Man Finnegan's arrival. The elder pulled up in his weathered cart, his equally ancient horse snorting and stamping its feet. "Hold up there, young Harper-Green!"

Pryce watched as Finnegan directed the loading of his horse and cart onto Tyler's boat. "Thought you might need some help with that overgrown lizard," he said, nodding towards Stormwing. "I've got some ideas about what dragons might fancy for dinner. Figured we could use the cart to haul in some game. Can't have your new friend going hungry, now can we?"

Pryce hurried over to Finnegan. "Glad to have you with us."

Finnegan clapped him on the shoulder. "Of course, lad. Someone's got to keep you out of trouble. Besides, I haven't seen a dragon up close in a long time. Just never thought I'd be feeding one instead of fighting it."

"What do dragons eat?" someone from the crowd called out.

"Fish, mostly," Finnegan replied. "Big ones, like the Moonshark from the lake."

From the barge, Pryce helped his father finish securing the last of the ropes tethering it to the Blue Horizon.

"Cast off!" Tyler called out, his voice carrying over the lapping waves.

As the Blue Horizon began to pull away from the dock, Pryce's eyes found his mother and sister standing at the edge. Pryce raised his hand, waving at them.

"We'll be back soon!" he called out. "Don't worry!"

Kai stood beside him on the barge, his white-blonde hair whipping in the wind.

Pryce leaned against the railing of the barge.

"So," Kai said, "a dragon trainer, huh? That's quite the career change from fishing."

Pryce couldn't help but chuckle. "Yeah, I guess it is. But you've got to admit, it's a bit more exciting than hauling in empty nets day after day."

Kai raised an eyebrow. "Exciting is one word for it. Dangerous is another. Just don't forget about the rest of us little people when you're off riding dragons and saving the world."

"As if I could ever forget about you, Frostborne. Someone's got to keep me grounded."

Pryce turned his attention to Stormwing, who lay bound and stressed on the barge. The dragon's chest heaved with labored breaths. "Hey, it's okay."

The dragon strained against its bonds, causing the barge to rock. Pryce gently stroked Stormwing's snout. "Whoa, easy there."

The dragon's breathing slowed a bit at Pryce's touch, but its muscles remained taut beneath the ropes. He continued to stroke Stormwing's snout, speaking in soothing tones as the barge was pulled further from shore.

The sail across Lake Dragontide to the Island of Emberfall was fraught with worry. Pryce couldn't tear his eyes away from Stormwing, who lay curled up on the hard planks of the barge. The dragon's occasional whimpers of pain were agonizing.

The island itself, when they finally reached its shores, felt as ill as his dragon. Wild and overgrown, it pressed in on the small beach. The remnants of buildings, barely visible beneath a tangle of vines and creepers, offered little comfort.

"I don't know how I'm going to live in such a place and train a dragon," Pryce said. "I've spent my whole life in Crystal Shores. This is my first encounter with a dragon, and now I'm supposed to heal it and train it here?"

"It does look pretty rough," Kai said.

The Blue Horizon glided toward the old dock of the abandoned Oceanrider outpost. The dock, weathered and covered in moss, jutted out into the water like a skeletal hand reaching for them.

Pryce stood at the edge of the barge. He glanced back at Stormwing, who lay bound and anxious, its blue eyes scanning the surroundings nervously.

"Get ready to cut the lines!" Finnegan's voice boomed from the stern of the ship. "Pryce, Kai, be prepared!"

Kai moved to Pryce's side. "I don't know how this is going to work."

"Me either."

As Tyler brought the ship closer to shore, a sudden jolt rocked the barge. Pryce saw a jagged rock scrape against the side of the barge, sending a shudder through the vessel. He tightened his grip on the railing.

"Hold on!" Tyler shouted from the ship.

The sudden impact startled Stormwing, who began thrashing violently against his restraints. Pryce could feel the dragon's powerful muscles straining, the ropes creaking under the pressure. The barge lurched dangerously, tipping to one side as the dragon's agitation threatened to capsize it.

"Stormwing, calm down!" Pryce pleaded. He reached out, trying to soothe the dragon with his touch.

But Stormwing's panic only intensified. The dragon's good wing flared out, catching the wind and adding to the barge's instability. With a mighty heave, the dragon broke free from some of his bindings. The sound of snapping ropes filled the air.

"No, Stormwing!" Pryce watched the dragon teeter on the edge of the barge. The vessel swayed perilously, and in a desperate attempt to regain control, Stormwing's tail lashed out, sending crates and equipment tumbling into the water with loud splashes.

"Hold on!" Pryce held out his hand as if he could will the dragon to calm down. But the panic in Stormwing was unmistakable, and he knew the dragon's instincts were taking over.

Then, with a final, frantic thrash of his wings, Stormwing tumbled off the side of the barge, disappearing into the deep, churning water below. Pryce watched the ripples spread across the lake's surface.

"Stormwing!" He leaned over the railing, his eyes scanning the dark waters for any sign of his dragon.

Pryce grabbed a length of rope and tied it securely around his waist, fastening the other end to the barge's railing. Taking a deep breath, he prepared to dive into the waters. With one last look at Kai, who was pulling on his arm, he dove into the turbulent lake.

4. The Final Cut

The murkiness of the lake made it difficult for Pryce to see more than a few feet ahead, but he could make out the faint outline of a rope still attached to Stormwing. He grabbed hold and followed it.

The dragon thrashed in the water, tangled in the remnants of fishing nets and ropes. Its broken wing flailed uselessly, adding to its distress.

He reached for his fishing knife from its sheath strapped to his belt and began cutting away at the ropes and netting that ensnared Stormwing. The dragon's powerful tail lashed out in its agitation, nearly clobbering Pryce and sending him spinning in the water.

"Easy, Stormwing," Pryce thought, though he knew the dragon couldn't hear him. He focused on cutting through another thick rope, his lungs burning for air.

Stormwing's struggles grew more frantic as Pryce worked. He narrowly avoided another swipe from Stormwing's tail, feeling the rush of water as it passed inches from his face.

His vision began to blur as he ran out of air, but he refused to give up. He could feel the tugging on his own rope—someone above was trying to pull him up. Probably Kai. But Pryce couldn't leave Stormwing like this.

But Pryce had to surface before he lost all his breath. His chest felt like it was about to explode, and his vision darkened at the edges. With a final push, he kicked upward, breaking through the water's surface, gasping for air.

Kai leaned over the edge of the barge. "Pryce! Are you alright? What's happening down there?"

"I almost have him free," Pryce panted, wiping water from his eyes. "Just need a few more moments."

From the ship, Old Man Finnegan shouted. "Pryce! You need to move faster or the dragon will drown!"

Pryce took one last deep breath and dove back under. The cold water enveloped him again as he swam down to where Stormwing continued to struggle.

He reached the spot where he'd been cutting through the ropes and netting. His fingers were numb from the cold, but he forced them to work, slicing through another thick rope that had wrapped around Stormwing.

The dragon seemed to sense Pryce's presence and calmed slightly, its thrashing less violent. Pryce worked with urgency, cutting away the last of the netting that held Stormwing captive.

With a final slash of his knife, the last rope fell away. Stormwing gave a powerful kick with its legs, propelling itself upward toward the surface. Pryce followed, his lungs burning once more.

As he broke through the surface of the water, gasping for breath, Pryce saw Stormwing already struggling toward the shore, his movements hindered by his broken wing.

Kai reached out from the barge, grabbing Pryce by the arm and hauling him aboard. "You did it!"

Pryce coughed. "Thanks, Frostborne."

Pryce heard his father shout from the ship. "Get the dragon into a cell before it escapes! I'll help as soon as I have the ship anchored and the barge secured to the pier!"

Pryce turned his gaze toward Stormwing, who sat motionless on the shore, looking worse for wear. The dragon's scales, once a brilliant blue, now appeared dull and lackluster. Its wing hung limply at its side.

"I don't think it's going anywhere," Kai said, quietly.

Pryce stood up and squeezed some of the water from his clothes. "I don't know if that's good or bad."

As soon as the barge was tied to the pier, Pryce and Kai sprinted down the dock toward where Stormwing still sat. The dragon's eyes followed Pryce's movements.

Pryce approached cautiously, placing a hand on Stormwing's snout. "You're safe now," he said, feeling the dragon's warm breath against his skin.

Kai shifted uneasily beside him. "Any idea where we can find a cell to hold it?"

Pryce stood up, his eyes scanning the abandoned Oceanrider base. The compound now stood eerily quiet. Its buildings now lay in disrepair, with weathered wooden structures and rusting metal equipment scattered about. Large cells lined one side of the base—remnants of a time when captured dragons were held there during the Dragonspine War.

Before Pryce could respond, he heard the clip-clop of hooves and turned to see Old Man Finnegan approaching with his horse and cart. Other ship hands hurried down the dock to where Stormwing lay. They hesitated, then slowly approached the dragon. The man carrying rope and chain began fashioning a makeshift collar around Stormwing's neck.

"There's an old dragon cell over there," another man called out, pointing toward the structure Pryce had noticed earlier. "Take it there."

Pryce felt a pang of sadness as he approached Stormwing once more. "Come on," he said softly, encouraging the dragon to stand. "Follow me." To his surprise, Stormwing complied, rising unsteadily to its feet. The broken wing dragged along the ground, and Pryce winced at the sight.

Finnegan followed along with his horse and cart. "We need to get that wing fixed," he said. "I can stabilize it until we get a doctor out here. Get him in the cell first; then I'll do what I can."

As Pryce guided Stormwing toward the cell, he glanced back at Finnegan and Kai, who were engaged in a hushed conversation. Snippets of their words reached his ears—"won't make it," "would be a miracle," "no doctor will come out to help fix the wing."

5. Whimpers

Pryce watched as Stormwing limped into the rusty cell. Its injured wing dragged along the dust-covered floor, leaving a trail.

As the dragon settled in the far corner of the cell, Pryce couldn't help but notice Stormwing's labored breaths. Each one was accompanied by a soft whimper that made Pryce wince.

"We need to close the door," Kai said.

Pryce tore his gaze away from Stormwing. Together, he and Kai grasped the heavy iron bars of the cell door. The metal was cold and rough against Pryce's palms. As they pushed, the door groaned in protest, years of disuse evident in its stubborn resistance. Pryce gritted his teeth, muscles straining as he and Kai fought against the rusted hinges.

Finally, with a loud, drawn-out creak, the cell door slammed shut. The sound reverberated off the stone walls, making Stormwing flinch. Pryce felt a pang of guilt.

"I'm sorry, Storm," Pryce said.

Old Man Finnegan approached, his cart laden with fish he had brought. He stopped at the feeding hatch, a small, barred opening next to the main door. "This'll have to do for now." He reached into the cart, grasping a slippery silver trout, and tossed it through the hatch. It landed with a wet slap in the trough.

Pryce watched as Stormwing's nostrils flared at the scent of food. But to Pryce's dismay, the dragon made no move to eat.

Finnegan frowned. "Come on, you need to keep up your strength."

Pryce watched Finnegan continue to feed Stormwing through the hatch. Each fish landed uneaten in the trough.

The dragon finally stirred. Stormwing slowly dragged himself toward the pile of fish.

"That's it," Finnegan said, nodding with satisfaction. "I'll come back tomorrow daytide to have a proper look at that wing. For now, let's give him some peace and quiet."

Pryce heard his father's distant voice. "It's getting dark. We need to set up camp for the night."

The sun had begun its descent, painting the sky in breathtaking hues of orange and purple.

"Those old barracks should provide decent shelter." Finnegan pointed with his walking stick toward a cluster of run-down buildings. "Not much, but it'll keep the night chill off our bones."

The group trudged toward the buildings. The once-sturdy wooden walls were now weathered and gray, with patches of moss creeping up from the foundation like green fingers. Several planks had fallen away, leaving gaping holes that exposed the building's skeletal frame.

Tyler pushed open the squeaky door and they filed inside. Pryce's eyes took a moment to adjust to the dim interior. Dust motes danced in the fading light that filtered through the cracks in the walls and roof.

The floor was littered with debris—broken furniture, tattered scraps of cloth, and what looked like animal droppings. Pryce wrinkled his nose at the smell, a mixture of decay and neglect. In one corner, a rusted bedframe stood, its mattress long since rotted away. Cobwebs adorned every corner and rafter.

"Well," Kai said, "it's not exactly the Dragontide Inn, but it'll have to do."

"At least it's got a roof," Pryce said, moving to help clear a space on the floor. He pushed aside the remnants of what might have once been a chair. As he worked, he overheard snippets of conversation between his father and the others who had come to help.

"Alright, gang, let's make this place somewhat livable before nightfall," Tyler said.

Pryce looked up, surveying the ragtag group his dad had gathered. Ana caught his eye, her stance and bearing suggesting combat experience. Next to her towered Jack, his gangly frame topped by a mop of ginger locks. In the background, Declan lingered, his mild-mannered presence seeming out of place in the dilapidated setting.

"Ana, can you and Jack check the perimeter?" Tyler asked. "Make sure there are no weak spots where wild animals might get in. Or worse, dragons looking for a midnight snack."

Ana rolled her eyes good-naturedly. "Always with the dragons, Ty. You'd think we were in a storybook or something."

Jack elbowed Ana playfully. "Come on, let's go dragon-hunting. I'll protect you from the big, bad beasties."

"In your dreams, Red."

Pryce watched them go. He turned back to see his father addressing Declan.

"Dec, let's see about getting a fire going," Tyler said. "This place is damp as a fish's backside. And speaking of fish, I don't suppose you've got any of that magic touch of yours to whip up some grub? I'm starving enough to eat a dragon."

"I'll see what I can do, Tyler. Though I can't promise dragon steaks on such short notice."

The fireplace was a sorry sight, choked with years of debris and ash. Pryce helped Declan set to work clearing it and the old iron stove out, using broken pieces of furniture as makeshift shovels.

As they worked, Pryce's fingers brushed against something smooth and round. He pulled it out, revealing a dragon scale. It was about the size of his palm.

"Well, would you look at that," Declan said, peering at the scale. "Seems this place has some history with dragons after all."

With the fireplace cleared, Tyler returned with an armful of driftwood he'd gathered from outside. "This should do for now," he said, arranging the wood in the hearth.

Pryce watched as his father struck a flint, sending sparks dancing into the dry kindling. After a few attempts, a small flame caught, growing steadily as Tyler carefully fed it more wood. The fire cast a warm, flickering light across the room, chasing away some of the gloom and dampness.

As the fire began to crackle and pop, Tyler stood up, brushing his hands on his trousers. He reached for a torch on the wall, striking it against the rough stone until it flared to life. "Pryce, come with me. We need to bring in the supplies from the ship."

He followed his father out into the chilled evening air, shivering slightly as the chill wind blew in from the lake. The sky had darkened considerably, transforming into a canvas of deep purples and blues. Stars were beginning to peek out, twinkling faintly in the twilight. As they made their way down to the shore where their boat was moored, Pryce couldn't help but cast worried glances back toward Stormwing.

"He'll be alright for now," Tyler said, noticing his son's concern. "Let's focus on getting everyone fed and settled for the night."

Declan jogged up behind them, his footsteps crunching on the gravelly path. "Thought you could use an extra pair of hands," he said, falling into step beside them.

"Appreciate it," Tyler said.

Pryce glanced at Declan. "So, Declan, how long have you known my father?"

"Oh, longer than I care to admit, lad. Your old man and I go way back."

"Declan here was green as spring grass when we first met."

"Aye, and you were just a pup yourself. But we've seen our fair share of adventures since then, haven't we?" Declan turned to Pryce. "We had to save your dad's butt more times than I can count. There was this one time, deep in the Dragonspine Reaches, when he got himself tangled in a nest of sea serpents. Thought we'd be having Tyler soup for dinner!"

Pryce couldn't help but smile, trying to imagine his usually composed father in such a predicament.

"Oh, come off it, you old sea dog. If I recall correctly, it was you who needed rescuing when that kraken decided your leg looked like a tasty snack." He looked at Pryce. "Don't let Declan fool you, son. Half his stories are tall tales, and the other half are pure fantasy."

Declan clutched his chest in mock offense. "You wound me, Tyler! I'll have you know every word I speak is the honest truth." He leaned in conspiratorially towards Pryce. "Your dad's just sore because I'm better looking than him, even after all these years."

As they reached the boat, they began loading their arms with supplies—dried meats, hardtack, and water-skins. Pryce grunted under the weight of a heavy sack of provisions, his muscles straining with the effort.

"Easy there, son." Tyler reached out to steady him. "No need to overdo it."

As they made their way back to the barracks, Pryce's eyes caught sight of something in the fading light. He squinted, making out the silhouette of an old ship, its mast tilting at an odd angle. "Hey, look at that."

Declan followed Pryce's gaze. "Well, I'll be. That looks like the Swiftwind sloop we used to save your pa from the Dragonkin Marauders." He winked at Tyler. "Remember that little adventure?"

"How could I forget? You nearly got us all killed with that harebrained rescue plan of yours."

Pryce took in the ship's condition, his imagination running wild with thoughts of the daring rescue his father had once been part of. The once-proud Swiftwind was a shadow of its former self.

"What happened?" Pryce asked. "How did it end up like this?"

Tyler sighed. "Time and tide wait for no man, son. Or ship, for that matter. The Swiftwind served its purpose, and now it rests here, a reminder of days gone by."

As they continued their trek back to the barracks, Pryce couldn't help but steal glances at the derelict ship. His mind raced with possibilities as he gazed at the Swiftwind. He could almost see it restored to its former glory, cutting through the waves of Lake Dragontide once more. "I bet I could fix her up."

His father's response was deflating. "Bad idea, son. That ship's seen better days. It'd be more work than it's worth."

But before Pryce could argue, Declan spoke up. "I don't know, Tyler. With a lot of elbow grease and some know-how, it might be possible. The bones of a good ship are still there."

Pryce envisioned the entire outpost transformed. The old barracks could become healing pens for injured dragons like Stormwing. The watchtower, now listing slightly to one side, could serve as a lookout point for spotting dragons in distress. And the Swiftwind . . . she could be the crown jewel, sailing out on rescue missions across the vast expanse of the lake.

But as quickly as the dream had formed, it began to crumble. Pryce caught sight of his father's face. The excitement deflated like a punctured balloon.

"Even if we could fix it up, where would we get the coin?" Tyler said. "The village coffers are as empty as our nets these days."

Declan added. "Aye, and materials don't come cheap. We'd need lumber, nails, tar . . . not to mention tools."

Pryce's shoulders slumped as they trekked back to the barracks. The supplies he carried seemed to grow heavier with each step, as if weighed down by his dashed hopes.

As they entered the barracks, Declan immediately set to work preparing supper, despite the less-than-ideal conditions. Pryce could hear him muttering under his breath, complaining about the state of the kitchen.

"Blasted stove's more rust than iron," Declan grumbled. "And these pots! I've seen better kept chamber pots in a pirate's galley."

Despite the cook's griping, the aroma of cooking fish and herbs soon filled the air. Pryce's stomach growled.

The door burst open with a bang, startling Pryce. Jack and Ana strode in, looking pleased with themselves.

Pryce watched as Jack announced their progress on patching up the barracks, his unruly red hair now adorned with cobwebs.

"Well, we've patched up every hole we could find," Jack declared, brushing at his hair. "Should keep the critters out, at least for tonight."

"Unless they're determined little buggers. Then all bets are off," Ana said.

Tyler chuckled. "Let's hope they're not. I'd rather not wake up with a raccoon for a bedmate."

"Speak for yourself. Might be an improvement over some of the company I've kept." Jack continued to fuss with his hair, muttering about "blasted spiders" and their "inconsiderate web placement."

"At least the raccoons would have better manners." Ana tossed a small pebble at Jack's head. "And probably smell better too."

Pryce couldn't help but laugh at the exchange.

"I'll have you know," Jack puffed out his chest, "that I bathed just last week. In a proper stream and everything!"

Tyler raised an eyebrow. "Was that before or after you fell into that mud pit trying to catch that 'monster fish' that turned out to be a log?"

The group erupted into laughter.

Pryce made his way over to where Kai and Old Man Finnegan were inspecting the beds. He watched as Kai tested the strength of the frames.

"Think these'll hold?" Pryce asked.

Kai shrugged. "They might. Or we might end up in a pile on the floor come morning."

Finnegan ran a hand over one of the threadbare mattresses. "In my day, we didn't have the luxury of beds. We slept on rocks and were grateful for 'em."

Pryce and Kai exchanged amused glances. Pryce couldn't resist the urge to tease the old man. "And I suppose you walked uphill both ways to get to those rocks?"

"You're darn right we did. And we liked it that way!"

Pryce heard the sound of metal clanging against metal. He looked up to see Declan standing near the makeshift kitchen area, banging a dented pot with a wooden spoon.

"Grub's up, lads!" Declan called out.

They gathered around the makeshift table, bowing their heads as Old Man Finnegan led them in an old Shorling prayer.

"Blessed be the waters that sustain us," Finnegan said. "Blessed be the fish that fill our nets and our bellies. Blessed be the family that surrounds us, whether by blood or by choice. May our bonds be as strong as the ancient oaks that line our shores. And blessed be the dragons that watch over our waters, reminding us of the power and mystery that dwell in this world."

As the prayer drew to a close, Pryce opened his eyes, catching Kai's gaze across the table.

"Now," Finnegan declared, "let's eat before this grub gets any colder!"

Pryce eagerly dug into the fish. Laughter and conversation filled the air, as Ana playfully attempted to steal food from his plate.

Pryce swallowed a mouthful of the fish, savoring the smoky flavor. He glanced around the table, taking in the warm smiles and lively chatter of his family and friends. His gaze settled on Old Man Finnegan, who was busy regaling Ana with one of his well-worn tales.

"You know," Pryce said, "I couldn't help but notice that bit in the blessing about dragons watching over our waters." He leaned forward. "Stormwing could do that, you know. I bet he'd make an excellent guardian for Crystal Shores."

"Ah, lad," Finnegan said, "that blessing's as old as the shores themselves. It harkens back to a time long past, when dragons and men lived in closer harmony."

Pryce opened his mouth to argue but thought better of it. Instead, he turned his attention back to his plate, pushing a piece of fish around with his fork.

As Pryce reached for another piece of fish, a faint sound caught his attention. He paused, fork hovering midair, and strained his ears. There it was again—a soft, mournful whimper. Stormwing.

Finnegan noticed Pryce's distraction. "I know that look, lad. But don't go getting any foolish ideas. Night's no time to be wandering about, especially not with what's out there."

"Finnegan's right, son. These parts can be dangerous after dark. More than you know."

"What kind of dangers?" he asked.

Ana plucked a slender bone from the fish she was eating. She held it up, gesturing with it as she spoke. "Well, there's the Thornveil Wolf for one. Nasty beast, that. Big as a horse, with teeth like daggers and claws that could tear a man in two."

Jack put his elbows on the table. "Aye, and that's not the worst of it. They say its howl can freeze a man's blood. I've heard tell of seasoned warriors dropping their weapons and fleeing at the mere sound of it."

Pryce's hand tightened around his fork. He'd heard tales of the Thornveil Wolf before. Now, in the flickering shadows of the barracks, those stories seemed far more plausible.

Another whimper drifted through the night, louder this time. He knew the dragon needed him.

The others continued to share tales of the dangers that lurked in the night. Declan spoke of ghostly lights that lured unwary travelers to their doom, while Tyler recounted a close encounter with a pack of shadow cats whose eyes glowed like embers in the dark.

But Pryce barely heard them. His mind was outside, with Stormwing, imagining the dragon alone and in pain.

6. The Sheila of Emberfall

Pryce stood abruptly, his chair scraping against the rough wooden floor. The sound cut through the conversation, drawing all eyes to him. "I have to check on him."

Kai pushed back from the table. "I'll go with you."

A muscle in Tyler's jaw twitched visibly. "Be careful out there, boys. The night holds more dangers than you know."

Ana leaned forward. "Watch for shadow cats. They're not as big as the stories say, but they're quick and silent. You won't hear them coming."

"And keep an ear out for the Thornveil Wolf," Jack added, his fingers drumming nervously on the table. "Its howl can freeze the blood in your veins."

"Don't forget the will-o'-the-wisps," Declan said softly. "They'll lead you astray if you're not careful."

Pryce rolled his eyes, trying not to show how irritated he felt at their obvious attempts to frighten him. He grabbed a torch from the wall, its flame sputtering to life as he lit it. "I wish I had my bow. You know, in case I run into any of those terrifying shadow cats or blood-freezing wolves you're all so worried about."

As Pryce and Kai stepped outside, the cool night air washed over them. A gentle breeze rustled through the leaves, carrying the scent of distant smoke. The moon peeked through gaps in the clouds, casting a silvery light over the abandoned outpost.

They set off toward Stormwing's cell, their footsteps crunching on the gravel path.

"Do you think Stormwing's in pain?" Kai asked.

"I don't know. But those whimpers . . . they sounded desperate."

They walked in silence. The waves lapped gently against the shore as a distant owl hooted mournfully.

"You know," Kai said suddenly, "this whole dragon thing . . . it's pretty incredible. I always thought of you as more of a gentle bookworm, not someone who'd be wrestling with dragons and diving into lakes to save them. I'm impressed."

Pryce glanced at his friend, surprised by the admission. "Thanks . . . I guess. I thought you thought I was crazy."

Kai chuckled. "Oh, I still think you're crazy."

As they approached the cell, Stormwing was there, seemingly unharmed. The dragon's blue eyes fixed on Pryce, and it let out a low, rumbling sound that was almost . . . welcoming?

They entered the cell and Kai watched as Stormwing approached Pryce. "You know, I think he might just be lonely. Look at how he's coming to you."

Pryce reached out, his hand finding the smooth scales of Stormwing's snout. The dragon leaned into his touch, and the whimpering they'd heard earlier ceased.

"I think you might be right." Pryce ran his hand along Stormwing's neck, feeling the powerful muscles beneath the scales. "Hey there, big guy. Did you just want some company?"

Kai checked the food and water troughs. "Everything looks fine here. We should probably head back before the others start to worry."

Pryce nodded, but he couldn't bring himself to leave just yet. He continued to stroke Stormwing's snout, murmuring soft words of comfort. The dragon's eyes began to droop, and Pryce could feel some of the tension leaving its body.

Finally, with a last pat, Pryce stepped back. "I'll be back in the morning," he promised Stormwing.

As they exited the cell, Pryce pulled the heavy door shut behind them. The clang of metal on metal echoed in the night, making both boys jump.

They had only taken a few steps back toward the barracks when a sound reached their ears. It was faint at first, barely distinguishable from the night sounds around them. But as they listened, it grew louder, more distinct.

It was a low, guttural growl, unlike anything Pryce had ever heard before.

"Did you hear that?" Kai whispered.

Pryce nodded, his mouth suddenly too dry to speak. They picked up their pace, the torch in Pryce's hand flickering wildly as they moved.

The sound came again, closer this time. It was a mix between a growl and a hiss.

Without a word, both boys broke into a run. The ground blurred beneath their feet as they sprinted toward the barracks, the terrifying sound seeming to chase them through the night.

They burst through the barracks door, slamming it shut behind them. Pryce leaned against it, his chest heaving as he tried to catch his breath. Kai slumped to the floor, his face pale in the lamplight.

The others jumped to their feet, startled by their sudden entrance.

Tyler rushed up to Pryce. "What happened? Are you boys alright?"

Pryce nodded, still trying to catch his breath. "There . . . there was something out there. Something chasing us."

"What was it?" Ana asked, her hand instinctively moving to the knife at her belt. "What did you see?"

Kai shook his head. "We didn't see anything, but we heard it."

"I think . . ." Pryce hesitated, looking at Kai for confirmation. "I think it might have been a pack of shadow cats."

A tense silence fell over the room. Then, Ana moved to the window, peering out into the darkness.

"Boys," Ana said, turning back to the group, "I think I've found your fearsome shadow cats."

Pryce pushed himself off the door and joined her at the window. There, illuminated by the moonlight, sat a small, ordinary-looking feline. Its fur was a mottled gray.

"That's . . . that's just a mouser," Pryce said, using the Shorling term for the small cats that kept rodents at bay in their village.

The tension in the room broke, replaced by laughter.

Jack slapped his knee. "Oh, lads, you should see your faces!"

Even Tyler cracked a smile. "Looks like our brave dragon trainer was bested by a little mouser," he teased.

Pryce felt his cheeks burning with embarrassment. He glanced at Kai, who looked equally mortified.

"It must have been left behind when the Oceanriders abandoned the outpost." Declan wiped tears of laughter from his eyes.

Pryce looked out the window again, studying the innocent-looking cat. Its tail flicked lazily as it watched a moth flutter by, completely oblivious to the commotion it had caused.

"Alright, alright," Tyler said, his voice still tinged with amusement. "That's enough excitement for one night. We need to get some sleep. We're heading back to Crystal Shores first thing in the morning."

As the others settled back into their makeshift beds, still chuckling and trading jokes at Pryce and Kai's expense, Pryce couldn't shake the feeling that what they'd heard was more than just the mouser. He lay down on his thin, lumpy mattress, and exhaustion began to overtake him.

***

The first rays of dawn crept through the cracks in the barracks' walls, casting long shadows across the room. Pryce stirred in his sleep, the lumpy mattress doing little to ease the ache in his back. A musty odor permeated the air. Suddenly, a hand shook his shoulder, jolting him awake.

"Rise and shine, lad," Old Man Finnegan's gravelly voice pierced through the fog of sleep. "We've got a dragon to tend to before we set sail."

Pryce rubbed his eyes. He sat up, wincing at his stiff muscles. "What time is it?"

Finnegan chuckled, his weathered face creasing with amusement. "Early enough for the fish to still be yawning. Now, up you get."

As Pryce stumbled to his feet, he noticed the others already gathered around the makeshift table. The clatter of utensils against tin plates filled the air as they finished their breakfast. Declan stood at the rusty sink, scrubbing dishes with a grimace.

"Son," Tyler called out. "We're shoving off soon. Best make haste with that dragon of yours."

Pryce nodded, grabbing a piece of hardtack from the table and shoving it into his mouth. The bread was tough and bland. He motioned to Kai, who was mid-yawn, his hair sticking up at odd angles. "Come on, Frostborne. Dragon duty calls."

They stepped outside into the cool morning air. Dew clung to the overgrown grass, soaking the hem of Pryce's trousers as they made their way to Stormwing's cell. Finnegan hobbled along behind them, a weathered leather satchel slung over his shoulder.

"Found this old doctor's kit in the barracks," Finnegan said, patting the bag. "Might come in handy."

As they approached the cell, a low rumble greeted them. Stormwing's eyes lit up at the sight of Pryce. The dragon pressed its snout against the bars, a puff of warm air ruffling Pryce's hair.

"Hey there, big guy," Pryce said softly, reaching through to stroke Stormwing's scales. They felt smooth beneath his fingers, like polished river stones. "Did you miss me?"

Kai opened the cell door with a rusty creak and moved to the water trough, refilling it from a nearby barrel. "At least someone's happy to see us this early."

Finnegan circled the dragon, his keen eyes taking in every detail. The dragon's wing dragged along the ground, and the dragon let out a pitiful whine.

"Hmm." Finnegan reached into his satchel. He pulled out a strange-looking instrument, all brass and leather. "Let's have a look at that wing, shall we?"

As Finnegan approached, Stormwing tensed, muscles rippling beneath its scales. Pryce moved closer, placing a reassuring hand on the dragon's neck. "It's okay, Storm. He's here to help."

With surprising gentleness, Finnegan manipulated the wing. Stormwing flinched but didn't pull away. After a few moments, Finnegan stepped back.

"Well, I'll be a barnacle's uncle," Finnegan said, scratching his chin. "That wing's not broken at all. Just a sprain, I'd wager. It'll heal up right quick on its own."

Kai's eyebrows shot up. "You mean it was all an act?"

Finnegan nodded with amusement. "Seems our scaly friend here has a flair for the dramatic. Been playing up that injury for a bit of extra attention, I'd say." He paused, studying Stormwing more closely. "And I'll tell you something else—this dragon's a sheila, not a fella."

Pryce blinked in surprise. "A sheila? You mean Stormwing's a girl?"

"Aye, lad. As sure as the tide rises and falls."

Kai burst out laughing, the sound echoing off the cell walls. "I knew it! You big drama queen."

As if on cue, Stormwing straightened her wing, the movement smooth and seemingly painless. The dragon's eyes darted to Pryce with what could only be described as a sheepish grin.

Pryce couldn't help but smile. He placed both hands on either side of Stormwing's face, looking directly into her eyes with affection. "You little trickster," he said with amusement. "I'm not mad, you know. But I do have to leave for a while."

A soft whine escaped Stormwing's throat.

"I know, I know," Pryce soothed, running his hand along the dragon's neck. "But I promise I'll be back soon. You be good while I'm gone, okay?"

As if understanding every word, Stormwing nuzzled against Pryce's chest, nearly knocking him over. The dragon's scales were warm now, and Pryce could feel the steady thrum of her heartbeat. He wrapped his arms around Stormwing's neck.

"Well, I'll be," Finnegan said, watching the exchange with wonder. "In all my years, I've never seen anything quite like this."

Kai nodded in agreement. "Looks like you've got yourself a friend for life, Pryce."

7. Negotiations and Nonsense

"So, lad," Finnegan said as they walked back to the barracks, "how exactly do you plan on managin' a dragon with no coin to your name? Not to mention helpin' your old man?"

"I've got a plan," Pryce said. "There's this wealthy fellow in town, Gavin Brooks. I'm going to ask him for a loan."

Finnegan's bushy eyebrows shot up. "A loan? For what?"

"To rebuild the barracks, fix up the old Swiftwind, and get everything I need to train Stormwing. I'll tell him how having a friendly dragon will protect Crystal Shores from marauders. It's a win-win."

"And your father?"

Pryce swallowed hard. "I'm old enough to make my own way now. Dad should understand that. He can hire someone to take my place at the docks and on the Blue Horizon."

"Now, hold on there, lad. Your pa might not have the means to hire help. And trainin' a dragon? That's no small feat, especially for someone who's never even been around the beasts before."

The old man's words stung. "Will you help me, Finnegan? I know you can't do much, but any advice would be helpful."

"Aye, I'll do what I can. But how do you plan on payin' back this Gavin character?"

"I could . . . I could sell my dragon training skills!"

"To who? There ain't no other dragons around these parts."

"Then I'll sell rides! People would love that, wouldn't they?"

Finnegan stroked his beard, considering. "It might work, but . . . Shorlings are scared of dragons now. Funny thing is, we used to be the best dragon trainers in all of Dragontide. But that was long ago, and no one remembers it anymore."

As they neared the barracks, Kai, who had been quietly listening, finally spoke up. "You know, Pryce, my uncle always says, 'The bravest step is the first one.' Maybe this is your chance to remind Crystal Shores of its heritage."

As they reached the barracks, everyone had already packed and was heading out to the ship.

Finnegan left the doctor's bag behind, and they made their way to the vessel. The journey back to the village was filled with unspoken worries and half-formed plans.

As they disembarked, Pryce turned to his father. "Dad, I'll be along shortly. I need to talk to someone about a dragon training loan."

Tyler's face clouded with concern. "Pryce, don't go getting yourself into debt over a dragon. We should take it to a far-off island and leave it there."

"No," Pryce said firmly. "I can't do that. I won't."

Finnegan cleared his throat. "I reckon Gavin's staying at the Rusty Anchor Inn, lad."

As the others dispersed—Finnegan and Tyler heading home, the crew going their separate ways, and Kai rushing back to his father's smithy—Pryce found himself alone as he set off toward the Rusty Anchor Inn.

But fate had other plans. As he rounded a corner, Pryce caught sight of Gordan Flintjaw, the bully who'd tormented him for years. Gordan wasn't alone; his equally unpleasant friend Dirk lurked nearby.

Pryce tried to slip past unnoticed, but Gordan's eyes locked onto him. "Well, well." Gordan sauntered over with Dirk in tow. "If it isn't the village weakling. Where you off to in such a hurry, Harper-Green? Running home to mommy?"

"Leave me alone, Gordan." Pryce tried to sidestep the larger boy.

But Gordan wasn't having it. He shoved Pryce hard, sending him stumbling. "What's the matter? Can't take a little rough-housing?"

As Pryce regained his balance, he felt something slip from his back pocket. His book. Gordan snatched it up, a cruel grin spreading across his face.

"What's this? A book?" Gordan laughed, holding it just out of Pryce's reach. "Look at the softshell, Dirk. Probably full of fairy tales and love poems."

"I'm not a softshell," Pryce said, lunging for the book.

But Dirk was quicker. He grabbed it from Gordan and began tearing pages out and tossing them into the air. "Oops. Looks like your precious book is falling apart."

Pryce felt something snap inside him. "You ignorant piece of shark bait!" he spat at Dirk. "That book's worth more than your entire future!"

The words had barely left his mouth when Gordan's fist connected with his jaw. Pryce staggered back, stars exploding in his vision. He swung wildly, but Gordan easily dodged the clumsy punch.

"Aw, look at the little fighter," Gordan taunted. "Maybe if you spent less time with your nose in a book, you'd know how to throw a proper punch."

Before Pryce could respond, another blow caught him square in the face. He hit the ground hard, too dazed to move. Through blurry eyes, he watched Gordan and Dirk amble away, their laughter echoing in his ringing ears.

A shadow fell over him, and a concerned voice cut through the haze. "By the tides, lad, are you alright?"

Pryce blinked, focusing on the face of a middle-aged man kneeling beside him. The stranger offered a handkerchief, which Pryce gratefully accepted, dabbing at the blood trickling from his nose.

"I'm fine," Pryce said, wincing as he sat up.

The man's eyes narrowed. "Those boys have been trouble for years. Want me to have a word with your father about this?"

"No." Pryce said quickly. The last thing he needed was for his dad to think he couldn't handle himself. "Really, I'm okay. Thank you for the hankie."

The man looked skeptical but nodded. "Keep it, lad. You might need it again."

As the stranger walked away, Pryce hauled himself to his feet, his body aching and his pride stinging worse than his split lip. He gathered what remained of his book, shoving the tattered pages into his pocket before continuing his journey to the Rusty Anchor Inn.

The smell hit him first—a pungent smell of cheap perfume, and spilled ale. Pryce had never set foot in a place like this before, and he felt woefully out of place among the rough-looking patrons and scantily clad serving girls.

Swallowing his nervousness, he approached the counter. The man behind it eyed him suspiciously. "You look like you've been through the wringer, boy. What happened to your face?"

Pryce ignored the question. "My name's Pryce and I'm looking for Gavin Brooks."

"Mr. Brooks doesn't see anyone without an appointment, and I don't see your name on the list, kid."

"Please. It's important. Can you at least tell me which room he's in?"

The man snorted. "He's in 2B, but you're not going up there. Mr. Brooks doesn't do business with children. Come back in a few years."

Pryce felt his frustration mounting. "Can't you just ask him if he'll see me?"

"Listen, boy, I told you to leave. Now scram before I—"

"Is there a problem here?" A sultry voice cut through the tension. Pryce turned to see a young woman in a dress that left little to the imagination. She smiled at him, her eyes kind despite her rough appearance. "You looking for someone, honey?"

Pryce nodded. "Gavin Brooks. I need to speak with him urgently."

The woman's smile widened. "Gavin? I can take you to him."

The man behind the counter sputtered. "Now see here, Rosie, Mr. Brooks—"

"Oh, hush," Rosie waved him off. "Follow me, sweetie. I'll get you sorted."

As they climbed the narrow staircase, Rosie chatted amiably. "So, what's a nice boy like you doing looking for old Gavin, hm? You're not in any trouble, are you?"

Pryce shook his head. "No, ma'am. I just have a business proposition for him."

"I see," Rosie said, but she didn't press further. They reached a door marked 2B, and she rapped her knuckles against it. "Gavin? You've got a visitor."

A muffled voice called from inside. "Come in."

Rosie pushed the door open and ushered Pryce inside. "This young man says he has some important business to discuss with you."

Gavin Brooks was a well-dressed man in his forties, with sharp eyes that took in Pryce's disheveled appearance. "Looks like you've had quite the day, lad. What happened to your face?"

Pryce straightened his spine. "Just a misunderstanding, sir. Nothing important. I'm here because I have a business proposition for you."

Gavin gestured to an armchair. "Is that so? Well, have a seat then. Can I offer you a drink?"

The casual offer of alcohol caught Pryce off guard. "Uh, no thank you, sir."

Gavin poured himself a glass of amber liquid and settled into the chair opposite Pryce. "So, what's this offer of yours?"

Pryce took a deep breath. "Sir, you've heard about the dragon that fell from the sky, right?"

Gavin nodded, his interest clearly piqued. "Of course. Quite the tale."

"Well," Pryce continued, his words tumbling out in a rush, "I've . . . I've bonded with it. The dragon, I mean. And I want to train it, but I need funds to rebuild the old barracks on the Island of Emberfall, and to get proper equipment like a saddle and reins."

Gavin's eyes widened, then narrowed thoughtfully. "That's quite the ambitious plan, young man. But how exactly do you intend to repay such a loan?"

Pryce leaned forward. "I could offer dragon rides! People would pay good money for that, wouldn't they?"

To Pryce's dismay, Gavin burst out laughing. "Dragon rides? My boy, the people of Crystal Shores are terrified of dragons. I doubt you'd find many takers. Besides, you haven't even trained this dragon yet, have you? Do you have any experience with dragon training?"

Pryce's heart sank. "Well, no, but I'm sure I can train Stormwing. I've read all about it."

Gavin's expression softened slightly. "Listen, lad. I admire your spirit, but this is far too risky an investment for me." He drained his glass and set it aside. "I'm sorry, but I can't help you. Come back when you've actually trained that dragon, and maybe we can talk business then."

Pryce felt the weight of disappointment settle in his chest. He'd been so sure this would work. As he stood to leave, he realized he was back at square one, with a dragon to care for and no means to do so.

8. Scales and Sapphires

Pryce stood to leave. As he reached for the doorknob, a sudden thought struck him. He turned back to Gavin.

"Mr. Brooks, I forgot to mention something important," Pryce said. "Stormwing could protect Crystal Shores from marauders. Surely that's worth a lot, right?"

Gavin leaned back in his chair. "Protection, you say? Well, that certainly would be valuable. But Crystal Shores hasn't been invaded in a long time."

Pryce noticed the fine quality of Gavin's clothes, and the sparkle of crystal decanters on the side table. This was a man who appreciated the finer things in life. And if Pryce wasn't mistaken, he had quite an ego to match.

Taking a chance, Pryce pressed on. "It could happen, though. And if it does, you'd be famous for protecting Crystal Shores and its people. Imagine the recognition, the gratitude . . ."

He watched as Gavin drummed his fingers on the armrest, clearly mulling it over. After a moment that felt like an eternity to Pryce, Gavin nodded.

"You make an interesting point, young man," Gavin said. "Very well. I'll give you a small loan to get started. But mind you, I expect to see results."

Relieved, Pryce scrawled his signature on the loan contract. With a pocket full of coin, he left the Rusty Anchor Inn, his spirits soaring. He decided to wait until he got back to the barracks before buying anything, wanting to assess how best to spend the precious funds.

As Pryce made his way home, a glint in a store window caught his eye. He paused, admiring a beautiful jewelry box on display. He made a mental note to buy it for his mother when he had more money. It would be the perfect way to thank her for everything she'd done for him.

The familiar scent of home greeted Pryce as he pushed open the front door. His family was just finishing their meal, and the sight of them gathered around the table made him smile.

"Pryce!" Ellie called out. "Get yourself a plate of food before I put it away. You look famished."

Pryce filled his plate to the brim. As he sat down, he felt his family's concerned gazes.

"What happened to your face, son?" Tyler asked. "You look like you've gone ten rounds with a Dryad."

Pryce shrugged, trying to downplay the incident. "It's no big deal. Just had a bit of a . . . disagreement with Gordan and Dirk."

Ellie sat a dish on the counter harder than expected. "Oh, Pryce. You need to stay away from those boys."

"Believe me, Mom, I tried," Pryce sighed, shoveling a forkful of food into his mouth.

Faye let out a laugh. "Bet you gave as good as you got, right?"

Tyler cleared his throat, clearly eager to change the subject. "So, did you manage to meet with Gavin Brooks?"

Pryce nodded, swallowing a mouthful of stew. "I did. He gave me a small loan to get started."

His father's expression grew serious. "Tread carefully, son. Borrowed money has a way of becoming a noose if you're not mindful."

"I'll be able to repay it. I've got it all planned out," Pryce said, then added, "Once I'm done eating, I'm heading back to the island. Mind if I borrow the skiff?"

"It's yours to use, but for the love of the old gods, be careful out there."

Suddenly, Faye's eyes lit up. "Oh! We have a surprise for you, Pryce!" She bolted from the room, returning moments later with a package wrapped in rough cloth.

Ellie smiled warmly at her son. "Your birthday's just around the corner. Since you'll be away on the island, we thought we'd give you your gift a bit early." Her voice softened. "You're of age now, nearly a full-grown Shorling. You're free to chart your own course, but please, promise me you'll stay safe."

Pryce unwrapped the gift, revealing a beautifully crafted quiver filled with arrows. ""This is . . . Incredible." He ran his fingers over the smooth leather.

"Your bow's still in good shape," Ellie said, "so we thought a new quiver and arrows would serve you well."

Tyler nodded approvingly. "Take it to the island with you. Keep honing your skills."

Faye leaned in. "Did you notice the blue sapphire sewn into it? It's not just for show. Mom told me it's Royal Sapphire—rarer than a dragon's tooth and twice as valuable. They say it holds ancient magic, giving its bearer wisdom beyond their years. And get this—it's a symbol of royalty. Whoever has it is said to have the blessing of the old kings."

Pryce looked at his mom. "Are you sure you want me to have this? Especially since it was a gift from Pip, that Quibnocket you told me about?"

"I'm sure. It might come in handy for you some-day." She reached for the necklace around her neck and unclasped it. Pryce had seen her wear countless times. It was a dragon pendant with a glass bubble filled with a red, sometimes glowing fluid.

"This pendant," Ellie said, holding it out to Pryce, "is a connection to our family's seafaring heritage and the mystical forces that have shaped our lives. I want you to have it."

Pryce took the pendant. "I remember you telling me about this. That fluid is our family's blood mixed with dragon blood, isn't it? Why are you giving it to me?"

"It is," Ellie said. "Keep it for now, and later, you can pass it on to Faye."

A half-forgotten memory stirred in Pryce's mind. "What about that compass you used to talk about? The Seafarer's Sigil?"

"My, my, brother dear. Aren't we getting a bit greedy? First the pendant, now the compass. What's next, Mom's wedding ring?" Faye teased.

Pryce felt his cheeks flush. "That's not what I meant. I just thought . . . well, with Stormwing and all . . ."

"Okay, you two," Ellie said. "The compass was lost in a river, in a cave in the Thornveil Wilds. It had the same Draconic essence as this pendant, and it could be used to find it, but . . . I never went back to that forbidden place again—and neither should you."

Pryce thanked his family for their support. The next hour passed in a blur of stories and laughter. As the conversation wound down, Pryce began packing his belongings, preparing for his journey back to the island.

His family gathered around him.

"Are you absolutely sure about this, Pryce?" Ellie asked. "Raising a dangerous dragon . . . it's not like training a hunting hound."

"Stormwing isn't dangerous, Mom. He's gentle, I promise. And I won't be alone—Finnegan and Kai will be there to help."

Despite his reassurances, Ellie nervously adjusted his collar and smoothed non-existent wrinkles from his shirt. Then she bustled around the kitchen, adding crusty bread and other provisions to his already bulging pack. "If there's even a hint of trouble, you come straight home, you hear me?"

With his bow across his back, the new quiver at his hip, and his pack full of supplies, Pryce set off through town toward the docks. As he approached Finnegan's cottage, the old man stepped outside, as if sensing Pryce's approach.

"Off to tame that beast of yours, are you?" Finnegan called out.

Pryce nodded, walking up to the weathered porch. "That's the plan. Say, Finnegan, I've been wondering—do young dragons hunt for themselves, or am I going to need to buy out half the fish market?"

Finnegan chuckled. "That dragon's wing isn't broken, lad. Stormwing can get all the fish it needs from Lake Dragontide. And since it's a freshwater lake, there's plenty to drink too." He fixed Pryce with a stern look. "Don't let that scaly devil take advantage of you. It's more than capable of fending for itself."

Pryce laughed. "No worries. Stormwing won't be pulling the wool over my eyes."

"Good lad. I'll drop by when I can to lend a hand, but if that dragon gives you any real trouble, you lock it up tight and hightail it back to the mainland, you hear?"

"I will, but I know there won't be any problems with Stormwing."

"I'm sure you're right, lad." He paused, then added with a wink, "Just remember, a calm sea never made a skilled sailor. It's the storms that teach us how to navigate."

With a grateful nod, Pryce climbed into his father's skiff. As he set out over Lake Dragontide, toward the Island of Emberfall, he felt the pendant against his chest and the quiver at his side, praying to whatever gods might be listening that he was making the right choice.

9. A Family of Misfits

As twilight approached, Pryce reached the shores of Emberfall Island. The soft splashing of water against his small boat created a calming cadence, causing him to question the wisdom of his choice to be alone on an island, become a dragon trainer, and accumulate debt.

He tied the boat securely to the weathered dock, the rough rope biting into his palms. "Ouch," he said before grabbing his bag of belongings, quiver, and bow. Then he made his way toward the barracks as the wooden planks creaked beneath his feet.

As Pryce walked, he heard unfamiliar sounds—rustling in the undergrowth, distant screeches, and the faint whistle of wind through abandoned buildings. It was a far cry from the familiar bustle of Crystal Shores. More than once he found himself whirling around, certain he'd seen something move in the corner of his eye.

Pryce clutched his bow tighter. "Get a grip, Harper-Green," he said to himself. "It's just an old outpost, not some haunted island."

Inside the barracks, Pryce fumbled with a flint to light a fire in the fireplace. "Come on, you piece of junk," he said, striking the flint again and again. Finally, a small spark caught, and he coaxed it into a flame. Warmth spread through the room as the fire grew, casting an orange glow across the walls.

Pryce set his belongings on the table where they had shared breakfast earlier, noticing a few crumbs and a forgotten spoon still lying about. He removed the ripped book from his pocket and placed it on the table. "Can't let those numbskulls win," he said, gently smoothing out a crumpled page.

Clutching a flickering torch, Pryce stepped outside to check on Stormwing's condition. As twilight descended, the air grew chilly, prompting him to tug his coat closer.

Pryce opened the cell door wide, not intending to close it. "Hey there, girl. Ready to be set free?"

Stormwing's eyes glowed in the torchlight. She pressed her snout against his body. "You can use this as your bed if you want, but you're free to roam."

Stormwing unfurled her wing, the movement smooth. Pryce couldn't help but chuckle, shaking his head in amusement. "Feeling better already, huh?" He reached out to stroke her scales. "You had me worried for nothing, you know that?"

As Pryce made his way back to the barracks, Stormwing followed. Her footsteps shook the ground slightly, and Pryce found himself marveling at her sheer size. It was easy to forget sometimes, just how powerful she really was. At the barrack's entrance, the dragon attempted to squeeze through, but her bulk prevented her from entering.

"Sorry, girl. You're a bit too big for indoors. Don't worry, though. I'll be right inside if you need me." He felt a pang of guilt at leaving her outside, but what choice did he have?

Stormwing let out a soft rumble, almost like a purr, and settled down just outside the door.

A commotion nearby caught Pryce's attention. The mottled gray cat he'd seen earlier had cornered something, its prey emitting high-pitched screeches. The cat's tail swished back and forth, its eyes fixed intently on its quarry.

"Hey now, leave that alone." Pryce shooed the cat away.

To his surprise, the cat's victim was a Tidewing gull, its feathers ruffled. The bird's plumage was a mix of soft grays and whites, with distinctive black markings on its wingtips. Around its leg was a small brass cylinder—a message capsule.

"Well, aren't you a sorry sight." Pryce carefully scooped up the bird. "Easy there, little fella. I'm not going to hurt you."

Pryce carried the cat and bird into the barracks. He set the gull on the table and turned his attention to the message capsule. He unlatched it, pulling out a slip of paper.

The message was old, the ink faded. It read: "Supplies running low. Send reinforcements. Marauders closing in."

"That's a really old message," Pryce said, setting the paper aside. He glanced nervously at the windows, half-expecting to see marauders peering in.

He rummaged through his meager supplies, tearing off a chunk of bread for the cat. "Here you go . . . Ash. That's what I'll call you." The name seemed fitting for the gray feline. The cat purred, rubbing against Pryce's leg before digging into the bread.

He pondered what to feed the seabird, eventually deciding to provide it with some water in a flat container. "I'll see about catching you some fish tomorrow . . . though I imagine you're quite capable of finding your own meals." Pryce added fishing to his expanding roster of chores, realizing it would benefit him as much as his newfound animal companions.

Glancing out the window, Pryce saw Stormwing drinking by the water's edge. The sight of her moving freely, without pain, brought a smile to his face. "At least she's settling in nicely."

The place was a mess—cobwebs in corners, dust on every surface, and who knew what kind of repairs the roof might need. "How am I going to make this work?" he wondered aloud, stoking the fire. "I'm no carpenter, that's for sure." Now, he wished he'd paid more attention when his father had tried to teach him basic repairs.

In the kitchen, Pryce discovered Declan had left behind some salt and dried herbs. "Thank you, Declan." A grin spread across his face. "Now I can make my awful cooking taste somewhat better."

Settling at the table, Pryce spread out the torn pages of his book as the fire crackled in the background. For a moment, it almost felt cozy. Ash eyed the bird with predatory interest, while the gull perched on the back of a chair.

"Ash, leave the bird alone. I mean it. No midnight snacks." He wondered if he'd have to separate them for the night.

Pryce watched as Ash sauntered across the room, tail held high, clearly at ease in the surroundings. The Tidewing gull, too, seemed unbothered by its new environment, preening its feathers as if it had always belonged there.

"You two seem right at home. The Oceanriders must've taken care of you, huh? But why'd they leave you behind?" Pryce asked, not expecting an answer from his furry and feathered companions.

"Well, whatever the reason," he said, "looks like you're stuck with me now. Hope you don't mind slumming it with a novice dragon trainer and his oversized lizard."

Pryce watched the bird flap its wings. I should give you a name . . . Stormy? No, too close to Stormwing. How about . . . Skye? Yeah, Skye works." The bird cocked its head at the sound of its new name, and Pryce grinned. "You like that, Skye? It suits you, I think." Naming the animals made them feel more like family than strays.

Pulling out a small notebook and a stub of charcoal, Pryce began listing his immediate needs and plans for the barracks. As he wrote, he knew his new housemates could largely fend for themselves. It was one less worry on his growing list.

"Look at us," he said to Ash and Skye. "A regular little family already. Who would've thought?"

Exhaustion setting in, Pryce moved his cot near the fire. As he lay down, Ash curled up beside him, the cat's warmth a small comfort. Skye settled nearby, its feathers rustling softly. Through the open window, he could hear Stormwing's heavy footsteps returning to her cell. It was beginning to feel like a new normal.

Deep in sleep, a noise jolted Pryce awake. He sat up, but saw nothing. Ash slept peacefully beside him, and the fire had died down to embers.

"Must've been a dream," he said, settling back down.

When morning light filtered through the windows, Pryce awoke to find Ash eyeing Skye hungrily. The cat's tail twitched back and forth, its gaze fixed on the bird. It was a reminder that despite their seeming friendship, nature had its own rules.

"Ash, no." Pryce scooped up the cat. "Skye's not breakfast. We talked about this, remember?" He set the cat down on the other side of the room, hoping the distance would be enough.

As he stretched, working out the kinks from sleeping on the hard cot, something on the table caught his eye. The torn pages of his book, which he'd left scattered, were now neatly stacked. Pryce froze.

"Did I do that in my sleep?" Pryce looked at Ash and Skye, but neither seemed bothered. "You two didn't see anything, did you?"

Shaking off his unease, Pryce made his way to the door. "From now on, this door gets locked at night. No more mysterious tidying while we sleep. Got it?" Ash meowed in response, while Skye merely ruffled its feathers. Pryce wished he could be as nonchalant as they were about the whole situation.

With that, Pryce stepped out into the morning light, Ash and Skye shooting out behind him. "Slow down, you two."

Pryce found himself glancing over his shoulder as he made his way towards Stormwing's cell, the dragon's pitiful lair.

10. A Cloak in the Shadows

Stormwing emerged from his cell, stretching his wings to their full span and shaking his head vigorously, sending a comical spray of morning dew and dragon drool splattering in all directions. The dragon's eyes fixed on Pryce, and he let out a low, rumbling purr that vibrated through the ground.

Stormwing padded toward him, his claws leaving slight indentations in the damp earth. As he approached, the dragon lowered his head and nuzzled Pryce's chest, nearly knocking him off balance.

Pryce laughed, the sound echoing across the quiet compound. "Easy there, big guy—I mean girl," he said, running his hand along Stormwing's neck. "You're not a little thing."

The dragon huffed, a puff of warm air ruffling Pryce's hair. Pryce grinned, scratching under Stormwing's chin. "Ready for some exploring, Storm? Who knows what we might find out here."

Stormwing's tail swished in response, and Pryce could feel the dragon's excitement. He set off toward the nearest outbuilding as Ash and Skye rushed past him. Skye chirped playfully as she fluttered around Ash, who was batting at her with his paw.

Pryce looked into the first structure, his eyes adjusting to the dim interior. Scattered about were ancient implements and discarded odds and ends. He realized some of these tools might prove useful down the line. As he scanned the cluttered space, peculiar instruments caught his attention. Their purpose eluded him. Could they have been crafted for dragon-related tasks? The possibility intrigued him as he continued his exploration.

As he approached the second structure, a large, tall shed, Pryce noticed Skye and Ash still trailing behind him. The gull hopped along, occasionally taking short flights, while the cat slinked through the tall grass. Pryce found himself chuckling at the comical sight of Stormwing's massive feet delicately navigating around the much smaller creatures, like a clumsy giant trying not to squash a village of tiny folk.

Pryce yanked on the corroded door handle, straining until it at last yielded with a resounding groan. Particles of dust danced in the beam of sunlight that penetrated the darkness within. He coughed, waving his palm to disperse the haze.

"Well, would you look at that."

Hanging from the ceiling beams, an old dragon saddle grabbed Pryce's attention, its leather worn and discolored but surprisingly whole. Foot supports swung from its edges, and a wide belly band hung underneath. Next to the saddle, a set of straps and bridles, all hooked onto sturdy iron pegs. Close by, he noticed a ragged saddle blanket, now thin and grimy. Pryce observed how the high-up storage would let a rider easily outfit a dragon without too much effort. The arrangement seemed to him both clever and oddly touching, a remnant of a time when Shorlings and dragons soared through the air together.

"This is perfect. With a little work, I might be able to use this for you," Pryce shouted through the door to Stormwing.

As Pryce examined his find, a commotion outside caught his attention. He stepped out of the shed to see Skye perched on a fence post, dropping small pebbles onto Ash's head. The cat hissed in annoyance, swatting at the air.

Pryce chuckled as he watched Skye repeat the action, clearly enjoying the game. Ash's tail puffed up in irritation, and he let out a low growl.

"So that's why you two don't get along," Pryce said, shaking his head. "Skye, leave Ash alone. He's not your personal target practice."

The gull cocked its head, looking almost innocent, before dropping another pebble. This time, Ash darted away, seeking refuge under a nearby wheelbarrow.

Pryce's laughter was interrupted by the sound of approaching footsteps. He turned to see Old Man Finnegan making his way up the path, leaning heavily on his gnarled walking stick.

"Morning, lad," Finnegan called out. "I see you've been exploring."

Pryce had not noticed Finnegan dock with his fishing boat.

Pryce nodded, pointing at the saddle. "I think it might come in handy for Stormwing."

"Ah, that's a good find. But you'll need to fix it up before it's of any use." He gestured towards the barracks. "Come on, I've brought some supplies that might help with that book of yours, too."

"How did you know about Legends of Dragontide being torn apart?"

"Ah, lad, word has a way of traveling in these parts."

Inside, Finnegan produced a small pot of glue and a needle and thread from his satchel. Pryce spread out the torn pages of his book on the table, carefully aligning the edges.

As they worked to repair the book, Finnegan peered at the contents. "Interesting reading material you've got there, lad. This section here is 'How to Train Your Dragon,' eh?"

Pryce nodded, his fingers sticky with glue. "It's got all sorts of information. The early steps seem simple enough—establishing trust, basic commands, that sort of thing. But it gets pretty complicated when it comes to battle training."

"Aye, dragons aren't simple beasts. You've got to start slow, build a bond. Respect goes both ways with dragons." He paused, studying Pryce's face for a moment before adding, "Seems to me you've already got that part figured out, lad."

"You're right about Stormwing and me. We've developed a real connection. It's like we understand each other without words sometimes."

Finnegan put the lid back on the glue. "Best we start trainin' that dragon of yours before it develops some unsavory habits. You don't want Stormwing decidin' your bedroom's the perfect spot for a midday nap, or worse, usin' your boat as a chew toy."

Pryce couldn't help but chuckle at the mental image. "I hadn't even thought about that. Are there really dragons that do those things?"

"Oh, aye. Had a mate once whose dragon thought the village well was its personal bathtub. Took weeks to get the scales out." He paused, stroking his salt-and-pepper beard. "Dragons can be domesticated, to a degree, but they've got minds of their own. Like tryin' to reason with the sea itself sometimes."

Finnegan groaned as he stood. "Oh, speaking of which, I brought along a little somethin' that might help. Got me a barrel of silver trout in the boat—a favorite for storm dragons, if I recall correctly."

"Really? That's perfect! I read that storm dragons love silver trout." He reached into his pocket and fished out a Thornveil piece. "I want to pay you for the fish. This is some of the coin I got from Gavin."

Finnegan waved him off. "Keep your money, lad. This time it's on me."

Pryce thanked the old sailor. Finnegan's kindness touched him deeply, and he made a mental note to find a way to repay the old seaman's generosity someday.

Finnegan jerked his thumb toward the docks. "If you fetch that barrel from my boat, we can get started on some basic trainin'. This shoreline here'll do just fine for now."

Pryce squinted as he and Finnegan emerged into the bright morning sunlight. Stormwing came into view as they walked, and suddenly Ash zipped between their legs. Pryce heard Skye's familiar squawk overhead as the bird dove close to the cat, nearly grazing its ears.

Finnegan shook his head. "Ah, to see a cat and bird at odds. Reminds me of an old saying: 'When the gull chases the mouser, the fish swim free.'"

Pryce raised an eyebrow. "I'm not sure that's actually a saying."

"It is now, lad."

Eager to begin, Pryce grabbed the old wheelbarrow that Ash had hidden under earlier and jogged down to the dock where Finnegan's boat gently bobbed in the water. He stepped onto the deck, spotting the barrel near the stern. It was heavier than he expected, and he grunted with effort as he lifted it out and onto the rickety contraption.

"Need a hand there, lad?" Finnegan called out, amusement clear in his voice.

"No, no, I've got it," Pryce said, his voice strained as he awkwardly shuffled back down the dock, hoping the wobbly wheel would not give out. The pungent smell of fresh fish wafted up from the barrel, making his nose wrinkle.

Finnegan nodded approvingly as Pryce set the barrel down on the pebbly shore. "Right then," he said, rubbing his hands together. "Let's see what that dragon of yours can do."

Stormwing approached, his nostrils flaring as he caught the scent of fresh fish. Pryce reached into the bucket he'd brought, extracting a plump silver trout.

"Alright, girl," Pryce said. "Let's see what you can do."

He held the fish out, remembering the book's advice about clear commands. "Stormwing, come."

The dragon tilted her head, regarding Pryce with an almost amused expression. She took a single step forward, then stopped.

"Oh, so that's how it's gonna be, huh? Come on, you know you want this tasty fish."

Stormwing's nostrils flared, and she inched closer, her long neck stretching out. Quick as lightning, she snatched the fish from Pryce's hand, tossing it into the air and catching it in her mouth with a satisfying crunch.

"Hey!" Pryce laughed, wiping his now-slimy hand on his trousers. "I didn't say 'eat' yet!"

Finnegan leaned against the fence. "Looks like you've got yourself a clever one there, lad. Might want to work on your timing."

Pryce nodded, reaching for another fish. "Alright, Stormwing. Let's try this again. Come . . . and stay."

This time, the dragon moved forward, her eyes locked on the prize. She stopped just short of Pryce, her breath warm on his face as she waited expectantly.

"Good girl." He tossed her the fish, which she caught easily. "See? We're getting somewhere already."

As Stormwing munched contentedly, Pryce turned to Finnegan. "The book mentioned flight training, but I guess that's a ways off, huh?"

The old man spat and wiped his mouth with the back of his hand, still leaning against the fence. "Aye, but don't you worry. With a bond like yours, you'll be soaring through the clouds before you know it. I reckon that beast can read your mind."

Pryce imagined himself and Stormwing gliding over Lake Dragontide, free as the wind itself. But for now, he had a stubborn, fish-loving dragon to train—and he couldn't have been happier about it.

Pryce continued the training throughout the day. Stormwing's progress was slow but steady, and Pryce found himself grinning every time the dragon responded correctly to a command.

Finnegan wandered back and forth along the shoreline, alternating between offering gruff advice and tinkering with an old fishing net. "Remember, lad, dragons are proud creatures. You've got to earn their respect, not demand it."

As the afternoon wore on, Finnegan busied himself with other tasks—repairing a loose plank on his boat, sharpening a collection of rusty hooks, and at one point, dozing off against a sun-warmed boulder. But his eyes always seemed to find their way back to Pryce and Stormwing.

"You're doing well, boy. Finnegan hobbled over, leaning heavily on his walking stick. "But remember, this is just the beginning. A dragon's not some pet you can train in a day."

Pryce wiped sweat from his brow. "I know. But we're making progress, right?"

Finnegan's wrinkled face cracked into a rare smile. "Aye, that you are. Now," he continued, glancing at the sun's position, "it's well past noonbell. That dragon of yours might have a bottomless pit for a stomach, but I'm famished. We'd best see to feeding ourselves."

Pryce felt a prickle on the back of his neck, as if someone was watching. He turned, scanning the treeline at the edge of the clearing.

There, partially hidden by the forest's shadows, stood a figure. A flowing cloak of midnight blue blended seamlessly with the darkness. It was a woman, tall and commanding, with long dark hair. Even from afar, her eyes seemed to bore right through Pryce.

The old man's gaze darted between Pryce and the treeline. "Pryce, we need to get inside. Now."

"Who is she?"

Finnegan's calloused hand clamped onto Pryce's forearm, yanking him toward the barracks with surprising strength. "That's Nymeria, queen of the Dragonkin Marauders. Vicious lot, those marauders—they'd sooner gut you than look at you."

Pryce stumbled as Finnegan dragged him along. "Dragonkin? I've heard mom and dad tell stories about them, but I thought they were creatures that existed only in far-off lands, beyond the edges of known maps."

"Aye, most folks do. Makes it easier to sleep at night. But they're as real as you and me, lad. And twice as dangerous."

Despite the old man's urgency, Pryce couldn't help but glance back. The spot where Nymeria had stood was empty, the shadows undisturbed as if she'd never been there.

"She's gone," Pryce said.

Finnegan grunted, maintaining his pace. "Don't let that fool you. Nymeria's like smoke—here one moment, gone the next. But make no mistake, boy. If she was watching us, she had a reason."

11. Crushed Wildflowers and Angels

Pryce followed Finnegan into the barracks. He kept glancing out the window, searching the treeline for any sign of movement, but Nymeria was not there.

"Stop your fretting and help me with these potatoes," Finnegan grumbled, pulling supplies from his pack, setting them on the crude wooden table.

Pryce joined him. "I thought you said we were having fish stew."

"Aye, and what's fish stew without potatoes? Unless you prefer eating like that dragon of yours—raw fish and nothing else. Though I suppose Stormwing has the right idea, skipping the cooking altogether."

"At least I know how to properly scale a fish," Pryce teased, watching Finnegan hack away at a trout with more enthusiasm than skill. "You're butchering it worse than a drunken sailor."

"Been scaling fish since before your father was born, you cheeky pup." Finnegan brandished his knife playfully. "Now, are you going to help or just stand there critiquing my technique like some fancy chef from the mainland?"

They worked side by side, Pryce chopping vegetables while Finnegan prepared the fish. The old man hummed an off-key sailing tune, occasionally breaking into snippets of bawdy verses that made Pryce's ears turn red.

"That's not how Mom taught me to cut onions," Pryce said, watching Finnegan's rough handling of the vegetables. The old man's technique seemed designed to create maximum chaos on the cutting board.

"And I suppose your mother's way doesn't end with tears streaming down your face?" Finnegan wiped his eyes with his sleeve, leaving a smudge of fish scales on his cheek. "Sometimes the old ways are the best ways, boy. Your mother learned to cook in a proper kitchen—I learned on the deck of a ship in the middle of a storm."

The stew came together quickly, filling the barracks with a smell that made Pryce's stomach growl. When they finally sat down to eat, the late afternoon light slanted through the windows.

"So," Pryce said between spoonfuls of the stew, "tell me about the Dragonkin."

Finnegan's expression darkened. "Some things are better left in shadow, lad. But since you've seen her . . ." He launched into tales of the Dragonkin's raids along the coast, their fearsome reputation, and their mysterious origins. His voice grew hushed as he described their ability to command dragons through ancient magic.

As night fell, Pryce let Ash and Skye inside. The cat immediately claimed a spot by the fire, stretching out like a furry king on his throne, while Skye settled onto a wooden stool, smoothing her ruffled plumage. Pryce fed them both—dried fish for Ash and some breadcrumbs for Skye.

"Your menagerie's growing," Finnegan said, helping Pryce set up a second cot near the fire. "Next thing you know, you'll be running a proper circus. Maybe we should charge admission."

They secured the barracks for the night, checking the locks twice before settling down to sleep. The fire crackled softly, and outside, Pryce could hear Stormwing's gentle breathing, punctuated by occasional snorts when she chased something in her dreams.

***

The next morning, Lune, dawned clear and bright. Finnegan insisted they observe the day of worship properly.

"Up with you, lad. We've got obligations to attend to," Finnegan said, already dressed in his cleanest shirt—which bore the marks of countless mends and patches.

Pryce groaned and rolled over, pulling his blanket tighter. "It's barely light out." Through bleary eyes, he watched Ash stretch lazily by the dying embers of last night's fire, clearly sharing his sentiment about the early hour.

"The sun waits for no man, and neither do the gods," Finnegan yanked Pryce's blanket away. "Your mother would string me up by my toes if she knew I'd let you sleep through morning prayers."

They made their way through the misty morning, boots squeaking against dew-laden grass. They walked past the sleeping dragon—Stormwing's massive bulk rose and fell with gentle snores. Skye followed them, gliding silently overhead.

"The Shorlings have always honored the old ways," Finnegan said, pausing to catch his breath at a moss-covered boulder. "It's what keeps us connected to the land and sea. Your ancestors understood that better than most—especially your mother's people."

The clearing overlooked the bay, where waves lapped against worn stones. Finnegan raised his arms. "Great spirits of tide and tempest. We stand before you as our ancestors did, humble before your might."

Pryce found himself remembering standing between his parents during ceremonies back home, his mother's voice mixing with his father's deeper tones.

"We thank thee for the bounty of sea and shore," Finnegan continued, "For the fish that fill our nets and the winds that fill our sails. For the dragons who share our skies and the wisdom of ages past . . ."

When the final prayer faded, Pryce turned to study the old man with new eyes. "I never knew you were so . . . religious."

"Don't look so shocked, boy. I'm not particularly religious, mind you, but there's value in remembering where we come from. Besides, your mother would sail straight across the bay if she heard you'd missed a single ceremony."

"She did always say missing prayers would bring bad luck."

"Smart woman. Though between you and me, I suspect she was more worried about keeping you lot in line than divine retribution. Nothing like a healthy fear of the gods—and your elders—to keep young ones from too much mischief."

They made their way back to the barracks, the morning sun now fully risen. Stormwing had awakened and was watching them, steam rising from her nostrils in the cool morning air.

"Right then," Finnegan said, clapping his hands together. "Now that we've properly honored the old ways, what say we honor our stomachs? I've got some salt pork that needs eating."

After breakfast, Pryce couldn't contain his excitement any longer. "Will you show me how to saddle Stormwing?"

"Aye, but mind you—no riding until you're both ready. Dragon riding isn't like hopping on a horse. One wrong move and you'll both end up in the lake . . . or worse."

They headed to the building where they'd found the saddle. Finnegan demonstrated the pulley system that raised and lowered it, the leather creaking like an old ship's rigging as Pryce practiced the motion.

"The leather's sound," Finnegan said, "but these spots here and here need mending." He pointed out worn areas in the reins and bridle. "If these snap mid-flight, you'll have no way to guide her. Might as well try to steer a hurricane."

Outside, Stormwing watched them through the wide doors, occasionally pawing at the ground or snapping playfully at passing insects.

Ash suddenly leaped onto the saddle, assuming a regal pose that made them both laugh.

"Look at that," Finnegan chuckled. "Seems your cat fancies himself a dragon rider, too. Better watch out—he might steal your glory."

"Maybe I could make him a carrier. Something secure enough for flying."

After Finnegan left, Pryce spent hours cleaning the saddle and shaking out the thick pad that would protect Stormwing's back. He fashioned a simple carrier for Ash from an old leather bag, testing it to ensure the cat would be safe. To his surprise, Ash seemed to enjoy being in it, purring as Pryce made adjustments.

Looking at the finished work, Pryce knew he should wait as Finnegan had advised. But the saddle seemed sturdy enough, and Stormwing had been so cooperative lately.

He raised the saddle and called Stormwing inside. The dragon entered cautiously, standing perfectly still beneath the hanging tack. It took longer than Pryce expected to secure everything properly, but finally, the saddle was in place, the bridle adjusted, and the reins ready.

Pryce placed Ash in his newly made pouch. Climbing the ladder, Pryce settled into the saddle. He instructed Stormwing to exit the building. The saddle shifted slightly—too loose, he realized with a bit of worry—but he pressed on anyway.

Instead of taking flight, Stormwing walked toward the water's edge.

"Don't be afraid. I know it's your first time flying with a rider."

Stormwing pawed the sand, then broke into a run along the beach. She made a small hop, wings spread wide, but remained earthbound. Ash peered out from his carrier, whiskers twitching with interest.

"Try again." Pryce leaned forward in the saddle.

This time, Stormwing's powerful legs propelled them forward faster. Her wings beat the air, and suddenly they were airborne. For one heart-stopping moment, her claws skimmed the lake's surface, but then she pulled up, climbing higher into the sky.

"Yes!" Pryce cheered as Skye soared alongside them. The view was breathtaking—Lake Dragontide stretched out below them like polished glass.

Pryce guided Stormwing over the island, taking in the stunning landscape. A vast meadow spread out below, dotted with wildflowers. Craggy mountains rose in the distance, their peaks shrouded in mist. A clear river wound through the terrain like a silver ribbon, disappearing into a dense forest that seemed to absorb the sunlight.

Ash had settled into a comfortable position in his carrier, seemingly unfazed by their altitude.

As they circled back toward the outpost, Pryce spotted someone in the meadow—a young woman with flowing blonde hair, watching their flight. Unlike Nymeria's threatening presence, this girl seemed almost angelic. Her face tracked their movement through the sky as her long, white dress rippled in the breeze.

Pryce raised his hand in greeting, then guided Stormwing toward the meadow. The landing proved more challenging than he'd anticipated. Stormwing's back legs touched down first, but her momentum carried them forward at an alarming speed. The loose saddle slipped sideways, and Pryce felt himself sliding.

"Steady!" he called out, but Stormwing was already stumbling, her wings flailing as she tried to regain balance. Pryce clung to the saddle with one hand while trying to protect Ash's carrier with the other. The cat yowled in protest as the carrier swung wildly.

Stormwing's left wing dipped, and suddenly they were tumbling. Pryce threw himself clear just as the dragon rolled, narrowly avoiding being crushed beneath her bulk. He hit the ground hard, rolling through the flowers as Ash's carrier went flying.

Stunned, Pryce found himself lying in a bed of crushed wildflowers, staring up at the afternoon sky. Stormwing had managed to right herself and was shaking her head as if embarrassed. Ash emerged from his carrier several feet away, fur puffed up to twice its normal size but otherwise unharmed.

Then a face appeared above him, framed by the sun—a girl with features so striking that his mind wondered if he'd died in the crash. "Are you an angel?"

12. Sweet Temptation

"Are you an angel?" Pryce squinted up at the figure haloed by the sun. His head spun from the fall, crushed wildflowers releasing their sweet perfume around him.

As his vision cleared, he saw her more clearly—a young woman with flowing blonde hair that caught the sunlight like spun gold. Her white dress rippled in the breeze, adorned with intricate dragon motifs in silver thread. But what caught his breath wasn't her beauty—it was the subtle shimmer of scales along her neck and temples, catching the light like tiny opals.

"Not quite," she said. She extended a delicate hand to help him up. "Though I imagine that fall was hard enough to make you see angels."

Pryce felt a strange pull as their eyes met—hers were an impossible shade of violet. The pendant his mother had given him grew warm against his chest, and he wondered if the dragon blood that flowed in his veins recognized something kindred in this mysterious girl.

A meow broke the spell. Ash emerged from his overturned carrier, fur standing on end like a puffed-up dandelion. Nearby, Stormwing shook herself like a massive dog, looking thoroughly embarrassed by their graceless landing.

"I'm fine," Pryce said, brushing crushed petals from his clothes as he stood. "Stormwing, you alright, girl?"

The dragon huffed in response. She ducked her head, looking about as embarrassed as a massive flying reptile could manage.

Skye circled overhead, letting out what sounded suspiciously like a mocking squawk. "Nobody likes a show-off, Skye."

"Your companions are . . . interesting," the mysterious girl said, watching as Ash attempted to groom his dignity back into place. Something in her tone suggested she found the whole menagerie beneath her notice. "A dragon who can't land properly, a mangy cat, and a common seabird."

Pryce felt a flare of defensiveness. "Stormwing's still learning. We all are." He stepped closer to his dragon. "And Ash and Skye are family."

"Of course. Forgive my rudeness. Perhaps . . ." She glanced at the dilapidated barracks in the distance. "Perhaps we could continue this conversation somewhere more comfortable? It looks like you could use a rest after that landing."

Pryce hesitated because of Finnegan's warnings about strangers, but something about this girl drew him in—like a tide he couldn't resist.

"The barracks isn't much, but you're welcome to come in. First, I need to get this saddle off Stormwing—"

"Leave it," she said. "The saddle can wait. I'd love to see your home, humble as it may be."

As they walked toward the barracks, Pryce couldn't help noticing how graceful she was, her white dress somehow remaining pristine. Stormwing followed at a distance, the loose saddle creaking with each step.

Inside the barracks, Pryce felt a little awkward at the sparse furnishings and rough conditions. "I don't have much to offer," he said, gesturing to the remains of breakfast—some hard bread and cold tea. "But you're welcome to—"

"You poor thing," she interrupted, genuine sympathy in her voice. "Living out here all alone, with so little." She turned to face him fully, and Pryce found himself transfixed by those violet eyes again. "But what if I told you it didn't have to be this way?"

"What do you mean?"

She smiled. "Allow me to properly introduce myself. I am Princess Seren of the Dragonkin, and I've been watching you, Pryce Harper-Green. You have a gift—a true connection with dragons. Mother was right about you."

"Mother?" Pryce's mouth went dry. "You mean . . . Queen Nymeria?"

"Yes, Queen Nymeria is my mother. She noticed your talent immediately. The way you bonded with Stormwing . . . it's rare, even among our people."

Pryce sank into a rickety chair. Through the window, he could see Stormwing attempting to scratch an itch around the loose saddle, looking thoroughly undignified. "Your mother . . . she was watching me yesterday."

"She sees potential in you, Pryce." Seren sat gracefully on the edge of the table, closer than he expected. The subtle scales along her neck caught the afternoon light filtering through the broken windows. "And so do I. Look at you—trying to train a dragon with nothing but an old book and cast-off equipment. Imagine what you could achieve with proper guidance."

His stomach twisted with excitement and dread. "What exactly are you offering?"

"Everything you've dreamed of. We have master dragon trainers who could teach you things that aren't written in any book. Stormwing could socialize with other dragons, learn from them. And you . . ." She gestured at the bare walls of the barracks. "You wouldn't be confined to this lonely island or bound by Crystal Shores' small ambitions."

Pryce's hand went to the dragon pendant at his neck, feeling its warmth. "But my family . . ."

"Would benefit enormously." Seren's violet eyes flashed for a moment. "The Dragonkin reward loyalty generously. Think of what you could send home to them. No more empty nets for your father. No more watching your mother stretch every coin until it screams."

Looking out the window again, Pryce caught sight of Skye landing near Stormwing. The gull had grown protective of the dragon, often bringing her small fish it had caught. Even now, it was checking the saddle straps with its beak.

"I can visit them? Come back whenever I want?"

"Of course. We're offering you opportunities, not a prison. Though," she added, "I suspect once you see what we can offer, you won't want to leave."

Pryce stood, pacing the squeaking floorboards. Everything she said made sense. Too much sense. A whisper of doubt made him pause by the kitchen doorway. "I . . . need a moment. To write a note for Old Man Finnegan. He deserves that much."

"Take your time," Seren said graciously.

In the kitchen, Pryce pulled out the coin purse Gavin had given him. Quietly, he tucked most of it into a loose floorboard, keeping only a small amount in his pocket. Finnegan's warnings about the Dragonkin Marauders echoed like a distant storm warning. Trust, but not blindly.

At the table, Pryce's hand trembled as he wrote:

Dear Finnegan,

I know this will disappoint you, but I've found a way to learn proper dragon training. Princess Seren of the Dragonkin has offered to help. I promise I'll make you proud and prove everyone wrong about Stormwing. Thank you for everything.

—Pryce

He left the note where Finnegan would find it, weighted down with a chipped mug. The old man's warning about the Dragonkin haunted him, but Pryce pushed the doubt away. This was his chance—perhaps his only chance—to become something more than just another struggling Shorling.

"Ready?" Seren asked from the doorway.

Pryce nodded, gathering his few belongings, including the new quiver and bow his family had given him. The pendant his mother gave him felt heavier than usual against his chest.

Outside, Stormwing greeted him with a gentle headbutt that nearly knocked him over. "We're going on an adventure, girl," he said, scratching under her chin. "A real one this time."

Ash had settled back into his carrier, seemingly resigned to more aerial acrobatics. Skye circled overhead, letting out concerned chirps.

"She can follow if she wants," Seren said, noticing Pryce's glance at the gull. "Though we have far better messenger birds among the Dragonkin."

Pryce spent several minutes adjusting and tightening the saddle straps, then climbed onto Stormwing's back. Seren mounted behind him, her arms slipping around his waist. The scent of her hair reminded him of storm winds over the lake.

"North," she said, pointing toward the distant mountains. "Beyond the Dragonspine Reaches."

As Stormwing spread her wings, Pryce turned for one last look at the rundown barracks, his temporary home with its leaky roof and creaking floors.

"Having second thoughts?" Seren's breath was warm against his ear.

"No," Pryce said. He gripped the reins tighter. "Let's go, Stormwing."

The dragon leaped skyward, stronger and more confident than before. As they climbed higher, Skye fell into formation beside them, her wings catching the same currents that carried them north. Below, the Island of Emberfall grew smaller, taking Pryce's old life with it.

He was no longer just Pryce Harper-Green, the fisherman's son who dreamed too big. He was Pryce the Dragon Trainer, heading toward a destiny that promised power beyond his wildest dreams.

If only he could silence the tiny voice that wondered whether he was flying toward that destiny—or into a carefully laid trap.

13. The Dragon's Palace

Pryce leaned forward against Stormwing's neck, squinting at the endless expanse of Lake Dragontide stretching before them. The sun hung low on the horizon as each beat of the dragon's wings came slower than the last, her muscles trembling with exhaustion.

"How much further?" he called over his shoulder to Seren.

The princess tightened her grip around his waist as Stormwing dropped several feet before catching herself. "Not far now. Look—there, where the clouds meet the water."

Pryce followed her gesture to a dark smudge on the horizon. Stormwing let out a whimper.

"She's tired," Seren said, her breath warm against Pryce's ear. "Storm dragons are strong, but this journey tests even the hardiest of them."

"Come on, girl." Pryce patted Stormwing's neck. "Just a little further."

The dragon's wing beats grew more labored. Every few strokes, she'd dip dangerously close to the water's surface. Pryce remembered his father's stories of ships lost in Lake Dragontide's depths.

"There!" Seren pointed. "Drakemere Island!"

The smudge on the horizon had turned into a magnificent cliff face that seemed to pierce the clouds. As they drew closer, Pryce's mouth fell open. An entire palace had been carved into the rock, its windows and balconies adorned with dragon motifs. Dragon-sized openings dotted the cliff face like honeycomb.

Above them, dragons wheeled through the air—not just one or two, but dozens. Storm dragons like Stormwing, their scales flickering with contained lightning. Sleek shadow drakes that seemed to bend the light around them. Even a massive fire drake, its wings trailing ember-bright sparks.

Stormwing's head lifted at the sight of her own kind. She let out a thunderous greeting call that echoed across the water. Several storm dragons broke from their aerial dance to escort them in.

"Welcome to my home," Seren said as they approached a vast landing platform jutting from the cliff face.

Pryce's wonder at the impressive sight clashed with his apprehension as he spotted the platform's greeting party. Unlike Seren's subtle dragon-scale markings, these Dragonkin bore prominent scales across their faces and arms.

As Stormwing landed heavily on the platform, her legs trembling with exhaustion, the assembled Dragonkin dropped into deep bows. Pryce scrambled to dismount, nearly stumbling on shaky legs.

"Your pets cannot enter the palace," Seren said, eyeing Ash and Skye with barely concealed disdain. "They can stay with your dragon in her stable."

"But surely Ash could—" Pryce began.

"No pets inside," Seren cut him off. "Palace rules."

Pryce paused, wanting to protest the palace rules. Instead, he said, "Where will Stormwing's stable be?"

Seren gestured to an elaborate structure jutting from the cliff face, level with the palace grounds. "There. I've arranged for her to have one of our finest stables, close to your quarters for easy access." She turned to a nearby servant. "Take the cat and bird to the dragon's stable."

The servant stepped forward, trying to corral Ash and Skye. The cat bristled, and Skye let out an indignant squawk.

"It's okay," Pryce told them. "Go to the stable. I'll visit soon."

He watched helplessly as his pets were led away, Ash's tail dragging low and Skye flying reluctant circles above. Beside him, Stormwing collapsed onto her belly with an exhausted huff, her wings twitching from the long journey. Her breath came in heavy pants, stirring his hair with each exhale.

"Princess Seren," the gathered Dragonkin said in unison.

"Rise," Seren said, her voice carrying an authority that surprised Pryce. "This is Pryce Harper-Green of Crystal Shores, a gifted dragon trainer."

A tall figure stepped forward from the group, and Pryce fought the urge to step back. The man's features were highlighted by subtle gray scales that looked like polished steel. Intricate dragon-scale tattoos wound up his arms.

"Master Kestrel," Seren said. "I trust you received my message about our guest?"

"Indeed, Your Highness." His voice was melodic, each word precisely chosen. "Young Master Harper-Green's reputation precedes him. Not many can bond with a storm dragon so quickly." His gray eyes studied Pryce with an intensity that made him feel uneasy. "Particularly not one so . . . untrained."

Before Pryce could respond, Stormwing let out a low rumble. Several of the airborne storm dragons had landed nearby, and she was watching them with interest.

"Go on," Pryce told her. "Make some friends."

Master Kestrel's eyebrows rose slightly as Stormwing immediately bounded toward the other dragons. "Interesting. Most storm dragons are far more territorial with strangers." He turned to Pryce. "Perhaps there's more to you than meets the eye, young man."

"The journey was long," Seren said. "Pryce should rest before tonight's feast."

"Of course." Master Kestrel gestured to a young Dragonkin with copper-colored scales. "Show our guest to the Azure Suite."

As Pryce followed his guide into the palace, his eyes widened at the grandeur around him. The corridors were vast enough for dragons to pass through comfortably, their walls adorned with luminous crystals that cast a warm glow. Elaborate tapestries depicted dragons and Dragonkin working together in harmony.

"Not quite the savage lair you expected?" the copper-scaled youth asked.

Pryce felt his face flush. "I . . . well . . ."

"Don't worry. We're used to outsiders' misconceptions." They stopped before an ornately carved door. "The feast begins at eveningbell. Someone will come for you." The young Dragonkin hesitated, then offered a slight bow. "I'm Aurix, by the way. Third-year apprentice to Master Kestrel."

Pryce found himself relaxing slightly at the other boy's friendly tone. "Pryce Harper-Green," he said, then added with an awkward laugh, "First-day apprentice to, well, everything, I suppose."

"First time away from home?"

"That obvious, huh?"

"Only to someone who remembers their own first day. The Azure Suite can be a bit overwhelming at first, but you'll get used to it. Just . . ." He glanced down the hallway before continuing in a lower voice, "don't touch the blue vase by the window. It's worth more than both our lives combined."

The Azure Suite took Pryce's breath away. The ceiling soared overhead, and one entire wall opened onto a private balcony overlooking the dragon nests below. The furniture was elegant yet sturdy, crafted from deep blue wood he'd never seen before. A massive bed dominated one corner, its covers embroidered with silver thread that mimicked dragon scales.

Pryce set his worn bag on an entry table, its surface inlaid with shimmering mother-of-pearl. The contrast between his meager belongings and the table's opulence made him self-conscious. He propped his bow and quiver against the wall beside it, careful not to scratch it.

Pryce walked to the balcony, gripping the railing as he watched Stormwing playing with the other storm dragons. They swooped and dove, occasionally releasing small bursts of lightning that crackled between them like a game of catch.

"She seems happy," Seren's voice came from behind him.

Pryce turned to find her leaning against the doorframe. "Storm dragons are social creatures," she said, joining him at the railing. "It's cruel to keep them isolated."

"I never meant to—"

"Of course not." She placed her hand over his on the railing. "You didn't know. Just as your people don't know the truth about us." She sighed, watching the dragons below. "Our people have been pushed to these islands, Pryce. We're not the monsters your stories make us out to be. We're fighting to preserve our way of life."

"The stories say you raid coastal villages, steal children—"

"Some do," she admitted. "There are extremists in every society. But most of us? We just want to live in peace, to maintain our connection to the dragons." Her violet eyes met his. "That's why you're here. To learn, to understand. To help bridge the gap between our peoples."

***

The feast hall pulsed with energy and laughter. Fire lamps cast light on walls covered in scales that Pryce realized, with a start, were real. The ceiling opened to the night sky where dragons occasionally swooped past, their silhouettes blocking out the stars.

Pryce tugged at the high collar of the formal attire he'd found laid out on his bed. He felt both overdressed and somehow still inadequate among the Dragonkin nobility.

"Wine, boy?" A scarred Dragonkin warrior thrust a goblet toward him. His grin revealed sharp canines. "Best vintage from the mainland." The warrior's words slurred slightly as he swayed on his feet.

"Thank you," Pryce said, accepting the goblet but only pretending to sip. These weren't the bloodthirsty raiders from his father's and Finnegan's stories. They seemed more like soldiers celebrating a long-awaited peace.

"Careful with Razorclaw's wine," Master Kestrel appeared at his elbow. "It's stronger than what you're used to in Crystal Shores." He guided Pryce away from the increasingly rowdy group of warriors. "Walk with me."

They moved to a quieter corner of the hall where a massive window overlooked the dragon aeries. Stormwing was curled up with two other storm dragons.

"She's remarkable," Master Kestrel said, nodding toward Stormwing. "Raw potential, like her rider. Tell me, what do you know of dragon training?"

"Only what I've read in books, and what seems . . . natural, I suppose."

"Natural." Master Kestrel smiled. "Yes, that's precisely what makes you interesting. Most trainers spend years learning rigid techniques, proper forms. But you?" He gestured to where Stormwing lay. "You achieved in days what takes others months. Pure instinct."

"Is that . . . good?"

"It's rare. And it could be very good indeed, with proper guidance." Master Kestrel turned to face him fully. "I'd like to train you, Pryce. Not here—Drakemere is too . . . political for real training. I have a facility on Dragon's Fang Island. It's where I work with our most promising riders."

Excitement surged through Pryce at the opportunity, then faded as he realized what it meant. "Even further from home?"

"Success requires sacrifice." Master Kestrel's voice softened. "I know it's not an easy choice. But think of what you could achieve. The wealth you could earn for your family. The bridges you could build between our peoples."

A burst of raucous laughter drew Pryce's attention back to the feast. Through the crowd, he spotted Seren speaking with a group of nobles, every inch the princess. She caught his eye and smiled, but something in her expression seemed strained.

"Think on it," Master Kestrel said. "But don't think too long. Opportunities, like the tide, wait for no one."

Later that night, Pryce stood on his balcony, watching Stormwing below. She was different here—more animated, more herself. A natural part of the storm dragons' social circle had immediately accepted her.

"What should we do, girl?" he whispered into the night air. "Master Kestrel's right about the opportunities, about helping my family. And maybe . . ." he thought of Seren's words about bridging the gap between their peoples, "maybe we could do some real good here."

Stormwing looked up at him and let out a soft chirp that echoed off the cliff face. In the shadows behind her, a darker shape moved—a shadow drake, seeming almost predatory.

Something was happening here, something bigger than his simple dream of becoming a dragon trainer.

14. Storm Warning

A bitter wind whipped across Lake Dragontide as Finnegan guided his boat toward the Island of Emberfall. Dark clouds roiled overhead, promising a storm.

He gripped the boat's wheel tighter as he approached the dock. Something felt wrong—the island's usual sounds were missing.

"Too quiet," he said, tying off his boat.

His walking stick tapped against the planks as he made his way to the barracks. He noticed Stormwing's empty cell, its door hanging open.

The barracks was dark. No smoke came from the chimney, no sign of Pryce or his pets. Finnegan approached the door.

"Pryce?" he called out, knowing already there would be no answer. "Lad?"

Inside, the hearth held nothing but cold ashes. No flapping of Skye's wings disturbed the silence. Ash's usual perch by the window sat vacant.

Finnegan looked around the abandoned room. "Oh, lad. What have you gone and done now?"

Finnegan shuffled further into the barracks, his walking stick catching on the uneven floorboards. A scrap of paper on the table caught his eye, weighted down by a mug. His fingers trembled slightly as he reached for it.

"What's this, then?" He squinted at Pryce's hurried handwriting.

"Princess Seren?" Finnegan spat the name like a curse. "Nymeria's daughter, no less." He crumpled the note in his fist and stuffed it into his pocket, remembering his warning to Pryce about the Dragonkin queen's appearance in the shadows.

A loose floorboard creaked under his foot as he paced. Finnegan paused, noting how it shifted differently than the others. Kneeling with effort, his joints aching, he pried up the board. A small pile of coins glinted in the dim light.

"Smart lad. At least you didn't trust them completely." He pulled out a coin, turning it over in his calloused palm. Most of Gavin's loan lay hidden here—a sign that some part of Pryce had doubts about his decision.

The memory of Nymeria watching from the treeline flashed through his mind. Her predatory stance, the way her cloak had melded with the shadows. He should have known she wouldn't leave the boy alone, not after seeing his gift with dragons.

"Should've kept a closer eye on you, lad. Should've known they'd send someone younger, prettier to turn your head."

The journey back to Crystal Shores felt longer than usual, each wave pushing against Finnegan's boat like a personal attack. He replayed the past few days in his mind, searching for signs he might have missed.

"The way the lad looked at that saddle," he said, adjusting his course against the strengthening wind. "Stars in his eyes, just like his mother at that age."

Dark clouds gathered overhead. A gull—not Skye, but similar enough to twist his heart—wheeled past, fighting against the growing storm. Thunder rumbled in the distance.

Finnegan remembered Pryce's questions about dragon training, his quick mastery of basic commands. The boy had a gift, no denying that. But gifts could be weapons in the wrong hands.

"Should've told him more about the mineral deposits. About why the Dragonkin really want Crystal Shores." He approached the shoreline. "They're not after some fishing village—they want what lies beneath."

The harbor came into view. Waves crashed against the pilings with growing force as the storm drew closer. Finnegan could see people hurrying to secure their boats, battening down against the weather.

His own vessel groaned as he guided it into its berth. There was no time to properly tie everything down—not with this news burning in his pocket. He had to reach the Harper-Greens before the storm broke.

"Hold together, old girl." He patted the boat's rail as he secured the minimum necessary lines. "Won't be long."

Thunder crackled overhead as Finnegan made his way through Crystal Shores' winding streets. His walking stick splashed through growing puddles. When he reached the Harper-Green home, he paused, gathering his resolve before knocking.

Ellie opened the door, her smile fading at his expression. "Finnegan? What's wrong?"

"Need to speak with you and Tyler," he said, his voice gruff. "About Pryce."

Tyler appeared behind his wife, drying his hands on a cloth. "Come in, old friend. You look like you've seen a seadrake."

Inside, Finnegan sank into a kitchen chair, his joints creaking almost as loudly as the wooden seat. He pulled out Pryce's crumpled note, smoothing it against the table.

Ellie snatched up the paper, her eyes darting across the words. "Seren? The Dragonkin princess?"

"What's this about?" Tyler moved to read over her shoulder." Those cursed books of his—filling his head with nonsense about dragon training and glory."

Faye crept down the stairs, drawn by the tension in their voices. She lingered in the doorway, her red hair a mirror of her mother's.

"It's not just the books," Finnegan said, clasping his walking stick. "Queen Nymeria herself appeared at the island. I warned the lad about her, but . . ." He shook his head. "That boy has a gift for talking to dragons. A rare gift. One the Dragonkin desperately want on their side."

"But why now?" Faye stepped fully into the kitchen. "The Dragonkin haven't bothered us in years."

Finnegan's expression grew grave. "Because they know what lies beneath Crystal Shores. The mineral deposits—dragon-magic ore that could make their forces unstoppable. We've had peace only because they couldn't access it. But with a talented dragon trainer like Pryce . . ." He let the implication hang in the air.

"They've been waiting," Tyler said quietly. "Waiting for someone like our son."

"He's been brainwashed," Ellie said, pacing the kitchen. Her fingers twisted the note until it was nearly shredded. "They must have fed him lies, twisted everything to make him think he was doing the right thing."

"He's of age now, Ellie," Tyler leaned against the counter, arms crossed. "Old enough to make his own choices, even if they're wrong ones."

"Choices?" Ellie faced her husband. "He's been sheltered his whole life. Maybe that's my fault. Maybe if I'd told him more about our bloodline, about the true nature of the Dragonkin—"

"Don't blame yourself," Finnegan interrupted, thumping his walking stick against the floor. "The dragon blood runs in his veins, just as it runs in yours. Some calls can't be ignored."

Rain lashed against the windows as the storm finally broke. Lightning flashed, illuminating Faye's worried face. "Will we have to fight him? If the Dragonkin come for the deposits?"

"No," Ellie said. "I'm going after him. I'll bring him home before it comes to that."

Tyler pushed away from the counter. "And how exactly do you plan to do that? Storm the Dragonkin stronghold single-handed?"

"Is his skiff still at the island?" Ellie asked Finnegan, ignoring her husband's question.

Finnegan nodded. "Aye. He must have flown off on that dragon of his. Took his pets with him too, I'd wager."

"El," Tyler's voice softened. "You can't just—"

"I can and I will." Ellie strode to the corner where an old trunk sat. "Grandpa Joe knew the secret ways to Dragonkin territory. He mapped them all."

Ellie opened her grandfather's trunk, the hinges squealed. She dug through layers of memories—old sailing charts, weathered logbooks, a compass with a cracked face—until she found what she sought.

"Here." She spread a yellowed map across the kitchen table. Finnegan leaned forward, squinting at the faded ink. Complex routes wound through the Dragonspine Reaches, marking hidden passages and secret coves.

A particularly violent thunderclap shook the house. Faye jumped, moving closer to her father.

"These routes," Finnegan traced one with a gnarled finger, "they're treacherous."

"I don't care. I won't let them use my son like some pawn in their games."

Tyler drew Ellie into his arms. "I'll go after him. Bring him back before—"

"No, I'm going. I just need to get the Seafarer's Sigil."

"Ellie," Tyler said. "You lost that compass in the Thornveil Wilds years ago. In that cave where—"

"Then I'll find it again," Ellie cut him off. "That compass can track dragon blood, and Pryce still wears my pendant. It will lead me straight to him."

The determination in her eyes reminded Finnegan of another headstrong Harper-Green who'd just flown off on a dragon.

"You can't stop him from making his own mistakes," Finnegan said. "Some lessons have to be learned the hard way."

Lightning split the sky again, and in that brief, brilliant flash, Ellie's features seemed to glow with something ancient. Something that spoke of dragon blood and old magic.

"Maybe." She tucked the map into her belt. "But I can stop him from making ones that'll get him killed."

Finnegan felt the time of peace was ending. And somewhere out there, beyond the storm, a young man with dragon blood in his veins was flying straight into the heart of an ancient conflict.

15. The Weight of Choice

Pryce had never seen so much food in one place. The breakfast spread before him in the Dragonkin palace's dining hall would have fed half of Crystal Shores. Golden pastries stuffed with exotic fruits. Smoked fish arranged in elaborate patterns. Steaming porridge dotted with berries and drizzled with honey.

He lifted a spoonful of the porridge to his mouth. It was perfect—and somehow that made it worse. His mother's porridge always had little lumps, places where the oats hadn't quite softened. He used to complain about those lumps. Now he found himself missing them with an intensity that surprised him.

"Is the food not to your liking?" Aurix asked from across the table.

"No, it's amazing," Pryce said, forcing himself to take another bite. "Just different from home."

A hush fell over the dining hall. Pryce looked up to see Princess Seren gliding between the tables, her white dress immaculate as always. Other young trainees scrambled to bow their heads, but she passed them without a glance, stopping beside Pryce.

"Ready for your first real day of training?" She smiled, resting a hand on the back of his chair. "Master Kestrel has great expectations for you."

Before Pryce could respond, a shadow fell across the table. A young man stood there, perhaps a few years older than Pryce, with features that seemed carved from stone. Dark scales traced patterns across his temples, and his eyes held a coldness that made Pryce's throat go dry.

"So," the newcomer said with disdain, "this is the prodigy everyone's talking about?"

"Thane Zharan," Seren said. "I didn't expect you back from patrol so soon."

Zharan? Pryce remembered his father telling stories of the brutal Dragonkin captain who nearly killed him during the war, and who'd sworn revenge on the Shorlings who'd defeated him. Captain Zharan, known for his ruthless combat and tactical mind, made him one of the most feared Dragonkin commanders. Thane had to be related to him.

Thane ignored Seren entirely. "Tell me, boy." His voice carrying the same cultured accent that seemed common among the Dragonkin nobility. "How does a simple Shorling come to ride a storm dragon?" The way he said 'Shorling' made it sound like something he'd scraped off his boot.

Pryce's hand instinctively went to the dragon pendant beneath his shirt. "Just got lucky, I guess."

"Luck? Is that what they're calling it now?" He leaned forward, placing both hands on the table. Up close, Pryce could see that his scales weren't just dark—they were scarlet, like war paint slashed across his skin. "I find it interesting that a fisherman's son suddenly appears with such . . . natural talents."

"Leave him be, Thane," Seren said. "He's here at my invitation."

Master Kestrel approached before Thane could respond. "If you're quite finished with breakfast, we have work to do."

Pryce scrambled to his feet, grateful for the interruption. As he followed Kestrel from the dining hall, he felt Thane staring at him.

"I trust you've checked on your dragon this morning?" Kestrel asked as they walked through the soaring corridors.

"I was about to—"

"No need. She's been fed and exercised. Your . . . pets as well." Kestrel's dismissive tone made it clear that the Dragonkin viewed pets the way most people viewed vermin. "We have more important matters to attend to."

They emerged onto a vast training ground carved into the very face of the cliff. Other dragons and their riders were already there, practicing aerial maneuvers that made Pryce dizzy just watching them.

"First, we assess your current capabilities." Kestrel gestured to where Stormwing was being led out by an attendant. "Show me your mounting technique."

Pryce approached his dragon, who greeted him with a gentle headbutt that nearly knocked him over. He heard Thane snort from somewhere behind him.

"Hey, girl." Pryce scratched her under her chin. "Ready to show them what we can do?"

What happened next seemed to surprise everyone except Pryce and Stormwing. Instead of using the formal mounting procedure—a complex series of steps involving specific hand and foot positions—Pryce simply stepped back, locked eyes with Stormwing, and nodded. The dragon immediately lowered her shoulder, allowing him to swing up smoothly onto her back.

"Interesting," Kestrel said. "Unorthodox, but effective. Your bond is . . . unusually strong."

"Strong enough to overcome proper training?" Thane called out. "Or perhaps to bypass it entirely?"

Kestrel held up a hand for silence. "Today, we focus on combat basics. A dragon rider must be able to defend himself and his mount." He drew a practice sword from a nearby rack. "You'll need this."

Pryce caught the thrown weapon awkwardly. The sword felt wrong in his hands—he was more comfortable with his bow. Above, dark clouds were gathering over the lake, rolling in from the direction of Crystal Shores.

"Focus," Kestrel commanded. "Your enemies won't wait for fair weather or better preparation. Now, show me your guard position."

Pryce raised the practice sword, trying to mimic Kestrel's stance. The weapon felt heavy, unwieldy.

"Wrong," Kestrel said, tapping Pryce's elbow with his own practice sword. "Your guard is too low. You're leaving yourself exposed."

Sweat trickled down Pryce's back as he adjusted his stance. Stormwing watched from nearby, occasionally letting out concerned chirps when Pryce took a particularly hard hit.

"Better," Kestrel circled him. "Now, the key to mounted combat is maintaining your balance."

They'd been at it for hours when Thane stepped forward. "Perhaps a demonstration would be more effective?"

"Very well. Thane, you may spar with the boy."

Pryce watched Thane select a practice sword, noting the casual familiarity he handled the weapon. This was no training exercise—this was an excuse to put him in his place.

"Remember," Thane's smiled, "this is just practice. No need to be afraid."

"I'm not afraid," Pryce said, but his voice cracked on the last word. Behind him, Stormwing growled softly.

They circled each other on the training ground. Thane moved like a predator. Pryce tried to remember everything Kestrel had taught him about guard positions and footwork, but his mind went blank when Thane eyes locked onto him.

The first strike came without warning. Pryce barely got his sword up in time to block, the impact jarring his arms. Thane pressed forward, each blow driving Pryce back toward the cliff's edge.

"Come now," Thane taunted, easily deflecting Pryce's clumsy counterattack. "Surely the great dragon prodigy can do better than this?"

Thunder rolled across the lake. Pryce risked a glance toward Crystal Shores, where the storm now raged. The momentary distraction cost him—Thane's practice sword caught him across the ribs, sending him stumbling.

"Focus!" Kestrel shouted. "Your opponent won't wait for you to gather your thoughts!"

Pryce regained his footing, panting. Something in Thane's expression—a flash of cruel satisfaction—reminded him so strongly of the stories about Captain Zharan that his next words slipped out before he could stop them.

"You fight like your father."

Thane froze mid-strike. "What did you say?"

Pryce immediately realized his mistake. "I . . . I just meant—"

"How do you know my father?" Thane's voice was deadly quiet. The practice sword in his hand trembled with barely contained rage.

"That's enough for today," Kestrel stepped between them. "Thane, you're dismissed. Pryce, we need to discuss your departure for Dragon's Fang Island tomorrow."

Pryce watched Thane stalk away with suppressed fury as the storm over Crystal Shores intensified.

"Dragon's Fang Island," Kestrel continued, "is where we conduct our advanced training. You'll learn things there that can't be taught here. Proper combat techniques, advanced dragon-handling, aerial warfare—"

"Actually," Pryce interrupted, "I can't go."

"Can't?" Kestrel's eyebrows rose. "This isn't a request, boy. Your training—"

"I need to return home. My family—"

"Your family will be fine," Kestrel's tone hardened. "This is about your future, about becoming something greater than a simple fisherman's son."

Thunder cracked overhead, closer now. Pryce thought of his mother's cooking, his father's quiet strength, Faye's laughter. He thought of Old Man Finnegan's warnings about the Dragonkin.

"It's not just that. I need time to think."

Kestrel studied him for a long moment. "Very well. You have until morning to 'think.' But remember—opportunities like this don't come twice."

As Kestrel walked away, Pryce stood alone on the training ground. Stormwing pressed her snout against his back, offering silent comfort.

"What have I gotten us into, girl?"

Evening found Pryce in the stables with Stormwing. Ash dozed nearby on a hay bale while Skye perched in the rafters above. The storm continued to rage over Crystal Shores, visible through the stable's wide openings.

"At least they've been taking good care of you all," Pryce said, running his hand along Stormwing's scales. His ribs still ached where Thane's practice sword had struck.

"They're well looked after," Aurix said, appearing in the doorway. "Princess Seren's orders."

Pryce watched as Aurix distributed the fish among the dragons. "Why would Seren care about my pets?"

"The same reason she brought you here," Aurix said, tossing the last fish to a shadow drake. "She sees something in you. But Pryce . . ." he lowered his voice, "Dragon's Fang Island isn't what you think."

"What do you mean?"

"The training there is . . . intense. Especially with Thane involved." Aurix glanced around before continuing. "And after what happened today—"

"I shouldn't have mentioned his father."

"No, you shouldn't have." Aurix set the empty bucket down. "Thane's been trying to restore his family's honor ever since Captain Zharan's defeat. He won't forget what you said."

Thunder boomed overhead.

"I just wanted to learn about dragons," Pryce said. "I never meant to get caught up in . . . whatever this is."

Stormwing nuzzled his shoulder as if sensing his distress. Ash stretched and padded over, rubbing against his legs. Even Skye fluttered down to land on the hay beside him.

"Sometimes the simplest dreams have the most complicated consequences," Aurix said. He started to say more but stopped at the sound of approaching footsteps.

Princess Seren appeared in the doorway. "I hope you're not letting today's . . . difficulties cloud your judgment about Dragon's Fang Island."

"I need to think about it," Pryce said.

"Of course. But remember, Pryce—you have a gift. It would be a shame to waste it."

As she glided away, Pryce turned back to the storm-darkened sky. Somewhere out there, his family was probably watching these same clouds, wondering where he was, if he was safe.

"What would you do?" he asked Aurix.

"I'd listen to my instincts. Dragons do. Maybe that's why they survive."

Pryce nodded, scratching behind Stormwing's ear ridge as another crash of thunder shook the stables. By morning, he would have to decide—continue down this path with the Dragonkin, or return to the simpler life he'd left behind.

But as he watched a shadow drake circling the palace towers like a dark sentinel, Pryce couldn't shake the feeling that his choice had already been made for him.

16. Dragon's Blood

Ellie shivered as the first rays of sunlight barely pierced through the morning fog on the Island of Emberfall. Her crossbody bag felt heavy against her hip as she stood on the dock; the old wood beneath her boots felt spongy. The humidity made every breath feel like drinking soup.

"Take these, lass." Finnegan extended a bundle wrapped in oilcloth. "Dried fish, hardtack, and some of that seaweed brew you fancy."

Ellie patted her bag. "I've packed my own supplies, but thanks."

"Aye, but an extra bite never hurt anyone where you're heading." He gazed past her toward the distant shoreline where Thornveil Wilds waited, a dark smudge against the horizon. "Those waters . . . they're not natural. Three ships lost last moon alone."

"I remember." Ellie's hand went to her neck where her dragon pendant used to rest—now around Pryce's neck, if he still wore it. "The Wavecutter went down near the southern point. They said the water just . . . opened up and swallowed her whole."

"And that's not the worst of it." Finnegan's said. "Something's stirring out there. The waters remember old magic, and they don't take kindly to visitors."

"The waters might not take kindly to visitors," Ellie said, checking the supplies in the small skiff's hold, "but they remember my bloodline. Dragon blood runs in these veins, thin as it might be."

"It's not just the waters I'm worried about, lass. That cave where you lost the compass . . ." Finnegan shook his head. "Aurathorn still claims those lands."

A memory flashed through Ellie's mind—the cave's darkness, the sound of massive wings, the desperate scramble through underground tunnels with the dragon's roar shaking loose stones from the ceiling. She'd dropped the Seafarer's Sigil there, its blue glow disappearing into the rushing waters of an underground river.

"I don't have a choice. My son is out there, being led astray by silver-tongued Dragonkin. Every moment I waste—"

"Is a moment he slips further from reach," Finnegan finished. He pressed the bundle of supplies into her hands. "At least take these."

Ellie tucked the bundle into her bag. "Thank you, old friend."

She untied the skiff and pushed off from the dock, Finnegan's voice carried across the water.

"Watch for the sunken ships, lass! They mark the safe channels—where there's room for one ship to sink, there's room for another to sail!"

Ellie adjusted the sail, catching the breeze. The canvas snapped taut, propelling the skiff away from the

Island of Emberfall and toward the forbidding shoreline of Thornveil Wilds. Somewhere in that darkness lay the compass that could lead her to Pryce.

The mist thickened as Ellie sailed, transforming the waters into an alien seascape. Through gaps in the fog, she caught glimpses of masts reaching up from the depths like grasping fingers—the graveyard of ships that had misjudged these treacherous channels.

"Keep the wreck of the Stormchaser to port," she said, recalling grandpa Joe's teachings. "Then three lengths past the Wavecutter's crow's nest . . ." Her voice trailed off as a dark shape loomed in the mist—the twisted remains of a merchant vessel, its hull split open like a rotten fruit.

A flash of memory struck her: five-year-old Pryce, sitting on her lap as she mended nets, asking about the ships that never came home. "But why do they sail here if it's dangerous, Mama?"

"Because sometimes," she'd answered, "the most important journeys are also the most dangerous."

The skiff scraped against something underwater, jolting her back to the present. Ellie's hands flew to the mainsheet, adjusting the sail's tension as she steered around a partially submerged figurehead—a woman with empty eyes and algae-draped hair.

The shoreline of Thornveil Wilds emerged from the mist like a wall of darkness. Ancient trees loomed overhead, their branches twisting together to block out the strengthening daylight. The air grew colder, heavy with the scent of something else—something old.

Ellie dropped the anchor over the bow, letting the rope play out until it caught. The skiff settled into position several yards from the pebbly shore. She released the dinghy tied to the stern, lowering herself into the smaller craft. The dragon blood in her veins, diluted though it was, might be enough to power the compass—if she could find it. But first, she needed to reach that cave.

The dinghy's bottom scraped against the stones. As Ellie stepped onto the shore, the pebbles shifted beneath her feet.

A distant roar echoed from the mountains, making the air itself tremble.

"Aurathorn." Ellie instinctively crouched lower. "Still guarding your territory, old one?"

The cave's entrance should be just ahead, hidden behind a curtain of moss. That's where she'd lost the compass, fleeing from Aurathorn. That's where it had fallen into the underground river, disappearing into the darkness.

Ellie paused at the cave's entrance. The moss parted like a beaded curtain as she entered the cave. The temperature dropped sharply, her breath forming clouds in the air. As her eyes adjusted to the gloom, ancient runes flickered to life along the cave walls—symbols visible only to those with dragon blood flowing through their veins.

"The old stories are true."

A pulling sensation grew stronger, as if the compass itself called out to her, beckoning her forward into the depths of the cave.

The runes along the cave walls glowed dimly, their ancient magic responding to Ellie's presence. "Come on, show me the way."

The cave remained silent except for the steady plip-plip of water dripping from the mineral-encrusted ceiling. Then she felt it—a warm pulse, like a heartbeat. The runes brightened, creating a path forward.

"Problems, dearie?"

Ellie whirled around, knife raised. There, perched on a boulder she could have sworn wasn't there a moment ago, sat a familiar figure. His patchwork cloak seemed to catch light that didn't exist, and a mischievous grin spread across his face.

"Pipwhistle," she said, lowering the knife. "Still appearing where you're least expected, I see."

The Quibnocket laughed. "Lost something shiny, did we? Again?" He produced a copper coin from thin air, making it dance across his knuckles. "Such a habit you have, dropping precious things in precarious places."

"I don't have time for games, Pip. My son—"

"Ah yes, young master Pryce." Pipwhistle's expression grew serious. "Flying off with dragons and danger, just like his mother. Though you at least had the courtesy to keep your feet on the ground."

He hopped down from the boulder, his movements fluid as water. "Been watching your progress, I have. Quite the show—blood magic in Thornveil Wilds!" He clucked his tongue. "Might as well ring a dinner bell for all the nasties lurking about."

A distant roar emphasized his point. Loose stones rattled on the cave floor.

"Aurathorn grows restless," Pipwhistle whispered. "And he's not the only one interested in your little treasure hunt. The Dragonkin have been sniffing about too, yes they have. Left their marks all over." He gestured to a wall where Ellie now noticed strange symbols carved into the stone.

"The compass. Do you know where it is?"

"Know where it is? Oh, my dear . . ." He reached into his cloak. "Sometimes the safest place for a treasure is in the hands of a thief."

Ellie gasped as Pipwhistle withdrew the Seafarer's Sigil from his cloak. The compass looked exactly as she remembered—tarnished bronze worked in sinuous, dragon-shaped designs, its central capsule dormant and dark.

"You've had it all this time?" Ellie stepped forward, then stopped as Pipwhistle danced backward, wagging his finger.

"Kept it safe, I did! Safer than the bottom of a river, wouldn't you say?" His laugh tinkled through the cave. "Though I must admit, watching you was quite entertaining.

Another roar shook the cave, close enough now that small stones rained from the ceiling. Pipwhistle glanced up, his smile dimming slightly.

"Big fellow's getting closer," he said. "And he's not alone. Can you feel them?" He cocked his head. "The Dragonkin scouts are moving through the trees like shadows. They know what you seek."

"Then help me, Pip. You obviously know something I don't."

"Don't I always?" He flourished his hands, and suddenly the air was filled with dancing lights—illusions of the compass spinning and multiplying until the cave looked like a starlit sky. "Dragon blood alone won't wake it, not anymore. The old magics are fading, diluting." The lights merged into a single point. "But there are . . . other ways."

"What do you mean?"

"Magic is like soup, dearie. Sometimes you need to add a little spice." He reached into his cloak again and pulled out a small vial filled with a silver liquid. "Moonflower dew, caught at midnight. Mixed with dragon blood . . ." His grin widened. "Well, that might just be potent enough to point you toward your wayward fledgling."

The cave trembled again. Closer. Much closer.

"Time grows short," Pipwhistle said, suddenly businesslike. "What say you, Ellie Harper-Green? Ready to make some real magic?"

"Do it."

Pipwhistle's movements became precise, almost reverent—so different from his usual theatrical flourishes. He uncorked the vial with his teeth, then held the compass over her palm.

"Three drops of blood," he said, picking her finger before she knew what happened. "Then three drops of dew. The old way. The true way."

As Ellie's blood dripped onto the compass, the carved dragon designs seemed to twist. The third drop hit the central capsule, and a faint blue glow sparked to life.

Pipwhistle added the Moonflower dew with expert precision. Each silver drop merged with her blood, creating swirls of luminescent blue.

A bone-shaking roar split the air—so close now that dust and pebbles cascaded from the cave ceiling. Pipwhistle's eyes darted to the entrance.

"Company's coming," he said. "Lots of company. Best hurry this along." He grabbed Ellie's bleeding finger and pressed it against the compass face. "Now, speak your blood's truth. Call to your son."

"I don't know the words—"

"Your blood knows. Let it speak!"

The compass grew warm under her palm. Words rose to her lips, words she somehow knew but had never learned.

"By blood and bone, by scale and sky," she heard herself say, "show me the path to my own."

The compass flared with brilliant blue light. The carved dragon coiled around its edge came alive, its tail sweeping around to point northeast.

"There!" Pipwhistle released her hand and backed away. "Follow that bearing, and you'll find your boy. But Ellie . . ." His smile faded completely. "What awaits you there . . . it's not just your son you'll have to save."

"What do you mean?"

Instead of answering, Pipwhistle cocked his head, listening. "They're here." He snapped his fingers, and suddenly the cave was filled with identical copies of Ellie and himself—perfect illusions scattering in different directions. "Run, dearie. I'll keep our guests entertained."

"Pip—"

"GO!"

Ellie clutched the compass and ran. Behind her, she heard Pipwhistle's musical laughter, followed by shouts of confusion from multiple voices—Dragonkin scouts, no doubt, trying to distinguish reality from illusion.

A massive shadow passed over the cave entrance—Aurathorn, descending. The dragon's roar shook the very ground, but Ellie didn't stop. She burst out of the cave into weak daylight, her feet finding the path back to the shore more by instinct than sight.

The compass burned against her palm, its blue light steady and strong.

She reached the shore and shoved the dinghy into the water and leaped in. When safely in the skiff, the current caught her, pulling her away from shore just as a terrifying screech split the air. Through the mist, she glimpsed Aurathorn landing at the cave entrance, massive wings stirring the fog into phantasmal shapes.

But the dragon didn't pursue. As Ellie finally sailed away, she heard Pipwhistle's voice carried on the wind: "Safe journeys, dearie! And remember—when the time comes, trust the blood!"

The words faded, leaving Ellie alone with the glowing compass. She set her course northeast, toward Drakemere Island.

17. Sealed with a Kiss

Pryce folded his spare shirt and tucked it into his worn traveling bag. His fingers brushed against the dragon pendant—his mother's necklace—and a wave of homesickness washed over him. He pulled it out, watching the red fluid shimmer in the morning light filtering through the Azure Suite's windows.

"Leaving so soon?"

Princess Seren stood in the doorway. She walked into the room, her movements as graceful as always.

"I have to," Pryce said, letting the pendant fall back against his chest. "My family—"

"Your family is precisely why you should stay." Seren unrolled several ancient scrolls across the table, their edges curling like dried leaves. The parchment crackled as she smoothed it flat. "Look at these."

Pryce leaned over the maps, inhaling their ancient perfume. They showed Crystal Shores, but unlike any charts he'd seen before. Strange markings crisscrossed beneath the village, forming intricate patterns.

"Dragon-magic ore," Seren said. "Rare minerals with incredible power, lying right beneath your home." She looked up. "The Seadrake Corsairs know it's there. They seek these deposits to forge weapons against us."

"Seadrake Corsairs?" Pryce remembered Finnegan's tales of massive serpentine creatures that could drag entire ships into the depths.

"Pirates who've learned to control seadrakes," Seren said, her voice dropping. "They've been raiding coastal villages for generations, growing bolder each year. With these minerals, they could forge weapons capable of cutting through dragon scales like paper." She straightened, her scales catching the light. "Your village would be defenseless against them."

She moved to the door and spoke quietly to someone outside. A servant entered carrying a leather pouch that clinked heavily.

"A small token of our commitment to Crystal Shores," Seren said as the servant placed the pouch on the table. "There's more where this came from."

Pryce thought of his father's fishing nets coming up empty day after day, of the worry lines creasing his mother's forehead as she stretched their meager coins to feed the family.

"Here," Seren said, drawing his attention back to the scrolls. "These runes detail the ore's properties." She stood close beside him, her arm brushing his as she pointed to the ancient writing.

Their hands touched as they both reached for the same section of parchment. Seren didn't pull away.

"You have a rare gift, Pryce," she said softly. "Like your mother's bloodline . . ."

She turned toward him, and before Pryce could react, she pressed her lips gently against his. The kiss lasted only a moment, soft as a feather's touch, but it left him stunned, his heart racing.

"Am I interrupting?" Master Kestrel's voice cut through the moment.

Pryce stepped back quickly, his face warm. Seren remained composed.

"We were just discussing the Seadrake Corsair situation," she said.

Kestrel stepped into the room. "Indeed. Our scouts report they're gathering forces. If they acquire the ore beneath Crystal Shores, their weapons would be unstoppable." He fixed his gaze on Pryce. "The time for training at Dragon's Fang Island is now. Today."

Pryce looked between them, then down at the maps showing his vulnerable village. He touched his mother's pendant again, feeling its warmth against his palm.

"I'll stay," he said finally. "For Crystal Shores."

Seren's triumphant smile was brief but unmistakable as she exchanged glances with Kestrel. The servant bowed and gathered up the pouch of gold.

"See that this reaches the Harper-Green family in Crystal Shores," Seren said.

As the servant departed, his footsteps fading down the corridor, Pryce felt like he'd just stepped into something he shouldn't have. But with Seren's kiss still tingling on his lips and the thought of his family's safety, he pushed his doubts aside.

He was doing this for Crystal Shores. What could possibly go wrong?

In the distance, a dragon's roar echoed off the cliffs, as if answering his unspoken question.

18. Terrors of the Undertow

Ellie looked at the compass, its blue glow steady as it pointed toward the distant horizon. A day had passed since leaving the Thornveil Wilds.

Her hand tightened on the skiff's tiller. Crystal Shores lay far behind her now, and ahead . . . ahead was Drakemere Island, though she'd never seen it herself. Only heard the tales of the Dragonkin queen's fortress carved into seaside cliffs.

The thinning morning fog revealed a massive shape. A warship emerged, its dragon-headed prow cutting through the waves.

"Well, what have we here?" The voice carried across the water. A figure stood at the warship's rail.

Ellie's hands moved swiftly, concealing the compass beneath a coil of fishing nets. "Just fishing," she called back. "These are open waters."

"Open waters?" The figure laughed. "You've strayed far from your fishing grounds, Shorling."

The warship drew alongside her skiff. Ellie could now see the figure clearly—a dragonkin commander, his scar stark against his dark scales, his armor gleaming with shadow drake scales.

Ropes snaked down from the warship's deck, and Dragonkin warriors descended. Their boots thudded against the skiff's planks. Ellie stood as they surrounded her, their scaled hands resting on sword hilts.

The commander landed last. He towered over her, studying her face. "You have the look of dragon blood about you," he said, his voice carrying the cultured accent of Dragonkin nobility. "Diluted, but there." He circled her slowly. "Now, why would someone of your . . . lineage be sailing these waters alone?"

"I'm free to sail where I please," Ellie said, meeting his gaze.

"Are you? We've been tracking you since the cave. Where is it?"

"Where's what?"

His hand shot out, grabbing her chin. "The Seafarer's Sigil. Don't insult us both by pretending ignorance."

Ellie jerked away from his grip. "I don't have it."

"Search the vessel. Tear it apart if you must."

His warriors moved with brutal efficiency. They ripped up floorboards, dumped out her supplies, scattered her food across the deck. One warrior kicked over her water barrel, letting precious fresh water drain into the bilge.

"Commander Shadowspear!" A younger Dragonkin held up the compass. "Found it beneath the nets."

Shadowspear took the compass. "Ah, there you are, old friend." He turned to Ellie. "You shouldn't lie to those who can smell deception."

"Kill her," one warrior suggested, drawing his blade. "Leave her body for the seadrakes."

"No." Shadowspear said. "She's entering the Undertow Sea. Without this compass, she'll never navigate the Dragon's Maws." He gestured at the horizon where dark clouds gathered. "The seadrakes will have her soon enough. A far more . . . fitting end for one of her bloodline."

The Dragonkin departed as swiftly as they'd arrived, taking her only means of navigation with them. Ellie watched their ship disappear, leaving her alone on the ravaged skiff.

Ahead lay the Dragonspine Reaches—a maze of volcanic islands with edges sharp enough to slice through hull wood. Massive whirlpools, the infamous Dragon's Maws, dotted the waters between the peaks. As clouds blotted the sun, she could see patches of eerie blue light marking the deep trenches where ancient things dwelled.

Ellie let out a breath and whispered one of her mother's old Shorling prayers: "Blessed tides guide me, ancient currents keep me." The familiar words steadied her nerves only slightly.

She surveyed the destruction on her small skiff. Most of her food was ruined, soaked with water and crushed underfoot by the Dragonkin warriors. She salvaged what she could—a few pieces of dried fish, some hard bread wrapped in oilcloth that had protected it from the worst of the damage. The fresh water was gone, all of it drained away when they'd kicked over her barrel.

"Think, Ellie," she said, gathering the scattered nets and coiling them properly. She had the knowledge to catch fish, but her water supply was running dangerously low. Unlike Lake Dragontide's clean, fresh waters back home, the Undertow Sea teemed with dangers. Luminescent jellyfish trailing poisonous tendrils drifted just beneath the surface. Worse were the microscopic seadrake spawn that could survive in a person's belly for weeks before growing large enough to kill. She'd heard tales of sailors who'd drunk the water out of desperation, only to be eaten from the inside out. Even the floating patches of seemingly harmless sea moss contained toxins that could cause hallucinations and madness. She glanced at the clouded sky. Perhaps rain would provide the safe water she desperately needed.

Hour by hour, the dark clouds hung overhead, neither advancing nor retreating, turning the day into endless twilight. When they finally drifted apart, the sun was already setting. One by one, stars emerged, their light distant in the vast darkness over the Undertow Sea.

She chose a bright star to navigate by, though the jagged silhouettes of the Dragonspine islands kept blocking her view. Strange lights danced beneath the waves—-some bioluminescent fish perhaps, or something worse. The splashing started soon after.

"Just waves," she told herself, but the sounds were too deliberate, too rhythmic. Something large moved through the water, circling her small craft.

A distant roar echoed off the volcanic peaks. Ellie's hands trembled on the tiller, wishing she had not set off for Pryce by herself.

Something bumped the skiff's hull.

Ellie grabbed a lantern, holding it over the side. The light revealed nothing but black water and swirling patterns of phosphorescence. Another bump, harder this time, nearly knocked her off her feet.

"Show yourself!"

As if in answer, a massive shape rose beside the skiff. A head larger than her entire vessel emerged. The seadrake's mouth opened, revealing rows of teeth as long as her arm.

Ellie could only stare. All the old stories, all the sailors' warnings about these creatures—none had done justice to the sheer terror of seeing one up close.

The seadrake's throat began to glow.

Steam rose from the creature's jaws. Ellie didn't think—she just moved. She dove to the deck as liquid fire streamed overhead. The mainsail caught the edge of the blast, flames racing up the canvas.

The seadrake's tail rose from the water like a massive serpent, then slammed down. The impact sent a wall of water over the skiff. The cold shock of it stole Ellie's breath, but at least it extinguished the burning sail.

Ellie scrambled to her feet.

The creature's head snaked down, jaws wide. Ellie grabbed an oar and swung with all her might. The wooden shaft cracked against teeth like swords, splintering in her hands. But the blow made the seadrake rear back, more surprised than hurt.

Its roar shook the air. The sound bounced off the nearby islands, amplified and distorted until it seemed to come from everywhere at once. Other calls answered from the darkness—more seadrakes, coming to investigate.

Massive shapes moved beneath the surface, their serpentine forms creating swirls of light in the black water. Three, no, four massive bodies circling her tiny vessel.

"No, no, no." Ellie looked frantically for anything she could use as a weapon. There was nothing that would help against a monster this size.

The seadrake circled her craft, each pass bringing it closer. Its scales scraped against the hull, the sound like knives on wood. Playing with her. Toying with its prey before striking.

Ellie touched her wedding ring, twisted it once for luck, and made a decision. The volcanic islands weren't far. If she could reach them.

But as she turned the skiff toward the razor-sharp rocks, all five seadrakes dove beneath the surface. The water went black.

The silence that followed was somehow worse than the roaring.

19. The Fang's Edge

Dawn painted Dragon's Fang Island in shades of blood and ash as Pryce guided Stormwing toward the landing area. The dragon's wings caught turbulent air currents rising from the volcanic peaks, making their descent tricky. Below them, the training grounds had been carved directly into the black rock, creating a series of terraced platforms where other dragons and their riders practiced aerial maneuvers.

"Easy, girl," Pryce said, patting Stormwing's neck as her wings trembled against another violent updraft. She let out a worried chirp as they passed a pair of fire drakes breathing streams of flame at moving targets.

They landed hard on the main platform, Stormwing's claws scraping against volcanic stone. Ash poked his head out from the carrying pouch, fur ruffled from the flight. Above them, Skye circled once before landing on a nearby rocky outcrop.

Master Kestrel stood waiting, his eyes narrowed at the sight of Pryce's companions.

"Welcome to Dragon's Fang Island," Kestrel said. "I trust your journey was uneventful?"

Before Pryce could answer, a shadow drake screamed overhead, its rider executing a perfect combat roll. The maneuver ended with the dragon's claws extended, ready to strike.

"Your pets will need to stay in the lower quarters," Kestrel said. "We can't have them disrupting training."

"They won't cause trouble," Pryce said, scratching behind Ash's ears. "They're part of my team."

"This isn't some village farm. This is a military training facility. Impressive, isn't it?" He gestured at the aerial display. "That's what you'll learn here. Real dragon riding, not just gentle flights over a lake."

A group of young riders approached, their dragons following behind. Pryce noticed their leather armor, so different from his simple fishing clothes.

"These are your fellow trainees," Kestrel said. "Though they've had somewhat more . . . extensive preparation than you."

A girl with short dark hair stepped forward. "I'm Raven," she said, offering a slight bow. "Don't worry about the fancy moves yet. Took me weeks just to stay on during basic maneuvers."

"I'm Pryce, and this is Storm—"

"Stormwing," a familiar voice cut in. "The dragon that can't even land properly."

Thane Zharan emerged from the group. His shadow drake curled around him protectively, yellow eyes fixed on Stormwing. Ash bristled in his carrier, and Skye let out a warning screech from her perch.

"Time for your first lesson," Kestrel announced. "Basic combat positioning. Raven, demonstrate the standard attack stance."

Raven swung onto her copper-scaled drake. With ease, she shifted her weight forward, one hand gripping the saddle's front ridge while the other held an imaginary weapon. Her dragon's neck arched, wings half-spread for balance.

"Your turn," Kestrel said to Pryce.

After securing Ash's carrier to a nearby post, Pryce mounted Stormwing. He tried to mirror Raven's position, but Stormwing fidgeted beneath him. The dragon's muscles tensed as another fire drake roared nearby.

"She's fighting you," Thane said, circling them on his shadow drake. "Dragons sense weakness. If you can't control her in basic stances, how do you expect to handle real combat?"

"I'm not weak. Storm's just not used to—"

"Not used to what? Being a proper dragon?" Thane laughed. "Face it, Harper-Green. You've made her soft, like everything else in that fishing village of yours."

The other trainees murmured, some nodding in agreement. Pryce felt his face grow hot. Below, Ash paced around his post while Skye swooped low over their heads.

"Perhaps," Kestrel said, "a demonstration is in order." He looked at Pryce and Thane. "Nothing teaches quite like experience."

"Master Kestrel." Raven stepped forward. "Pryce just arrived. Maybe we should—"

"He's had time to bond with his dragon," Kestrel said. "Now we'll see what that bond is worth." He turned to Pryce. "Unless you'd prefer to return home?"

The word 'home' carried a weight of shame. He remembered Seren's kiss, her words about protecting Crystal Shores. How could he face her if he couldn't even handle basic training?

"No," Pryce said, sitting straighter in the saddle. "I'll do it."

"Simple rules," Kestrel said. "First to force their opponent to yield or lose position wins. No direct attacks on the dragons." He stepped back, raising his arm. "Begin!"

Thane's shadow drake launched into the air with explosive force. Stormwing followed more hesitantly, her powerful wings carrying them skyward in wide spirals. Skye followed the battle from a safe distance.

Thane struck first, his drake diving from above. Pryce yanked on the reins, and Stormwing barrel-rolled away from the attack. The sudden maneuver nearly unseated him.

"Sloppy," Thane called out, banking for another pass. "Your drake has potential, but you're holding her back."

Stormwing growled, electricity crackling along her scales. Pryce felt her muscles bunch beneath him. Above them, Skye kept pace, her warning calls marking Thane's position whenever the shadow drake tried to use its natural camouflage.

"Now," Pryce said, "Show them what you can do!"

Stormwing shot upward, surprising both Thane and his drake. They climbed until the training grounds below looked like a child's toy, Ash a mere speck beside the training post. Then, without warning, Stormwing tucked her wings and plunged.

Wind screamed in Pryce's ears as they dove past Thane, close enough to see his startled expression. Stormwing's natural storm magic left a trail of crackling energy in their wake, disrupting the shadow drake's flight.

"Better!" Kestrel's voice carried from below. "But a real enemy won't be so easily rattled!"

As if proving the point, Thane's drake recovered quickly. It vanished into its own shadow—a trick Pryce hadn't known was possible—only to reappear directly above them.

"Too predictable," Thane said as his drake's talons nearly scraped Pryce's back.

Stormwing jerked away, her movements dissolving into chaos. She bucked and twisted, fighting against Pryce's commands as terror overtook her. Above them, Skye screeched.

"Storm, please!" Pryce fought to regain control. "I know you're scared, but—"

The shadow drake struck again, this time catching Stormwing's wing with its tail. They began to fall, spinning toward the rocky ground below.

At the last possible moment, Stormwing snapped her wings open. The sudden deceleration slammed Pryce against the saddle. They pulled up mere feet from the volcanic rock, sending loose pebbles scattering.

"Yield!" Kestrel shouted. "Before someone gets killed."

Pryce raised his hand in surrender. Thane's drake landed nearby. Skye descended to perch on Stormwing's saddle.

"Not bad for a fisherman's son," Thane said. "At least you didn't fall off."

The other trainees gathered around as Pryce dismounted on shaky legs. Raven approached, offering a waterskin.

"You lasted longer than I did my first time," she said.

"Enough rest," Kestrel called out. "Formation training. Everyone in the air—including you, Pryce. Your real work begins now."

The afternoon dissolved into a blur of drills. From his perch on a high rock, Ash watched the aerial training. Skye had taken to following their maneuvers, occasionally letting out warning squawks when other dragons flew too close to Stormwing.

They practiced attack formations, defensive patterns, and coordinated strikes. With each passing hour, Stormwing grew more agitated. Her usually smooth movements became jerky.

"Higher!" Kestrel shouted from below. "Dragons are weapons of war! They must learn to strike without hesitation!"

Pryce felt Stormwing's muscles trembling beneath him. When she tried to execute a diving attack, her wing clipped another trainee's dragon.

"Control your beast, Harper-Green!" Thane's voice cut through the chaos. "Or do you need another demonstration?"

By evening, Stormwing was refusing commands entirely. She landed hard on a lower terrace, away from the other dragons, and wouldn't budge. Ash padded over from his watching spot, rubbing against her leg while Skye landed on her back, preening the dragon's scales in a gesture of solidarity.

"Storm?" Pryce slid from the saddle, noticing how she flinched at his touch. "What's wrong, girl?"

A pained screech echoed from somewhere below. Stormwing's head snapped up, her eyes fixed on a cave entrance partially hidden by volcanic steam. Ash's ears flattened at the sound, and Skye took flight.

"It's nothing," Pryce said, but Stormwing was already moving. "Storm, wait!"

She led him down a narrow path, past the official training grounds. The cave opening belched hot air and the sounds of suffering dragons. Ash slunk beside them into the cave.

Inside, rows of injured dragons lay chained to the walls. Some bore fresh wounds from training accidents. Others showed signs of older abuse—scars, badly-healed wings, broken spirits. Skye fluttered from injured dragon to injured dragon, as if trying to offer comfort.

"What have they done to you?" Pryce said, reaching for a young fire drake with a crudely splinted leg. The dragon whimpered.

Stormwing pressed closer to Pryce, her wings drooping as she gazed at the injured drake sympathetically.

Then the hair on Pryce's neck prickled. An unnerving sound vibrated through the cavern—a throaty growl that seemed to shake the rock walls. It was a noise of raw might.

Pryce gulped. He willed his legs to move, each step a monumental effort. The deeper he advanced, the more the air pulsed with the dragon's threatening sound. Ash remained glued to his heel.

Emerging into a sprawling grotto at the cavern's heart, where torches on the walls cast jittery shadows. Pryce froze. The source of the sound was a titan, unlike anything in the legends he had read. The dragon was gargantuan, its scales the hue of polished night. Massive chains, as thick as a ship's mast, shackled the creature to the cave's rear wall.

The beast's eyes locked onto Pryce. They were eyes that spoke of a spirit unbroken by its captivity. A furious roar tore from its throat, the chains clanged as the dragon surged forward. Drool dripped from its fangs, sizzling when it touched the cold stone of the cave floor.

"By the Ancients," Pryce said with dread as he backed up hastily.

20. Stranded

The water was eerily still, a deceptive mirror reflecting the faint starlight of the graveyard watch hours of Ryxe. The skiff drifted, a tiny speck of wood and sail on the vast, dark expanse of the Undertow Sea.

The silence pressed in, far more unnerving than the seadrakes' roars had been. They had vanished beneath the surface as quickly as they had appeared. Where are they now? She wondered, looking at the water around her. She felt a lurking dread, a primal awareness of unseen predators beneath the waves, as if she was a small mouse in a room full of cats.

With no compass to guide her—the darned Dragonkin had taken that—Ellie focused on the distant silhouettes of the jagged volcanic islands on the horizon. Just reach the shore, she told herself, and then you can worry about the next step. She relied on the feel of the wind on her face, the subtle push and pull of the waves against the hull, as she steered toward what she hoped was safety.

The skiff moved through the black water, her only source of light was the lantern casting a dim circle around the boat. She shivered, not entirely from the cold. Then, a subtle ripple broke the water's surface, a reminder that she was not alone, and the seadrakes still lingered. She tightened her grip on the tiller, as she scanned the darkness for any sign of the beasts below.

The rocky shoreline loomed before her, and she maneuvered the skiff towards it.

"Almost there."

The vessel shuddered as it scraped against the jagged rocks, the noise jarring. The hull groaned as water began to seep in. Ellie scrambled to drag it further up the shore, ignoring the pain in her shoulders as she heaved. She knew that the skiff wouldn't last long and that she had no other way to leave the island.

No. Don't think about it, she thought, as she pulled with all of her might. Just get through this night.

As far as she could tell, the island was a desolate landscape under the dim starlight. Volcanic rock and loose gravel stretched out before her, a barren wasteland. The air was humid, a suffocating blanket clinging to her skin. A thick fog from the sea and the dark night clung to the land, obscuring everything beyond her small pool of lantern light.

It was difficult to see, her vision limited, making the island appear more terrifying than it already was. She strained her eyes, trying to look through the gloom, but the fog seemed to swallow the light, rendering the world into a series of shifting shadows.

Thirst became an insistent ache in her throat. Ellie knew she had to find fresh water soon or she wouldn't survive long. She could see no sign of life until her gaze caught on a slender vine clinging to a rock face—a water plant. Its leaves holding droplets of the morning dew.

She drew her knife and cut the vine, and carefully coaxed the water from the plant to her lips, letting each precious drop linger on her tongue. "Just enough to get me through."

The fog that clung to the island, creating a sense of isolation. She wrapped her arms around her body. "What was Grandpa Joe's saying for staying warm?" she asked herself, but she couldn't remember. Never mind, that's not important right now. Shelter first, she thought, trying to be practical.

The limited circle of light from her lantern and each rustle of the damaged sail made her jump. Ellie tried to shake off her unease, her hand instinctively moved to the knife at her belt. Okay, Ellie, she said to herself, Just breathe and think. She had to focus on finding shelter. She had to survive.

Using the ruined sail, she managed to create a crude shelter, shielding herself from the night's chill and the unseen dangers. It offered minimal protection, just a few layers of tattered canvas secured to rocks and broken pieces of the skiff. She worked quickly, not wanting to spend any longer in the open than she had to.

As she worked, her fingers brushed against a strange shape—a peculiar crystal embedded in the rock, unlike anything she'd seen on the mainland. It seemed out of place on the volcanic landscape, and she made a mental note to examine it later, when survival wasn't her immediate concern.

As the fog swirled and the night settled around her, Ellie became acutely aware of the feeling of being watched. The darkness was alive with movement, faint whispers and rustling leaves. Just the wind, Ellie, she thought. Just the blasted wind. They sounded like murmurs from the rocks. Something felt familiar about the place, like a forgotten dream, a whisper of an old song. It was as if the island itself was watching her.

A deep unease settled in. She'd felt this before, a strange familiarity that made her uneasy. She looked at her finger, to the simple silver ring that rested there, a reminder of home and family.

Then, as she huddled beneath her makeshift shelter, she heard it: a single, chilling sound. It was a cry, almost Shorling, and yet something about its tone suggested something not quite of this world. It was distant, but clear, and echoed eerily across the rocks, seeming to come from everywhere at once. Was someone else on the island, or was this just a trick of the night?

21. The Sculptor's Hand

The air in the grotto was the scent of sulfur and something else—a musky odor that made Pryce's nostrils flare. The enormous dragon, strained against his chains, the metal scraping against the volcanic rock as the beast let out a low, rumbling growl that vibrated through the stone floor.

He hates it here, Pryce thought, looking at the massive creature. He felt a strange kinship with the beast.

"Impressive, isn't he?" Master Kestrel's voice came from behind, making Pryce jump.

Pryce turned to face Kestrel, who had entered the grotto without a sound.

Kestrel kept a respectful distance from dragon, his gray eyes studying Pryce's interaction with the beast.

"What is he?" Pryce asked, his gaze returning to the chained dragon. "Why is he chained up like this?"

"This," Kestrel said, "is Ragnarok. A rare and powerful specimen." He gave an almost apologetic shrug. "He requires a . . . certain level of restraint, for everyone's safety." He paused, letting the words settle. "Ragnarok seems to have a particular dislike for Dragonkin. It's why we have struggled so much."

"Restraint?" Pryce asked. "He looks tortured."

Kestrel's face hardened for just a moment, then shifted back to its practiced calm, like a mask that slipped and then settled back into place. "He is . . . spirited. He needs proper guidance, someone who understands dragons as you do, Pryce. Most of us here have been trained, but you . . . you seem to have a natural bond, a gift. A gift that is rare." He paused, his eyes locking with Pryce's. "That's why you're here, isn't it?"

Pryce looked over at Ragnarok, the beast watching him intently, its gaze filled with distrust, not just anger. "And the other dragons?" Pryce asked. "Why are they so hurt?"

"Training accidents, mostly," Kestrel said, his tone dismissive as he gestured with a gloved hand. "We push our riders, and sometimes their dragons, to their limits. It is the only way to become stronger." He walked closer to Pryce, and placed his hand on Pryce's shoulder, his grip firm but gentle, his eyes locking with Pryce's. "You will understand soon enough. You need to be strong, both of body and mind."

Pryce was not satisfied, but he knew that pressing the issue would get him nowhere. Kestrel didn't seem like someone who liked to be questioned, and Pryce knew it was best not to provoke him just yet. "Right," Pryce said, letting the matter go for now, "then let's get started."

***

The first rays of dawn barely pierced the volcanic haze of Dragon's Fang Island as Pryce found himself on the training grounds. It was still early, the sky a dull gray, the air heavy with the smell of sulfur. This was Ryxe, a day that was typically devoted to study, but here, it was a day of battle.

The ground vibrated with the constant roar of dragons taking to the sky, and his muscles ached from yesterday's training. He was still wearing the Dragonkin training leathers that had been placed in his room for him, the leather stiff and uncomfortable, like a cage. They want me to be like them, he thought. His personal belongings and his own clothes were tucked away in the corner of the small space. His room, located at the far end of a large hall where the other trainees stayed, was small, private and functional, but it felt like a prison.

"You're late." Kestrel's voice was sharp as he approached. "Discipline is key to becoming a dragon rider." Kestrel stepped in front of Pryce.

Pryce felt his jaw tighten, but he did not say anything as he watched Kestrel begin. He is not just a trainer, Pryce thought, focusing on the way Kestrel held the sword. He is a sculptor, molding me, and I am but a piece of clay. Kestrel did not care about the individual, he was only concerned about the end result, and the idea made Pryce uneasy. It was as if Kestrel was working on Pryce to make a masterpiece, a weapon, and he wouldn't stop until the job was finished, and there wasn't anything Pryce could do to stop it.

"Today, we focus on mounted combat," Kestrel said as he gestured to the training area. "A dragon rider is not a mere passenger. You must become one with your dragon, anticipating its movements and controlling your environment." He gestured to a training area filled with obstacles, fire pits, and moving targets, all designed to test their agility and balance. They were expected to maneuver their dragons through tight spaces, execute rapid attacks, and to avoid the simulated debris fields that could cause them to fall from the sky, all while keeping their focus and composure.

A young Dragonkin, with scales of a deep, earthy brown, led Stormwing towards him. Jorr, Pryce remembered the young man's name from the previous day, handed Stormwing's reins to Pryce. He wore a mix of leathers and hides as he checked Stormwing's tack. He patted Stormwing's muzzle, a strange contrast to the harsh ways of the other Dragonkin.

"She's been fed and watered, young master," Jorr said respectfully. "She has a good heart." Then he returned to the other dragons.

Pryce mounted Stormwing, feeling uneasy. He knew Stormwing, her quirks, her needs, but she was changing. Here, she was just another dragon, a weapon in the making. He wanted to take her away from this place, to protect her from the Dragonkin and all of their madness, but he had to complete the training, if only to keep his family safe. "Just a little while longer," he whispered to Stormwing.

The drills were relentless, designed to push him beyond his limits. Kestrel's words, though seemingly focused on training, were laced with subtle jabs at Pryce's background.

"Focus, Shorling," Kestrel said as he corrected Pryce's posture for what felt like the tenth time, the tip of the practice sword sharp against his ribs. He was strong and agile, but he wasn't the same as the others, and Kestrel made sure he knew that he was different. He was something different, something Kestrel kept telling him was special, but he only felt isolated and alone.

"Your form is sloppy. You must control your movements," Kestrel said as he circled Pryce and Stormwing. "Dragons respond to strength, not hesitation."

He is trying to break me, Pryce realized. He wants to mold me, make me one of them. And that's when he understood, Kestrel didn't really care about dragons, he only cared about their power, how he could control them, how he could use them. He was a tool, that's what Kestrel wanted him to be. And he would never be a tool.

He pushed through the drills, each swing of his sword, each flight maneuver, a battle against exhaustion. He moved like Kestrel wanted him to, with precision and power, but he knew that it was a performance, something that he had to do to survive.

During a short break, Pryce was heading for a waterskin when he saw Thane watching him from the edge of the training grounds. He was no longer openly ridiculing Pryce, but had a look of cold fury that made the fine hairs on his arms rise. Pryce could feel that Thane's resentment was growing, feeding on Pryce's success as it became more apparent that Pryce was a threat, and that his natural talent would make Thane seem less special.

"Impressive progress," Thane said with a harsh undertone. He stopped a few feet away, arms crossed as he watched Pryce. "For a Shorling."

Pryce bristled, his fists clenching. "I'm learning."

Thane chuckled, making the other trainees glance over. "Learning quickly, it seems. But natural talent can only take you so far, can't it? There's no substitute for real training." He leaned forward, his voice dropping to a whisper. "I've heard tales of your father, Harper-Green. He brought shame to my house, and now his son is here, showing us up." Thane paused. "Perhaps, you should honor his memory by staying on the ground." Thane glared at him.

Pryce felt a tremor of fear, knowing how much Thane hated him. He is just trying to provoke me, Pryce thought, trying to stay calm.

"My father was a hero to his people," Pryce said, meeting Thane's gaze. "And I will honor his name."

Thane laughed again. He had succeeded in his goal, he had gotten under Pryce's skin, and Pryce knew he couldn't let him win.

Thane focused on something behind Pryce before he turned abruptly and left, leaving Pryce staring at his retreating back.

That afternoon, Pryce was led back to the cave where Ragnarok. The other trainees, and Kestrel, followed closely behind.

"We have all tried to tame Ragnarok, Pryce," Kestrel said, his voice echoing in the large space. "None of us have succeeded. Now it is your turn. Perhaps, you will finally be able to break him."

Pryce's attention was drawn toward the giant dragon. He could see Ragnarok straining against its chains. It was clear the Dragonkin were trying to control the beast by force, trying to break him with fear and pain.

He stood before Ragnarok, and this time it didn't snarl or roar, it just watched him. He hesitated, then slowly, cautiously approached the beast.

22. What Once Was

Ellie woke beneath her makeshift shelter, her throat parched and her muscles aching from yesterday's encounter with the seadrakes.

As she emerged from her shelter, her boots crunched on the volcanic gravel. The island's terrain was a maze of sharp ridges and deep valleys, with ancient ruins peeking through the morning fog like the bones of some long-dead creature.

Strange crystalline formations jutted from the volcanic rock, rainbow-like refractions colored the landscape. Some crystals were as small as her finger, others tall as ship's masts.

In the distance, ruins of what might have been towers or temples rose from the mist, their broken spires wrapped in crystalline growths like frozen lightning.

"Water first. Everything else can wait."

Ellie picked her way through the maze-like terrain. The volcanic gravel shifted treacherously under her feet. She paused at what appeared to be an ancient archway, its surface etched with symbols. Something about this place felt wrong—as if the usual rules of nature had been suspended.

Walking back to her ruined skiff, she surveyed the damage. The hull was split in three places, the wood warped beyond repair. Without proper tools and materials, the vessel would never sail again.

A flash of movement caught her eye—something colorful darting between the rocks. She reached for her knife, then relaxed as a familiar laugh echoed across the stones.

"Still jumping at shadows, Ellie-belly? And here I thought marriage might have steadied those nerves of yours."

Ellie turned, finding the Quibnocket perched on a crystal formation. His patchwork cloak rippled with colors, and his wiry hair seemed to dance in a wind that wasn't blowing.

"Pip?" She blinked, wondering if thirst was making her hallucinate. "How did you—never mind. Of course you're here. You're always where you shouldn't be."

Pipwhistle grinned, revealing teeth that needed brushed. "Now, is that any way to greet the one who gave you such a lovely wedding gift?" He produced what looked like a Royal Sapphire from thin air, then made it vanish again. "It's good that you've passed your dragon pendant on to young Pryce. It suits him better anyway, wouldn't you say?"

"Pip, I don't have time for—"

"Time!" He lept down from his perch. "Oh, but you do, dearie. This is Aetheria, where time plays tricks and the past mingles with the present like tea leaves in hot water." He snapped his fingers, and suddenly the air was filled with dancing lights that formed images—seadrakes swimming through air, ancient ships sailing stormy skies.

"I need water," Ellie said, trying to stay focused despite the mesmerizing display. "And my skiff is beyond repair."

"Beyond repair?" Pipwhistle skipped over to the ruined vessel. "Oh yes, quite beyond repair. But then, some things must break before better things can be built." He tapped the crystal embedded in the nearby rock. "See these? They're not just pretty baubles. They're memories, dearie. The seadrakes' memories, to be precise."

Ellie stepped closer to examine the crystal. Within its depths, she could almost see shapes moving, like shadows beneath ice. "What do you mean, their memories?"

"The seadrakes weren't always what they are now," Pipwhistle said. "The Dragonkin did that—twisted them, bound them with blood magic and false worship. But here on Aetheria . . ." He gestured at the ruins around them. "Here, the truth still echoes."

"Stop speaking in riddles, Pip," Ellie said, the dryness in her throat making her voice crack. "I need water, and I need to reach my son."

"Water flows where water wills, but sometimes—" He paused, nose twitching. "Oh, very well. No riddles. Come along, Ellie-belly." He gestured for her to follow as he skipped between the rocks. "The spring's this way, unless it's moved since yesterday. Places have a habit of wandering on Aetheria."

Ellie followed him through a narrow passage between two crystalline formations. The rocks here were smooth, worn by something other than wind or rain. Ancient carvings covered their surfaces—images of seadrakes and Shorlings, not fighting, but dancing together through waves that curved up into the sky.

"Here we are!" Pipwhistle spread his arms wide as they emerged into a sheltered cave. Crystal-clear water bubbled up from somewhere deep beneath the volcanic rock, collecting in a pool.

The cave walls weren't just smooth—they were polished to a mirror finish, reflecting the pool's light. Ancient pictographs decorated the ceiling.

"Drink up, but mind you don't swallow any memories. They tend to disagree with Shorling digestion."

Ellie knelt beside the pool, cupping the cool water in her hands. "What happened here, Pip? What's the truth about the seadrakes?"

"Ah, now that's the proper question!" Pipwhistle settled onto a rock. "Before the Dragonkin came with their blood magic and binding spells, seadrakes were guardians of the deep places. They sang to the tides, kept the balance." His voice took on a sing-song quality:

"When dragons rode the winds above,
And seadrakes swam below,
The world was kept in balance true,
'Till pride did overthrow."

"You're saying the Dragonkin corrupted them?" Ellie asked, wiping water from her chin.

"Corrupted, bound, enslaved—such ugly words for an ugly truth." Pipwhistle produced a piece of glowing crystal from his cloak, rolling it between his fingers. "But bonds can be broken, songs can be relearned. The seadrakes remember, deep in their bones, what they once were. That's why they fear this place—too many memories in these crystals."

Ellie stood, her thirst quenched. "Are you saying I could communicate with them? Find a way past them to reach Drakemere Island?"

"Perhaps." Pipwhistle's grin widened as they left the cave and walked back to the shore. "But first, you'll need to learn their song. And for that—" He held up the glowing crystal. "—you'll need to see what they once were."

"How?" Ellie asked, eyeing the crystal. "Just looking at it won't—"

"Oh, but it will!" Pipwhistle pressed the crystal into her palm. "Close your eyes, feel its warmth. The memories want to be seen, want to be known."

Ellie hesitated, then closed her eyes. The crystal pulsed in her hand like a tiny heartbeat. Images flooded her mind—seadrakes gliding through pristine waters, their scales not the dull black she knew, but iridescent with colors that had no names. They sang to each other in voices that could shake mountains or whisper secrets to shells.

"I see them," she whispered. "They're beautiful."

"Keep looking," Pipwhistle urged. "See how it changed."

The vision shifted. Dragonkin sorcerers stood on clifftops, their hands raised as they chanted in ancient tongues. Dark magic poured from their fingers, seeping into the waters, wrapping around the seadrakes like chains. The creatures' songs turned to screams, their scales darkening as the magic corrupted them.

"Enough!" Ellie opened her eyes, her hand shaking. "How do I reach them? How do I make them let me sail to Drakemere unharmed?"

"The old songs still echo in their bones," Pipwhistle said. "But singing them comes with a price." He produced another crystal, this one dark as storm clouds. "The memories of pain are just as strong as those of beauty."

Before Ellie could respond, a massive shape broke the surface of the nearby sea. A seadrake's head rose from the waves, water cascading from its scales. But this time, Ellie saw it differently. Beneath the corruption, she glimpsed its true nature.

The creature's eyes fixed on her, and suddenly her mind filled with a vision—Pryce standing before a chained dragon of immense size, its scales black as midnight. The dragon's eyes burned with fury as Master Kestrel urged Pryce forward. "Break it," Kestrel was saying. "Prove your worth by breaking its will."

"No!" Ellie shouted, the vision shattering.

The seadrake reared back, its throat beginning to glow with deadly fire. But Pipwhistle stepped forward, his voice rising in an otherworldly song that made the crystals around them vibrate in harmony.

"Quickly now," Pipwhistle said between notes, holding out both crystals. "You'll need their complete song—both the light and dark of it. The seadrakes must know you understand not just what they were, but what they lost." His voice dropped lower. "But remember, Ellie-belly—once you take these crystals, once you learn their songs, you can't unlearn them. And some memories have teeth."

23. Sweet Poison

Ragnarok's scales gleamed in the torchlight as Pryce approached. The massive dragon pulled against his chains, but in his eyes now—not just fury, but a wary assessment.

"Closer," Kestrel commanded from behind Pryce. "Show no fear, or he'll sense it."

Pryce took another step forward. The dragon's head snaked down, bringing one fierce eye level with Pryce's face. This close, Pryce could see old scars beneath the scales, likely from previous "training" attempts.

"That's close enough," Kestrel said. He gestured to several handlers who carried heavy leather restraints. "We'll need to muzzle him before moving him to the training yard."

Jorr stepped forward, he held out a massive muzzle reinforced with metal bands. "Easy now," he said, though whether to Ragnarok or Pryce wasn't clear.

"He's never let anyone this close before," Raven whispered from somewhere behind them. "Not without trying to burn them."

"Perhaps he's finally broken. About time," Thane said.

Ragnarok's growl resonated through the cave, but he kept his eyes on Pryce. There was intelligence in that gaze, and something else—a deep, smoldering resentment that wasn't directed at Pryce himself, but at what he represented.

"I'm not here to break you," Pryce said softly, pitching his voice so only Ragnarok could hear. "But I need you to work with me, just for now."

The dragon's nostrils flared, releasing a thin stream of smoke. But he didn't pull away when Pryce reached for the muzzle in Jorr's hands.

The muzzle was heavier than Pryce expected. He held it carefully, letting Ragnarok see it, smell it.

"Get on with it," Thane snapped. "He's not some pet needing coddling."

Ragnarok's muscles bunched, scales rippling with tension. Pryce shot Thane a warning look. "Maybe if you'd tried coddling instead of breaking, you wouldn't have failed."

Silence fell in the cave. Even Kestrel raised an eyebrow at Pryce's boldness.

Jorr cleared his throat. "The chains, young master? We should secure them before—"

Ragnarok lunged. Not at Pryce, but toward Thane. The old chains groaned against stone as the dragon's massive head snapped forward. Pryce stumbled back as handlers rushed forward with poles and hooks.

"Control him!" Kestrel shouted.

But Pryce stepped between the handlers and dragon. "Wait! Let me—" The words died in his throat as Ragnarok's head swung toward him. Those eyes fixed on him with frightening intensity.

"Remember what you are," Thane said. "A fisherman's son playing at being a dragon rider."

Something shifted in Ragnarok's gaze—recognition, perhaps, of another soul who'd been judged and found wanting by the Dragonkin. The dragon lowered his head, not in submission, but in what felt like a temporary truce.

Working quickly, Pryce secured the muzzle. The handlers attached guide chains, and slowly they led Ragnarok toward the cave's outer chamber. The dragon moved with coiled grace.

The afternoon sun cast long shadows as they reached the training yard. Pryce's heart hammered as handlers removed the muzzle, replacing it with a lighter battle bridle. This was the moment of truth.

"Mount up," Kestrel ordered. "Show us this special bond you supposedly have."

Pryce grabbed the guide rope, using it to pull himself onto Ragnarok's massive back. For one breath, everything was still. Then Ragnarok exploded into motion.

The world became a blur of sky and stone as the dragon bucked and twisted. Pryce clung desperately to the rope, his muscles screaming. Each impact rattled his teeth. A particularly violent twist nearly sent him flying.

"Stay with him!" Kestrel's voice seemed distant. "Assert your dominance!"

But dominance wasn't what Pryce wanted. As Ragnarok reared again, Pryce leaned forward, pressing his palm against the dragon's scales. "I know," he said. "I know they hurt you. But I'm not them."

The dragon's movements became less violent, though still far from calm. That's when Pryce caught a flash of white from the corner of his eye.

Princess Seren stood at the yard's edge, her presence like a beacon in the chaos. He sensed something cold in her eyes before being replaced by warmth so quickly Pryce wondered if he'd imagined it. Their eyes met, and something shifted in his chest. He had to succeed. Had to prove himself worthy.

Ragnarok must have sensed the change in Pryce's determination. The dragon's next move was almost playful—a half-hearted buck that Pryce easily rode out.

"Enough for today," Kestrel called as darkness crept across the yard. "A promising start."

As handlers rushed to secure Ragnarok, Seren approached Pryce. "Walk with me," she said, her voice soft but commanding. "We have much to discuss about Crystal Shores' future."

Pryce's legs trembled as he walked beside Seren. His muscles ached from the battle with Ragnarok, but he straightened his spine, not wanting to appear weak.

"You have a remarkable gift," Seren said, leading him toward a balcony overlooking the training yards. Below, handlers guided Ragnarok back to his cave. The massive dragon glanced up at where Pryce stood.

"He fought me every step of the way," Pryce said, running a hand through his sweat-dampened hair.

"And yet you stayed on."

Seren turned to face him, close enough that he could see the subtle shimmer of scales along her temples. Her hand touched his arm with a grip that felt more reptilian than Shorling.

"Do you know how many riders Ragnarok has thrown? How many he's injured?" She reached up, her fingers ghosting over a scrape on his cheek. "But with you, he shows . . . restraint."

Pryce's skin tingled where she touched him, though whether from attraction or unease, he couldn't tell. "Maybe he's just tired of fighting."

"Or maybe he senses what I do." She produced a heavy pouch that clinked with coins. "Your worth to us. To Crystal Shores."

"What do you mean?"

"Our scouts report increased Seadrake Corsairs activity near your village. The Corsairs grow bolder."

Her violet eyes held his with an intensity that should have warned him, but he was already falling.

"Time grows short, Pryce. We need Ragnarok ready, and you're the key to controlling him."

"I don't want to control him. I want to—"

"To work with him? Of course." Seren smiled. "That's exactly why you're perfect for this task." She pressed the coin pouch into his hands. "I've had you moved to better quarters. Closer to mine."

Pryce's heart raced at her proximity. "Princess, I—"

"Seren," she corrected, stepping closer. "When we're alone, call me Seren."

The kiss caught him off guard—soft at first, then deepening with an intensity that made his head spin. When she pulled back, her eyes seemed to glow in the gathering darkness with a predatory gleam he chose to ignore.

"Your family will be protected," she whispered against his lips. "Your village will prosper. All you have to do is trust me." She kissed him again, briefly. "Trust us."

As Seren's footsteps faded down the corridor, Pryce touched his lips. Below, Ragnarok let out a low rumble that might have been a warning. But all Pryce could think about was Seren's kiss, and the promise of glory it held.

That night, Pryce's new quarters felt luxurious after his previous sparse room. Moonlight filtered through stained-glass windows, casting dragon-shaped shadows across a bed large enough for three. Ash curled contentedly on a velvet cushion while Skye perched on an ornate stand near the balcony.

He emptied the coin pouch onto a desk. More money than his father made in a year of fishing. His fingers found his mother's pendant, warm against his chest.

"We're doing the right thing," he told his pets. "Protecting Crystal Shores from the Corsairs."

Ash's ear twitched, but the cat didn't look convinced.

A distant roar echoed through the night—Ragnarok, still restless in his cave. Pryce walked to the balcony, looking out over the moonlit training grounds. Tomorrow they'd work together again, and this time . . .

His hand drifted to his lips, remembering Seren's kiss. She believed in him. Saw his potential when everyone back home had dismissed him as just another fisherman's son.

A knock at his door startled him. "Enter."

Jorr stepped in, carrying fresh training leathers. "Begging pardon, young master. For tomorrow."

"Thanks." Pryce noticed how the young handler's eyes kept darting toward the shadows. "Something wrong?"

Jorr hesitated. "It's not my place, but . . ." He lowered his voice. "Be careful with Ragnarok. The last rider who got close . . . Master Kestrel said it was an accident, but . . ."

"What happened to them?"

"No one knows. They just . . . disappeared." Jorr backed toward the door. "Some say Ragnarok's not meant to be tamed. That he knows things. Secrets about—" He cut off as he walked into the hall. "Good night, young master."

After Jorr left, Pryce stared at his reflection in a mirror. His father's eyes stared back, but everything else had changed. The Dragonkin leathers suited him now. He looked stronger, more confident.

"I won't disappear," he said to his reflection. "I'll succeed where others failed. For Crystal Shores. For Seren."

But as he turned away, Stormwing's worried chirp carried from her stable, harmonizing with Ragnarok's distant call. The sounds merged into something that might have been a warning, or a lament.

Pryce closed the balcony doors, shutting out the night as Seren's kiss burned on his lips like a brand.

Like a promise.

Like a chain.

24. The Crystal City

The seadrake towered before her, water cascading from its scales. Its throat began to glow with deadly fire, the heat almost singeing her eyebrows. The stench of sulfur stung her nose—like the volcanic vents near Emberfall, but fouler.

"By the tide's grace," Ellie said, clutching the crystals with trembling hands. The song Pipwhistle had sung seemed to fade like morning mist. "I know what you were . . . before they changed you."

The seadrake's head snaked closer, steam rising from its jaws. Its eyes held no recognition—only fury. Around her, the crystals began to crack from the heat, their surfaces splintering with the sound of breaking glass.

"Pip?" The Quibnocket had vanished into whatever space between moments he called home. Ellie backed away slowly, sweat trickling down her spine. "I'm not your enemy, great one."

The creature's roar shook the ground beneath her boots. Ellie turned and ran, feeling the scorching heat as the seadrake's fire melted the stone where she'd stood moments before. The air behind her crackled, and she caught the smell of her own singed hair—like the time she'd leaned too close to the hearth at the Rusty Anchor Inn.

She pushed through dense vegetation, her boots slipping on crystal shards as she scrambled up the slopes. The heavy thud of the seadrake pushing onto shore echoed through the strange forest, each impact making the ground shudder. Branches whipped her face as she ran, but she didn't slow until the sounds of pursuit faded.

"Ruddy depths," she panted, slipping the useless crystals into her bag. Her hands shook as she wiped sweat from her face. "Some dragon blood I turned out to be." She touched her wedding ring for luck, twisting it once as she caught her breath. She'd have to figure out the songs later—assuming she survived long enough to try again.

A sweet scent caught her attention—like honey, but with an undertone that reminded her of the poisonous sea moss that sometimes drifted into Crystal Shores harbor during storms. Through the twisted trees, she glimpsed something moving, something that belonged in her mother's nightmarish tales rather than the waking world.

"A Sweetsnare," she whispered. "By the lake's depths, the old texts were true . . . ." Her mother's botanical scrolls in Tidelore Hall had described these monsters.

The massive flower swayed before her, its petals deep crimson with veins of purple running through them like river tributaries. The bloom gaped wide enough to swallow a person whole. As she watched, mesmerized, the petals rippled with an almost hypnotic rhythm—like a jellyfish dancing in dark waters.

Something brushed her ankle. Ellie looked down to see a thick tendril wrapping around her boot, as strong as the mooring lines on the Blue Horizon.

"Not today, you ruddy plant!" She slashed with her knife, the blade barely cutting through the vine's rubbery flesh. More tendrils reached for her, their movements deliberately slow, almost gentle—like seaweed caressing a drowning sailor. Sweet-smelling fluid oozed from the cut vine, splattering her forearms. Pain blazed where it touched her skin.

The flower's petals spread wider, revealing row upon row of crystalline teeth. The honey-sweet scent grew stronger, making her sick. Another tendril caught her wrist, trying to pull her closer to that waiting mouth.

"I didn't survive the ruddy Undertow Sea to end up plant food." Ellie sawed at the vine around her wrist. Each cut released more of that burning sap, raising welts on her skin. Her knife arm struggled as she hacked at the thickest tendril, remembering Tyler's lessons about finding the weakest point.

The massive bloom lunged toward her, petals spreading wide. Through the teeth, Ellie caught a glimpse of something half-dissolved in its depths—bones, she realized with horror. Animal bones, bleached white.

With desperate strength, she drove her knife deep into what looked like a central vine. The plant recoiled with a sound like tearing silk, its tendrils releasing her as it twisted in apparent pain.

Ellie stumbled backward. Her forearms felt like she'd plunged them into boiling chowder where the sap had touched them. She needed water—her skins were still on the ruined skiff, but with that seadrake patrolling the shore . . . .

"Think," she said, forcing herself to keep moving despite the pain. Through the strange, twisting vegetation, she spotted something that didn't belong in any natural forest—spires rising against the daytide sky like ship's masts in fog.

Through the thinning vegetation, massive structures emerged, their crystalline towers catching the sunlight in ways that made her eyes water. An entire city spread before her, its buildings seeming to have grown from the ground rather than been built—like the limestone formations that rose from the depths of Lake Dragontide.

Crystal formations had overtaken much of the stonework, creating strange hybrid structures that defied description. Even the grandest tales she'd heard of Drakemere Island's palace—with its dragon-sized corridors and carved spires—seemed mundane compared to this alien cityscape.

"Pip?" she called out. "A little guidance would be welcome right about now." The burns on her arms throbbed in time with her pulse, reminding her of her urgent need for fresh water.

Only the wind answered, carrying the distant sound of waves. She pressed on, following what might once have been a road, now half-reclaimed by transparent growths that sparkled. Her boots crunched on fragments that might once have been cobblestones.

Movement caught her eye—quick, darting shapes between the buildings. Not quite Shorling, they kept their distance but watched her with unsettling intensity. When she turned to look directly at them, they disappeared into the shadows.

"I mean no harm," she called out, but the watchers remained hidden.

The ancient city opened into what must have been a marketplace, its stalls now partially merged with the crystal formations. Dried fountains stood in empty squares, their basins etched with scenes that made her pause. Shorlings and seadrakes, dancing together through waves that curved up into the sky. Not fighting, not hunting—celebrating like the festivals of her childhood in Crystal Shores.

"By the old kings . . . what happened here?" she wondered aloud. "The Dragonkin must've done this."

A sound drew her attention—the splash of water, as welcome as a freshening breeze to a sailor. In the center of the marketplace, a spring still flowed, its water clear. Ellie approached cautiously, remembering Finnegan's warnings about drinking from strange waters. But the spring looked pure, and the pain in her arms had become nearly unbearable.

Kneeling beside the fountain, Ellie pushed up her sleeves to examine the damage. Red welts marked her skin from wrist to elbow, some already beginning to blister like a bad scald from the cookfire. She cupped the cool water in her hands and let it run over the burns, sighing with relief as it eased the stinging.

As she drank deeply from the spring, her peripheral vision caught movement. One of the watching creatures had ventured closer—a child-sized being with skin that seemed to shift between flesh and crystal, like sunlight playing on waves. It studied her with eyes like polished moonstones before vanishing again into the shadows.

A weathered map caught her eye, preserved behind a sheet of crystal that had grown over the wall like ice on a winter pond. Despite its age, she could make out familiar landmarks—and there, marked among the intricate routes through the Dragonspine Reaches, was Drakemere Island. It wasn't far at all.

"Thank you," she said to the hidden watchers, though she wasn't sure they understood. "I need to find my son before the eveningbell."

Following the streets toward the sound of waves, she emerged into a harbor unlike any she'd seen in all her years of sailing. Crystal growths had consumed most of the docks, creating a forest of translucent spires that chimed softly in the breeze.

But there, nestled between two crystalline formations, lay a lone fishing vessel. The ship's weathered hull was bleached gray from countless suns, but its lines were as familiar to her as her own reflection—the kind of craft she'd grown up sailing on Lake Dragontide.

Two masts still stood, their rigging intact though stiff with age. Nets hung like forgotten spider webs from the railings, and rusted hooks dangled from weather-worn lines. The vessel had the deep hull of a fishing boat, but the sleek lines of something built for speed—the kind of craft that could outrun a storm or slip past seadrake patrols.

"The Tidedancer," she read from the faded name on the bow.

"Please be seaworthy," she said, climbing aboard. The deck planks creaked but held her weight. She moved methodically through her inspection, checking the rigging as Tyler had taught her, testing the rudder's response, examining the sails stored below for signs of rot.

The ship's hold yielded unexpected treasures—preserved supplies, dried fish that looked as fresh as if it had been caught during last tide's run, hard biscuits sealed in waxed paper. Even an old compass that still pointed true, as far as she could tell. In the captain's cabin, she found charts marked with safe passages through the Dragon's Maws, though the paper was so delicate she barely dared touch it.

But taking the boat without asking felt wrong, like stealing from her own kin. "Hello?" she called out, voice carrying across the harbor. "I need this boat and supplies to reach my son at Drakemere Island. Please . . . is anyone here who can grant me passage?"

The strange inhabitants remained hidden, though she caught glimpses of forms moving between the spires. They neither helped nor hindered as she prepared the vessel.

She hauled fresh water from the spring, washing out the old waterskins she'd found before filling them for the journey ahead. Every movement was watched by unseen eyes—she could feel them.

In the boat's small cabin, Ellie spread the fragile charts across the mounted table, comparing them to the compass readings. The workspace reminded her of Tyler's cabin on the Blue Horizon—cramped but efficient, with a narrow bunk built into one wall and storage compartments beneath. She traced possible routes, her father's lessons flooding back like a rising tide.

"Keep the whirlpools to starboard," she said, following the faded ink lines. "Follow the deep water markers where the old ships rest." Strange symbols marked certain passages—warnings perhaps, or signs only the ancient mariners would have understood.

Back on deck, she checked the rigging one final time, testing each rope as methodically as her mother had taught her to mend nets. The ropes were old but sound, and the sailcloth, though weathered, showed no tears. She hoisted the mainsail partway, testing how it caught the wind. The boom creaked but held steady.

Finally, she untied the mooring lines, using a pole to push away from the crystal-encrusted berth. The Tidedancer's hull groaned like an old sailor rising from his chair, but then the vessel slid smoothly into deeper water.

Ellie looked back at the shore as she guided the boat toward open water. For a moment, she glimpsed the watching creatures gathered at the harbor's edge—-dozens of them. One raised a hand in what might have been farewell.

"Thank you," she called back, though the wind carried her words away. Ahead lay the Dragon's Maws and beyond them, Drakemere Island.

She adjusted the sails, feeling the familiar thrum of wind and wave through the deck planks. The Tidedancer responded eagerly, like an old horse remembering its youth. Together, they set course for the treacherous waters ahead, leaving the mysterious island to its secrets.

25. Dragon Whispers

Pryce rubbed sleep from his eyes as he stepped onto his balcony, the chill of Kaalm's dawn raising goosebumps on his arms. Above, Skye circled with a pebble clutched in her beak, while below, Ash stalked through the training yard, his gray fur bristling as he tracked the bird's shadow.

"Don't you two ever get tired of this game?" Pryce called out, but neither pet paid him any attention.

Skye let out a mischievous squawk and released the pebble. It bounced off Ash's head with perfect accuracy, causing the cat to yowl in indignation. Ash's tail puffed up to twice its size as he batted at the air uselessly.

"Serves you right," Skye seemed to say as she landed on a nearby weapon rack.

Ash hissed something that sounded suspiciously like a curse, if cats could curse, and slunk behind a practice dummy.

Pryce couldn't help but smile at their antics. His muscles ached from yesterday's training with Ragnarok, and the massive dragon's roars filled his dreams. He touched his mother's pendant, drawing comfort from it.

"Young master?" Jorr's voice came from the doorway. The young handler's earth-brown scales caught the morning light. "Master Kestrel expects you at the dragon caves shortly. He says he wants you alone to lead Ragnarok from the cave to the training ground. He says today is . . . important."

"When isn't it?" Pryce said, but he nodded to Jorr. "How's Stormwing this morning?"

"Your storm dragon is doing well. She's been fed and exercised already. Quite gentle for such a powerful beast." He shifted his weight. "But Master Kestrel awaits. Best not keep him waiting."

"I'll be there soon."

As Jorr left, Pryce caught movement in the corner of his eye. Princess Seren stood on her own balcony, her white dress rippling in the morning breeze. She raised a hand in greeting. The memory of their kiss still made his head spin.

A roar echoed from the dragon caves—Ragnarok, calling him to another day of training. Or perhaps warning him. Lately, the massive dragon's cries had begun to sound less like mindless rage and more like . . . words. Almost as if . . .

"Stop it," Pryce told himself. "Dragons don't talk. They're just . . ." But he couldn't finish the thought. Not after what he'd seen in Ragnarok's eyes.

The walk to the dragon caves felt longer each morning. Ash trailed behind Pryce, still shooting dirty looks at Skye, who glided overhead. The volcanic stone was warm beneath Pryce's boots, and steam rose from cracks in the ground, carrying the ever-present scent of sulfur.

Master Kestrel waited at the cave entrance. "You're late."

"Sorry, I was—"

"Save your excuses." Kestrel's voice carried the cultured accent of Dragonkin nobility, but there was an edge to it today. "Ragnarok grows restless. Perhaps he senses your . . . distraction."

Pryce followed Kestrel into the cave. Other handlers moved about, carrying feed and water to the injured dragons still chained in their cells. One young fire drake with a splinted wing whimpered as they passed.

Ragnarok's chains rattled as he turned to face them, and Pryce felt something brush against his mind—like fingers trailing through water.

"Begin," Kestrel commanded, stepping back to observe.

Pryce approached Ragnarok slowly, maintaining eye contact.

"Easy," Pryce said softly. "We're not enemies, you and I."

Ragnarok's head snaked down, bringing one fierce eye level with Pryce's face. The dragon's breath was hot against his skin.

Then it happened.

A flash of memory—not his own—crashed through Pryce's mind. He saw Dragonkin warriors with burning brands, heard the screams of younger dragons being "trained." Felt chains biting into scales for the first time, tasted blood and fury and helplessness.

Pryce stumbled backward, gasping. "What was—"

They break us, a voice rumbled in his head. *Break us, bind us, make us weapons for their war.*

"Ragnarok?" Pryce whispered, too softly for Kestrel to hear.

The dragon's eye fixed on him with intelligence. *You hear me, young one. As she did, before they broke her too.*

"Who—"

"Is there a problem?" Kestrel's voice cut through the moment. "Perhaps you need more motivation."

"No, Master Kestrel," Pryce said. "Ragnarok and I are . . . understanding each other."

Kestrel's eyes narrowed. "Are you? Then perhaps it's time for the next phase of training." He gestured to someone in the shadows. "Thane, join us."

Pryce's stomach clenched as Thane stepped into the torchlight, his scarlet scales gleaming like fresh blood. The older trainee carried a cruel-looking prod—the kind used to "encourage" difficult dragons.

"Remember," Kestrel said, "some beasts only understand pain."

Ragnarok's muscles bunched beneath his scales. *They come with their burning sticks, thinking pain breeds loyalty.*

"We don't need that," Pryce said quickly. "He's responding well to—"

"He?" Thane sneered. "It's a beast, nothing more. My father understood that before your kind killed him." He jabbed the prod toward Ragnarok's flank.

Without thinking, Pryce grabbed Thane's wrist. "Don't."

The cave went silent except for the rattling of Ragnarok's chains. Even the injured dragons in their cells seemed to hold their breath.

"Take your hand off me, Shorling," Thane said.

"Enough." Kestrel's command cracked like a whip. "Thane, wait outside. Pryce . . . continue with your training. Show us this special bond you claim to have."

As Thane stalked away, Pryce turned back to Ragnarok. The dragon's eyes held a new light—something almost like approval.

You are not like them, the voice whispered in his mind. But be careful, young one. They will try to make you so.

"I won't let them hurt you.".

It is not my pain you should fear. Ragnarok's mental voice said. The princess with dragon scales speaks with a forked tongue. Her mother's blood runs cold as the depths.

"Seren? But she—"

"Stop whispering to it and show me progress," Kestrel interrupted. "The dragon must be ready when the Seadrake Corsairs attack Crystal Shores."

Ragnarok's thoughts flooded with images of battles long past. They twist truth like they twist dragons. Listen with your blood, not your heart.

Pryce touched his mother's pendant. Everything he'd dreamed of was within reach—glory, power, Seren's love. But at what cost?

"The chains," Kestrel said. "Remove them."

Pryce's hands trembled as he worked the heavy locks.

Careful now, Ragnarok's voice whispered in his mind. They expect violence. Let us show them something else.

The final chain fell away with a thunderous clang. Kestrel stepped back, his hand moving to the weapon at his belt. But Ragnarok simply stretched, his massive wings unfurling like storm clouds, and lowered his head to Pryce's level.

"Impossible," Kestrel said.

"Mount him," came Seren's voice from the cave entrance. She stood like a vision in white. "Show them what you can do, my prince."

Pryce's heart soared at her words. He placed his hand on the dragon's scales, feeling the heat beneath. With practiced grace, he swung onto Ragnarok's back.

They see what they wish to see. A weapon tamed. A boy seduced by power. Let them believe.

Pryce gripped the riding harness as Ragnarok moved toward the cave's exit—a predator playing at being tame. Outside, dawn had given way to full morning. Ash and Skye watched from their perches as dragon and rider emerged into the training yard.

Thane stood with the other trainees. "This proves nothing. A true test requires combat."

"Perhaps you're right." Seren smiled. "A demonstration then?"

She plays her game well, Ragnarok observed. But remember who you are, son of Crystal Shores.

"I accept," Pryce said.

Thane mounted his shadow drake and took to the air first, climbing into the volcano-warmed thermals above the training yard.

"Show them all," Seren called up to Pryce. "Show them what we can accomplish."

Ragnarok's muscles tightened beneath Pryce. Ready, young one?

"Ready," Pryce whispered, and they launched into the sky.

The wind rushed past as Ragnarok climbed, his powerful wings cutting through the air. Below, the training yard shrank to the size of a game board, the watching Dragonkin mere pieces upon it. Thane's shadow drake circled above, almost invisible against the morning clouds.

He will strike from behind, Ragnarok warned. It is their way.

Sure enough, the shadow drake seemed to vanish completely. Pryce felt rather than saw Thane's approach—a disturbance in the air, a shift in the wind.

"Now!" he called, and Ragnarok rolled just as Thane's drake slashed through the space they'd occupied.

"Lucky dodge," Thane said, his voice carrying on the wind. "But luck won't save you, Shorling."

Ragnarok's response was a roar that shook the air, sending nearby birds scattering. They gave chase, matching Thane turn for turn. The shadow drake was faster, more agile, but Ragnarok's raw power made up the difference.

Watch his pattern, Ragnarok instructed. Like all Dragonkin, he repeats himself.

Pryce studied their opponent's movements. Three beats up, fade to shadow, strike from above. Again and again, like a dance whose steps never changed. On the fourth repetition, Pryce was ready.

"Dive!" he called, and Ragnarok plunged toward the earth. The shadow drake followed, just as predicted. At the last moment, they pulled up, using their momentum to loop behind their pursuers.

"What—" Thane's shock was visible as Ragnarok's tail swept past his drake's wing, sending them tumbling through the air.

They recovered quickly, but something had changed. The confident sneer was gone from Thane's face, replaced by something darker. He drew a blade from his saddle—not a practice weapon.

He means to end this permanently, Ragnarok warned.

"Thane, stand down!" Kestrel's voice carried from below. "This is a demonstration only!"

But Thane wasn't listening. His drake vanished again, and this time Pryce felt the killing intent behind Thane's approach.

Ragnarok moved with great speed for something so large. His wing caught the shadow drake's attack, and for a moment, the two dragons grappled in midair. Pryce could feel Ragnarok's muscles straining, feel the heat building in the dragon's chest.

Trust me, Ragnarok's voice filled his mind.

Pryce nodded, gripping the harness tighter. Ragnarok's jaws opened, and a blast of flame hot enough to melt stone erupted—not at Thane and his drake, but at the air around them. Steam exploded outward as the moisture in the clouds flash-boiled.

The shadow drake's camouflage vanished in the superheated air, leaving them exposed. Before Thane could recover, Ragnarok's tail swept his blade away, sending it spinning toward the earth.

They landed in the training yard, Ragnarok's claws leaving deep marks in the volcanic stone. Steam still rose from his scales, and small electrical discharges crackled between his teeth. Thane's shadow drake touched down moments later, its sides heaving with exhaustion.

"Treachery!" Thane shouted, leaping from his saddle. "He used forbidden magic!"

"The only treachery was your blade," Pryce said, sliding from Ragnarok's back. "This was supposed to be a demonstration."

Seren came forward, placing herself between them. "Enough. Pryce has proven himself beyond question." She turned to face the gathered Dragonkin. "Here stands a true dragon rider, worthy to join our ranks . . . and perhaps more."

Her hand found Pryce's. Ash wound between their legs, purring, while Skye landed on Ragnarok's horns with a triumphant chirp.

"Well done," Kestrel said. "The boy has talent, Your Highness. With proper guidance—"

"My guidance," Seren interrupted. "Pryce will train with me from now on."

She moves her pieces across the board, Ragnarok observed silently. And you, young one, are her queen's gambit.

But Pryce barely heard the warning. Seren's touch, her smile, the admiration of the crowd—it was intoxicating. This was what he'd dreamed of, wasn't it? Power, respect, a place among the mighty.

"Come," Seren said softly. "There's much to discuss about your future. Our future."

As she led him away, Pryce glanced back at Ragnarok.

Remember, that deep voice sounded in his mind. Remember who you are, when the time comes.

Thane's voice carried across the yard: "This isn't over, Shorling."

But Pryce was already following Seren, past his old room in the trainee barracks where he'd spent his first night on Dragon's Fang Island. Her dress rippled like dragon wings as they walked beyond the weathered building toward the grand stone residence where she had moved him.

The corridors grew darker as Seren led him deeper inside. Their footsteps echoed off volcanic rock walls, and the luminous crystals cast strange shadows through steam that seeped from nearby vents. Finally, she drew him into a secluded alcove overlooking the dragon aeries.

"You were magnificent today," she said, her violet eyes reflecting the crystal light. "Everything I knew you could be."

"The blade Thane drew—it wasn't practice steel."

"Thane will be disciplined." She stepped closer, her hand finding his cheek. "But let's not speak of him. There are more important matters to discuss."

"Like what?"

"Like your future. Our future." Her fingers traced his jaw. "The Dragonkin need new blood, Pryce. Fresh perspectives. Those like Thane cling to old hatreds, but you . . . you could help forge a new path."

"What do you mean?"

"My mother grows old. Soon, the Dragonkin will need new leadership." She smiled. "Imagine it—you and I, ruling together. Crystal Shores would prosper under our protection. No more empty nets, no more struggling to survive."

The scent of storm winds always seemed to cling to her. "Your mother wouldn't approve."

"Mother sees your value. Why else would she have sent me to find you?" Seren's lips brushed his ear. "You're special, Pryce. Meant for greater things than fishing."

Greater things, Ragnarok's warning filled his mind. Or greater chains?

But Seren was kissing him, and the dragon's voice faded beneath a wave of desire. Her scales were smooth beneath his fingers as he pulled her closer.

"Say yes," she whispered against his mouth. "Be my prince. Rule with me."

"Yes," he breathed, though somewhere deep inside, a voice that sounded like his mother's urged caution.

Seren's smile held triumph. "Then let's begin."

Seren pulled away slowly, her fingers lingering on his chest near his mother's pendant. "How are you finding your new quarters? Much better than that dreadful trainee room, isn't it?"

"It's perfect," Pryce said. "Though Ash and Skye are still adjusting to the change."

"Oh, darling." She laughed softly, but the sound held no warmth. "You still insist on keeping those common creatures? I thought we discussed this. A prince of the Dragonkin has no need for such . . . pets."

Something cold settled in Pryce's stomach. "They're not just pets. They're—"

"Family?" Her voice held gentle mockery. "You have a new family now. One worthy of your gifts." She gestured to the dragons in their aeries below. "These magnificent creatures will be your true companions. Your weapons."

Listen, Ragnarok's voice whispered in his mind, though the dragon was far below. *Listen to what she does not say.*

"The Seadrake Corsairs," Pryce said. "When will they attack Crystal Shores?"

"Soon enough." Seren's hand found his again. "But don't worry about that now. Come, there's someone I want you to meet. Someone who can help unlock your full potential."

She led him through twisting corridors until they reached a door carved with dragon motifs. Inside, an elderly Dragonkin sat at a desk covered in ancient scrolls. His scales were dull with age, but his eyes burned with intensity.

"Pryce, meet Master Vex," Seren said. "He's going to help you . . . evolve."

The old Dragonkin smiled, revealing teeth filed to points. "Welcome, young prince. Shall we begin your transformation?"

Remember who you are, Ragnarok's voice came again, urgent now. Remember before it's too late.

But Seren's hand was warm in his, and the promise of power thrummed in his veins like dragon fire. As Master Vex approached with a crystal vial filled with swirling darkness, Pryce thought he heard his mother's pendant pulse once, like a warning heartbeat.

The vial's contents reflected like oil on water. Master Vex held it up to the light, and for a moment, Pryce thought he saw shapes wiggling within—dragons in miniature, fighting against their crystal prison.

"One small drink," Vex said, "and your transformation begins. The dragon blood in your veins will awaken fully."

"You know about my bloodline?"

"Why do you think the princess chose you?" Vex's laugh was dry as old scales. "You're already part dragon. This will simply . . . complete the process."

Seren squeezed his hand. "Think of it as stepping into your destiny."

The pendant grew warm against his chest—almost hot enough to burn. From somewhere far below, Pryce felt Ragnarok's consciousness brush against his mind. They offer power, but at what price? Look closer, young one.

"What exactly will this do to me?" Pryce asked, studying the vial.

"Your scales will emerge first," Vex said, running a finger along his own facial ridges. "Then the other changes. Strength. Power. You'll be one of us completely."

"And if I refuse?"

Seren's grip tightened painfully. "Why would you refuse such a gift?"

Because gifts from serpents often bear poison, Ragnarok whispered in his mind. Choose wisely. Your mother's blood or their poison. But know this—you cannot be both.

26. Through the Dragon's Maws

Ellie winced as she smoothed medicinal salve over her forearms. The Sweetsnare's burns had blistered overnight, leaving angry red welts from wrist to elbow. She'd found the jar of ointment in the Tidedancer's captain's quarters, tucked away with other medical supplies.

"Just like Tyler's kit on the Blue Horizon," she said, remembering her husband's meticulous organization of salves and bandages. The familiar scent of wintergreen and dock leaf filled the cabin.

The ship's deck rolled beneath her as she secured the last bandage. Through the cabin's weathered windows, she could see the first of the Dragon's Maws churning ahead—a massive whirlpool that made the legendary tide-races of Lake Dragontide look like ripples in a pond. Even from here, she could see the eerie blue light pulsing in its depths.

Ellie tucked the jar away and climbed to the deck. The old charts she'd found marked a narrow safe passage between the maelstroms, but one wrong turn would drag the Tidedancer into the abyss. She'd seen smaller vessels caught in whirlpools before—watching helplessly as they spiraled down into darkness.

"Not today," she said, gripping the ship's wheel. The wood was smooth beneath her palms, worn by countless hands before hers. "I've got a son to save."

The morning wind caught the mainsail, pushing them closer to the Dragon's Maws. Ellie could feel the subtle pull of the current already, trying to draw them off course.

The crystals from Aetheria clinked in her bag, but those songs would have to wait. Right now, she needed all her focus to thread this needle of calm water between death's teeth.

The first whirlpool loomed larger with each passing moment. Ellie eased the wheel to starboard, following the faded markings on the ancient charts. According to the cryptic notations, she needed to stay in the deep water channel marked by the wreckage of old ships.

She spotted the first marker—a broken mast jutting from the waves like a skeletal finger pointing skyward. Beyond it, barely visible through the morning haze, other pieces of shattered vessels formed a morbid trail through the Dragon's Maws.

"Keep the Wavecutter's crow's nest to port," she said, recalling her father's tales. "Then three lengths past the merchant galley's bones."

The current grew stronger, making the Tidedancer's timbers creak. Ellie felt the subtle shift in the deck beneath her feet as competing forces pulled at the hull. To her left, the massive whirlpool's rotation created its own wind, trying to snatch her sails.

A deep thrumming sound vibrated through the ship. Ellie frowned, moving to the port rail. Far below the surface, that strange blue light pulsed like a massive heartbeat. Something about its rhythm seemed almost familiar.

The wheel suddenly jerked in her grip. The current had caught them, dragging the Tidedancer's bow toward the whirlpool's edge. Ellie threw her weight against the wheel, muscles straining.

"Not here," she said through gritted teeth. "Not when we're so close."

She remembered Tyler teaching her about fighting crosscurrents near the ice flows of Lake Dragontide. "Don't fight the water directly," he'd said, demonstrating with gentle adjustments rather than forceful turns. "Work with it, let it help you find the path."

Ellie relaxed her death grip on the wheel slightly, feeling how the current wanted to pull them. Instead of fighting it entirely, she used its force to help swing the Tidedancer's bow toward the next marker—the broken hull of what had once been a merchant vessel.

The ship responded, cutting through the waves more smoothly now. They were halfway between the first two whirlpools when something massive moved beneath the surface. A shadow passed under the Tidedancer, larger than any seadrake she'd seen before.

"Stay below," she whispered, though she knew the creatures couldn't hear her. "Just let us pass."

The shadow moved on, but Ellie's hands remained tight on the wheel. She still had four more sets of whirlpools to navigate before reaching open water again.

And somewhere beyond them lay Drakemere Island—and Pryce.

She glanced at the approaching vortex, its spiraling surface mesmerizing in its deadly beauty. The strange blue light pulsed again, stronger now.

The second set of whirlpools flanked the channel like twin sentinels. Their roar filled the air—a deep, hollow sound that seemed to resonate in Ellie's bones. Between them, the safe passage narrowed to barely twice the Tidedancer's width.

A sheet of spray hit her face as the bow crashed through a wave, but she didn't dare release the wheel to wipe her eyes. Even a moment's distraction could send her spiraling into the abyss.

The blue light pulsed again, closer to the surface now. It cast strange shadows across the Tidedancer's deck. The thrumming grew stronger, vibrating through the hull until her teeth ached.

"Depths take you," she said, blinking water from her eyes. The next marker—what looked like the stern of an ancient warship—was barely visible through the spray.

Something struck the hull with enough force to make the whole ship shudder. Ellie stumbled, keeping her grip on the wheel only by wrapping her arm through the spokes. That same massive shadow passed beneath them again, but this time it was close enough to the surface that she could make out scales the size of barrel lids.

The creature circled back, and now she could see it clearly through the water—a seadrake larger than any in the stories. Its scales weren't the corrupt black of the others, but rather an iridescent blue.

"Hold steady," she told herself, forcing her attention back to the channel markers. "Just hold—"

The seadrake breached, its massive head rising from the waves like a mountain of scales and teeth. Water cascaded from its fins as it twisted in the air, its body passing so close to the ship that Ellie could have reached out and touched it.

For one heartbeat, its eyes met hers. In their depths, she saw something that stole her breath—not mindless fury like the others, but intelligence. Wisdom. Pain.

Then it crashed back into the sea, sending a wave that nearly capsized the Tidedancer. Ellie spun the wheel hard, fighting to keep the ship from being pushed into the nearest whirlpool.

The impact knocked something loose in her bag. The crystals from Aetheria spilled across the deck, their surfaces catching the strange blue light. As they rolled toward the scuppers, the seadrake's thrumming changed pitch—almost like a response.

The crystals skittered across the deck with each roll of the ship. Ellie couldn't risk releasing the wheel to grab them—not with the whirlpools pulling at the Tidedancer's hull. One crystal tumbled through the scupper, disappearing into Lake Dragontide's with a tiny splash.

The seadrake dove after it, its massive body creating a wake that pushed the ship dangerously close to the whirlpool's edge. The blue light pulsed faster now, almost like a warning.

"Come on," Ellie urged, spinning the wheel to counter the current. Her burned arms strained. The Tidedancer groaned.

The remaining crystal rolled toward the port side as the ship tilted. It produced a sound that cut through the whirlpools' roar. The seadrake's humming changed pitch again, harmonizing with the crystal's tone.

Ellie remembered Pipwhistle's words about the creatures' true nature, about songs that could reach past centuries of corruption. But there was no time for songs now—not with the next set of whirlpools approaching fast.

These were worse than the others. Three massive whirlpools formed a triangle, with the safe channel snaking between them like a thread through needles. The blue light pulsed from all three simultaneously, making the water itself seem to glow.

"Sweet depths," she said, seeing how narrow the passage was. The charts showed this as the most dangerous stretch—where most ships were lost.

The seadrake surfaced again, this time off the starboard bow. It moved with grace, its body creating a pattern in the water that caught Ellie's attention. The creature was swimming against the whirlpools' pull, forming an eddy that actually helped push the Tidedancer toward the safe channel.

Was it... helping?

A memory surfaced—her mother teaching her to read the water's moods while fishing near Crystal Shores. "The lake remembers," she'd said. "It remembers what was, what should be. Sometimes, if you listen close enough, it tries to remind us too."

The seadrake surfaced again, closer now. In the blue light, Ellie could see patterns etched into its scales—symbols similar to those in the ruined city. Its massive body continued to cut through the current, forming a barrier between the ship and the nearest whirlpool.

"You're not like the others, are you?" she said, adjusting their course to follow the path the creature created. "You remember what you once were."

The dragon's thrumming shifted pitch again as Ellie noticed the whirlpool's pull seemed to weaken wherever that resonance touched the water.

Through the spray, she spotted the next marker—the shattered bow of a merchant ship. But this time, she didn't need it. The seadrake's wake formed a clear path through the maelstroms, its body carving a safe channel through the deadly currents.

"The lake remembers." She let the wheel move more freely, trusting the path the ancient creature revealed.

The Tidedancer picked up speed, riding the edge of the current. They passed between the three whirlpools so close that Ellie could feel the spray from all of them. The blue light pulsed one final time, illuminating the seadrake's eye as it turned to look at her.

In that moment of connection, Ellie understood. The Dragon's Maws weren't just a barrier—they were a test. The whirlpools' pull weakened as the Tidedancer cleared the last eddy, and the seadrake dove deep, its task complete.

Ellie let out a breath. She retrieved the crystal from the mast's base, its surface warm to the touch as she placed it back into her bag. Far ahead, though still obscured by haze, dark cliffs rose from the water—- Drakemere Island.

As the haze thinned, Drakemere Island's true scale became clear. The cliffs didn't just rise from the water—they towered, their black stone faces riddled with cave openings like a giant honeycomb. Near the top, elaborate architecture had been carved directly into the rock—spires and balconies that seemed to defy gravity.

Ellie's mouth went dry. The Dragonkin palace was larger than all of Crystal Shores. Dragons wheeled through the air around the higher levels, their scales catching the late morning light. She counted at least a dozen before giving up.

"Where would they keep you, Pryce?" she wondered aloud, studying the cliff face. The dragon pendant he wore would lead her to him if she was close enough, but first she had to gather information.

The Tidedancer's bow cut through the waves as Ellie searched for a safe approach. She needed somewhere hidden from the dragons that patrolled the skies.

A dark shadow beneath the cliffs caught her eye—a natural arch of black stone, barely visible unless you knew where to look. The opening seemed large enough for the Tidedancer, and the overhang would hide them from the dragons circling above.

Ellie guided the ship carefully through the narrow entrance. The space opened into a sheltered cove, its walls riddled with smaller caves. Symbols had been carved into the rock, weathered by centuries of waves.

Perfect. She dropped anchor in the deepest part of the cove, where the Tidedancer's mast wouldn't show beyond the arch. A sentry dragon passed overhead, its shadow briefly darkening the water, but the ship remained hidden in the gloom beneath the stone.

Somewhere in that fortress, she would find Pryce. She just had to figure out how to get inside without being spotted by the dragons that wheeled overhead.

The burns on her arms throbbed, reminding her to reapply the salve before doing anything else.

Ellie formed a plan. The Dragonkin would have supply ships, messengers, servants—someone would know where they were keeping her son. She just had to find the right person to ask.

Ellie retreated to the cabin and pulled out the jar of salve. Her burns had started bleeding again during the difficult passage through the Dragon's Maws. As she unwrapped the bandages, she studied charts spread across the captain's table.

The Dragonkin palace's defenses were formidable from the water, but these old diagrams showed something interesting—a network of sea caves beneath the main fortress. Supply vessels would need a way to deliver goods even in bad weather. If she could find one of those caves . . .

A splash outside made her freeze. She crept to the cabin window, staying in the shadows. A small fishing boat passed by the arch, its crew dressed in the simple clothes of servants rather than the elaborate armor of

Dragonkin warriors. They were hauling in nets full of fish—probably to feed the dragons.

Ellie watched them work. The servants would know the palace's layout, its routines. And more importantly, they'd know where prisoners were kept.

She finished wrapping fresh bandages around her arms, then began searching the Tidedancer's storage compartments. There had to be something she could use.

Her hand struck a bundle of cloth. She pulled it out—simple fishing clothes, worn but sturdy, much like the ones the servants wore. A plan began forming in her mind.

"Sorry, Tyler," she said, thinking of all the times he'd warned her about taking unnecessary risks. "But sometimes the best way through a dragon's den is straight through the front door."

She began cutting cloth. The burns needed to be hidden—no servant would be allowed to work with open wounds. As she worked, she memorized the cave systems shown in the charts. She would have one chance at this.

A horn sounded from above, its deep note ringing off the cliffs. The fishing boat outside quickly hauled in its last net and began rowing toward one of the larger cave openings.

Change of watch, Ellie realized. Perfect. She could use the shift change to slip in among the returning servants.

Now she just needed to get up there without being spotted by the dragons above.

Ellie changed quickly into the servant's clothes she'd found. The rough fabric irritated her burns, but at least the long sleeves hid the bandages. Her red hair would stand out like a signal fire among the dark-haired Dragonkin. She searched the cabin's storage, finding a battered fisherman's cap with a deep brim. It wasn't perfect, but tucked up carefully, it would hide her distinctive hair.

"Think like a servant," she told herself, practicing the stooped walk she'd seen the fishermen use. "Eyes down, shoulders bent. Don't draw attention."

She gathered into her bag only what she absolutely needed—the medicine jar, a waterskin, and some dried fish wrapped in cloth. The servant's trousers hung loose, threatening to slip down her hips. She threaded her knife belt through the loops, as both protection and practicality. The bulky shirt draped over the belt, hiding everything beneath its coarse fabric.

The horn sounded again, longer this time. Through the cabin window, she watched another fishing boat row past, heading for the same cave as the first. The shift change wouldn't last long.

Ellie took one last look around the Tidedancer's cabin. The old ship had served her well, but now she needed to move on foot. She touched the worn timber of the door frame, silently thanking the vessel.

"Well," she said, adjusting the cap lower, "time to walk into the dragon's mouth."

27. Two Bloods

The vial's contents swirled like storm clouds in Pryce's palm, dark liquid moving with an unsettling life of its own.

Master Vex's laboratory reeked of potions and worn scrolls. Its stone walls were lined with shelves of mysterious ingredients. Dried herbs hung from the ceiling, their bitter fragrance barely masking an underlying smell of decay—like thunderstorms mixed with grave dirt. The only light came from a small window, and luminous crystals set in iron brackets, casting everything in shifting shadows that made the scales on Vex's face seem to move.

Seren's hand remained warm against Pryce's back. The subtle scales at her temples flexed with her smile as she leaned closer.

In the corner of Vex's study, Ash had pressed himself against the wall, his gray fur standing on end. Outside the room's single window, barely wider than an arrow slit, Skye scratched at the ledge with her talons, as if trying to reach Pryce.

"Drink, my love," Seren whispered, her lips brushing his ear. Her breath was warm. "Become who you were meant to be."

Pryce remembered Ragnarok's warning, but Seren's touch scattered his thoughts like leaves in a storm. Her fingers traced circles on his back, each movement sending warmth through his body that made it hard to think clearly. When she pressed closer, the scent of rain-washed skies filled his head. This was everything he'd dreamed of—power, acceptance, and a princess who saw him as more than just a fisherman's son. Each soft brush of her fingers weakened his resolve, drowning out the dragon's warning in a tide of longing.

Pryce lifted the vial to his lips. Somewhere in the back of his mind, a voice that sounded like his mother's whispered caution, but Seren's other hand found his cheek, turning his face toward hers. Her violet eyes held such promise, such certainty. How could something that felt this right be wrong?

The first drop hit his tongue like a bolt of lightning. The liquid burned like ice, then blazed into fire that spread down his throat and into his chest. He managed three desperate swallows before his mother's pendant flared with sudden heat, searing him. The pain made him gasp, his fingers going numb. The vial slipped from his grasp, shattering against the stone floor in a spray of dark liquid and crystal shards.

"No matter," Vex said. "You've taken enough to begin."

The first wave of pain dropped Pryce to his knees. It felt like molten glass flowing through his veins. Every heartbeat sent fresh agony coursing through him. Through the haze of pain, he heard Ash yowl—a sound of pure terror—and saw the cat scramble up a bookshelf, sending scrolls and vials tumbling to the floor.

"Wretched beast!" Vex lunged for Ash, scattering more vials in his haste. "That was three months' work, you mongrel vermin! I'll have your hide for a potion bag!"

The cat darted between shelves as Vex hurled a crystal at him, missing and shattering it against the wall.

"Control yourself," Seren snapped at Vex. "The transformation is more important than your experiments."

Vex turned back, chest heaving, but his eyes still tracked Ash's movement along the highest shelf. "These beasts are a plague," he spat. "Like all common animals, they have no place among the Dragonkin. When the boy is fully changed, he'll see that too."

Seren knelt beside Pryce, her fingers brushed his forehead. "The transformation can be . . . uncomfortable. But it will pass, my love. Like a snake shedding its old skin to reveal something more beautiful beneath."

Pryce tried to respond, but the words tangled in his throat. His vision swam, turning the room's crystal lights into smears of color. Through the haze, he watched in horror as his hands began to change. The skin split along his knuckles, revealing scales that pushed through like spring buds breaking soil. They spread across his fingers, each new scale bringing fresh waves of agony.

The pain intensified. One moment it burned like molten metal, the next it chilled him to the bone. His teeth ached, and something shifted beneath the skin of his face, pulling tight across his cheekbones.

"Something's wrong," Vex said sharply, moving closer to examine Pryce's face. "The reaction shouldn't be fighting itself like this. The scales, yes, but this resistance—"

"What's happening to him?" Seren gripped Vex's arm. "Fix this!"

Pryce could barely focus on their voices. Two distinct sensations warred within him—one familiar and pure, like the waters of Lake Dragontide, the other alien and corrupt, like poison seeping through his veins. The dragon blood of his ancestors clashed with Vex's tainted potion, turning his body into their battlefield.

He clawed his way toward the window on hands and knees, desperate for fresh air.

"Help me get him to his quarters," Seren ordered. She gestured to two guards outside the door. "Quickly, before anyone sees him like this. The wedding announcement hasn't even been sent—we can't risk rumors about his condition spreading through the ranks."

The world tilted and spun as they half-carried him through the winding corridors. Stone walls blurred past, the luminous crystals leaving trails of light across his vision. Pryce's feet dragged against the floor, his boots scraping stone. Through waves of pain, he caught fragments of conversation—servants stopping their work to stare, their whispers following like shadows.

"The princess's chosen one . . ."

"Did you see his face? The scales . . ."

"They say the wedding will be held at Drakemere . . ."

"So soon?"

Each word floated past like debris in a storm tide. He tried to swallow, but his throat had changed, making even that simple action strange and painful.

When awareness returned fully, he lay on his bed, the silk sheets cool against his burning skin. The late afternoon sun slanted through the stained-glass windows, casting dragon-shaped shadows across the blankets. He lifted his hands, turning them in the light. Scales covered his palms now, spreading up his wrists and forearms in patches that disappeared beneath his torn sleeves. The transformation had shredded parts of his clothing where the scales had pushed through.

"Rest, my prince." Seren sat on the edge of his bed. "The worst is over. Soon you'll be perfect."

Perfect for what? he wondered as she left the room. His mother's pendant still burned against his chest where scales hadn't yet appeared, but the searing pain had dulled to a persistent ache.

On the balcony, Skye paced back and forth, her wings half-spread as if ready for flight. She wouldn't meet his gaze directly. Near the door, Ash had wedged himself beneath a heavy chair, only his gray tail visible. Every few moments, the tail would twitch, as if the cat fought between the instinct to flee and loyalty.

"I won't hurt you," Pryce tried to say, but his voice came out wrong—deeper, with rough edges that made both animals flinch.

He forced himself up. The room swayed as he stumbled to the washbasin, catching himself on its marble rim. Water sloshed over the sides as he steadied himself. Slowly, dreading what he might see, Pryce raised his eyes to the mirror.

Scattered patches of scales traced his jawline like frost on a windowpane. More had emerged at his temples, spreading back toward his hairline. He touched them with a scaled finger, feeling their smooth hardness. But his eyes remained unchanged. They were still his father's eyes, now staring back at him from an increasingly unfamiliar face.

A burst of laughter in the corridor drew his attention. Pryce pushed away from the basin, his new scales catching on the fabric of his sleeve. He moved to the door, pressing his ear against the wood.

"Did you see the size of the mining equipment they're moving through the sea caves?" The voice belonged to one of Thane's training partners. "The crews will be ready once we control Crystal Shores—"

"Quiet, fool!" Kestrel's voice commanded. Boot steps halted abruptly. "The boy might hear. These walls carry sound."

"What does it matter now?" A third voice—Pryce recognized him as one of Seren's personal guards. "He'll be too busy with wedding preparations to notice anything. The princess has him thoroughly enchanted." The guard chuckled. "And afterward, it won't matter. Once he's fully transformed and married to the princess, Crystal Shores' resources will be ours legally. The mining rights alone will fund our armies for years."

"And what of the Seadrake Corsair threat?" The first voice again, lowered now. "The villagers grow suspicious."

"A convenient fiction," Kestrel said. "The simple fools will welcome our protection from an enemy that doesn't exist. They'll thank us while we strip their lands bare."

Pryce's scaled hands curled into fists. All those battle formations they'd practiced, the defensive strategies he'd learned—they weren't meant to protect Crystal Shores. They were invasion plans, disguised as salvation.

Pryce staggered away from the door, his newly heightened senses overwhelmed by the lingering scents of Kestrel's passage—smoke and something else, something that made his transformed nose twitch.

A draft whispered across his scales, so faint he might have missed it before the change. He turned, following the sensation to an elaborate tapestry depicting dragons in flight.

The weaving rippled, ever so slightly, against the stone wall.

There—a seam in the stone, barely wider than a knife's blade. He pressed against different stones until one shifted with a grinding sound. The wall swung inward, revealing a narrow passage.

The secret room beyond served as a war chamber. A massive table dominated the space, its surface covered with maps and documents weighted down by chunks of crystal. Training schedules, patrol reports, and tactical drawings covered every surface. But these weren't defense plans—they were detailed attack formations, invasion routes that led straight to Crystal Shores.

A map larger than the others caught his eye. It showed his village, but marked with strange symbols he'd never seen in his navigation studies. Notes in Kestrel's precise handwriting filled the margins: "Primary ore deposits here" and "Deep mining required" and "Estimated yield: enough dragon-magic ore to arm three battalions."

Beneath the map, a leather portfolio contained surveys of Crystal Shores' underground resources. The diagrams showed vast mineral deposits, each carefully measured and marked in red ink. Page after page of calculations detailed the anticipated yields.

These weren't the plans of protectors. This was a systematic strategy to strip his home of everything valuable, using him—using his marriage to Seren—to make it all legal.

A noise in the corridor made him freeze. Footsteps approached his room. Pryce grabbed the most damning documents and slipped back through the hidden door, careful to seal it behind him. He had just straightened the tapestry when someone knocked.

"Young master?" Jorr's voice called. "Are you well?"

No, he wasn't well at all. And neither was Crystal Shores, unless he found a way to stop this.

"Enter."

Jorr stepped in. His eyes widened at Pryce's transformation, though he tried to hide his reaction. "Feeling better, young master? The princess sent me to check on you. She's concerned about your comfort."

"I'm fine." Pryce turned away, pulling his collar higher to hide the scales creeping up his neck. "Just tired."

"Of course." Jorr shifted his weight, clearly uncomfortable with Pryce's changed appearance. "Oh, and Master Kestrel wanted you to know—the wedding announcement is being sent to Drakemere Island today. A shadow drake rider left an hour ago with the news. They say it will be the grandest celebration since Queen Nymeria's coronation."

Everything was moving too fast, like a ship caught in a tide race. "Thank you, Jorr."

After the handler left, Pryce sank into a chair, the documents crinkling in his hand. Ash finally emerged from his hiding place beneath the furniture, whiskers twitching as he approached his transformed friend. The cat's steps were cautious, testing each pawfall as if the floor might disappear. When he reached Pryce, Ash stretched his neck forward, sniffing the scaled hand that rested on the chair's arm. After a long moment, the cat butted his head against Pryce's fingers—still trusting, still loyal, despite everything.

Skye landed on the balcony rail, her wings settling against her sides. Her message capsule caught the dying light.

The dragon blood of his ancestors still resisted Vex's corrupted magic, but for how long? The transformation crept further with each passing hour. Soon he would change completely, marry Seren, and become the weapon they needed to strip Crystal Shores of everything valuable. His own people would welcome their destroyers, thanks to his betrayal.

Somewhere beyond the Dragon's Fang's peaks, Crystal Shores waited, unknowing, while its doom was planned in these dark halls. In his scaled hands, Pryce clutched the proof of their deception—maps and surveys that showed the Dragonkin's true intentions.

28. Kitchen Whispers

Ellie watched from the Tidedancer's shadow as another fishing boat approached the hidden cove. Like the others she'd observed, this one rode low in the water, heavy with the evening catch. Two women and a man worked the oars while an elderly fellow managed the nets.

The burns on her arms throbbed as she adjusted her borrowed servant clothes. She'd need a story; something simple but believable. The fishing crews had been coming and going all afternoon, delivering their catches to the palace above. Some boats seemed understaffed, their crews struggling with the heavy nets.

When the next boat passed close to her hiding spot, she made her move.

"Need an extra hand?" she called, making her way along the cove's edge. "Saw you struggling with them nets."

The elderly man squinted at her. "Who's asking?"

"Sara," Ellie said, using her mother's name. "Just finished my shift with Torren's crew, but could use the extra coin if you're hiring."

The man glanced at his struggling crew, then back at Ellie. "You know silver trout? Storm drakes won't eat nothing else."

Ellie nodded. "Worked the lake since I was old enough to hold a net."

"Three coppers for the evening run," he said. "Mind you do exactly as told. Dragonkin don't take kindly to mistakes with their dragons' dinner."

"Fair enough." Ellie climbed carefully into their boat, mindful of her hidden injuries. The other workers barely glanced at her as she took position near the nets.

The elderly man—who introduced himself as Roan—showed her their system. "Sort by size here," he demonstrated. "Biggest ones go to the royal dragons. Smaller ones for the trainees. Any that ain't silver trout, we keep for ourselves."

Ellie settled into the rhythm of sorting fish, grateful her years on the Blue Horizon made the work second nature. Her bandaged arms protested each movement, but she kept her expression neutral as she worked.

"You're quick with them fish," one of the women said, pausing to wipe sweat from her brow. "Most new ones fumble about."

"Had a good teacher," Ellie said, remembering Tyler's patient lessons. She glanced up at the palace towers looming above them. "How many deliveries you make each day?"

"Three or four," Roan said. "More when they're training new dragons. Them storm drakes eat enough for ten men each."

The boat rounded the cliff edge, revealing the main harbor. Ellie's breath caught at the sight. Dozens of vessels crowded the water, from tiny fishing skiffs to massive supply ships. Dragons perched on carved stone ledges above, watching the boats below.

"Keep your head down," Roan warned as a shadow drake swooped low over the harbor. "Best not to draw their attention."

They tied up at a weathered dock where other crews already unloaded their catches. Servants scurried back and forth with baskets and carts, carrying fish up the endless stone steps carved into the cliff face.

"Here." Roan handed her a wooden token stamped with a dragon's head. "Shows you're cleared for delivery duty. Don't lose it, or the guards'll have you in chains faster than a seadrake can swallow a ship."

Ellie tucked the token into her pocket. One wrong move would expose her as an impostor.

"Sara, help Mira with them baskets," Roan called, pointing to where the older woman struggled with a heavy load. "Then follow her up to the kitchens. She knows the way."

Ellie hurried to help, catching the basket before it could slip from Mira's grip.

"You're favoring them arms something fierce," Mira said quietly. "Nets catch you wrong?"

"Something like that," Ellie said, adjusting her grip to hide her wince.

Mira studied her face. "Well, them kitchen fires'll help with the ache. Come on then—Cook Marta hates waiting on her deliveries."

They joined the line of servants climbing the steps. Ellie counted the landings as they ascended, noting how each branch led to different parts of the palace. Their path took them through torch-lit corridors where the stone walls still showed tool marks from their carving.

Steam billowed from massive doorways carved into the rock. The kitchen's heat hit Ellie like a wave. She followed Mira past rows of cooking fires where servants tended bubbling pots and turned spits laden with meat.

"New girl, eh?" A round-faced woman appeared through the steam, her arms dusted with flour to the elbows. Cook Marta, Ellie guessed from the way other servants quickly stepped aside. "Let's see what Roan sent us."

Ellie kept her head down as Marta inspected their baskets. The cook's eyes missed nothing, categorizing each fish with efficiency.

"These'll do for the storm drakes," Marta said. She jabbed a thumb toward a line of workers breaking down larger fish. "Join that lot. You done this before?"

"Yes, ma'am." Ellie set her basket down at an empty station. Her fingers found the familiar grip of a scaling knife, but she forced herself to use cruder movements. A skilled fisherman's daughter would give her away as surely as her red hair.

"Storm's coming," someone muttered nearby. "Can feel it in my bones."

"That's not storm weather," another servant replied. "That's them dragons stirring things up. Getting worse every day with all this fuss about the wedding."

Ellie's knife slipped, nearly cutting her finger. Wedding? She kept working, straining to hear more.

"Hush now," Marta called sharply. "Less gossip, more fish. Them drakes won't feed themselves."

A crash from the corridor scattered conversations as two Dragonkin strode through the kitchen, surveying the workers. One stopped near Ellie's station, nostrils flaring.

"You smell like the lake," he said, eyes narrowing.

"Been fishing all day, m'lord," Ellie mumbled, remembering how the palace servants deferred to their masters.

"Hmph." He moved on, but Ellie's hands trembled as she returned to her work. One wrong word, one slip of her cap, and all would be lost.

"Don't mind them," Mira whispered when the Dragonkin had passed. "They're all stirred up lately. What with the princess's big announcement and all."

"Announcement?" Ellie kept her voice carefully casual.

"Where you been, girl? Princess Seren's getting married! To some dragon trainer from out past Crystal Shores way. They say he's special—got the old blood in him. Being transformed and everything."

The scaling knife clattered from Ellie's numb fingers.

"You alright there?" Mira touched Ellie's shoulder. "Gone white as a ghost, you have."

"Just . . . the heat." Ellie retrieved her knife with shaking hands. The burns on her arms felt like they were on fire again. "This dragon trainer—where is he now?"

"Oh, he's up at Dragon's Fang Island with Master Kestrel." Mira lowered her voice. "Heard tell he's got a way with the big ones. Even that beast they keep chained in the caves."

A young servant hurried past with a message clutched in his hand. "Cook Marta! Princess Seren needs more supplies at Dragon's Fang for the training feast. Says they're celebrating the dragon trainer's progress tonight, before bringing him back for the grand ceremony."

Marta swore under her breath. "They expect us to get supplies up that mountain tonight? With a storm brewing?" She pointed at two workers. "You and you—start packing preserves. They'll have to make do with what we can send."

"Progress," Ellie whispered. She scraped her knife against the fish with more force than necessary.

"Aye," Mira said, clearly enjoying having a fresh audience for the gossip. "Heard tell he's mastering them dragons faster than anyone expected. Even that black beast they keep chained up. Though some say . . ." She glanced around before continuing. "Some say the changes are happening faster than normal too."

"Changes?"

"That's what comes of drinking dragon potions, don't it?" Another servant joined their conversation, her voice dropping to a whisper. "My cousin's friend works in the laboratories there. Says they're turning him into one of them. Scales and all."

Ellie's vision blurred. The knife slipped again, this time drawing blood from her palm. She barely felt it through the horror of what she was hearing. Her son—her Pryce—was being transformed into one of them?

"Here now," Mira pressed a clean cloth into her hand. "You're having a rough go of it. Come help me with the stores instead. Quieter there, and cooler too."

Ellie followed numbly as Mira led her away from the busy kitchen and into a storage room lined with shelves. Salted fish and dried herbs hung from the ceiling.

"Sit." Mira guided her to a crate. "You've been pushing too hard with them injured arms. Let me see."

"No, I—"

But Mira was already pushing up her sleeve, revealing the bandages. The older woman's eyes widened at the marks of the Sweetsnare's burns.

"Those ain't from no fishing nets," Mira said quietly. Her eyes moved to where Ellie's cap had slipped, revealing a strand of red hair. "And you ain't no ordinary servant neither, are you?"

Ellie's hand moved to the knife at her belt. Mira noticed and shook her head.

"Put that thought right out," the older woman said. "If I meant you harm, I'd have called the guards already." She reached up and pulled down a bunch of dried herbs, crumbling them between her fingers. "These'll help with them burns. Sweetsnare got you, didn't it? Nasty things, them flowers."

"You know about Sweetsnares?"

"Know about a lot of things. Including why a woman with warrior's calluses and a mother's eyes might be sneaking into Drakemere." Mira began mixing herbs in a small bowl. "He's your boy, ain't he? The one they're changing?"

A crash from the kitchen made them both jump. Voices raised in argument about the supplies for Dragon's Fang.

"Yes," Ellie whispered. What was the point in denying it now? "His name is Pryce."

"Thought as much." Mira pressed the herb mixture into Ellie's hands. "Put that on them burns when you can. Now listen close, 'cause we ain't got much time before they notice we're gone."

"Why are you helping me?"

Mira's face hardened. "Because I had a boy once too. Till the Dragonkin decided he had the right blood for their experiments. Never saw him again after the changes started." She glanced at the door. "Your Pryce . . . they say he's different. Stronger. The changes ain't killing him like they do most. That's why the princess chose him."

"Chose him for what?"

"For their plans, of course. Crystal Shores sits on something they want bad. Mining crews been gathering equipment for months. But they need a legal claim to the land." Mira's voice dropped lower. "What better way than a royal marriage to a local boy? Especially once he's fully changed—more dragon than Shorling."

"The villages that fell to them before . . ." Ellie began, remembering Finnegan's warnings about the Dragonkin's conquests.

Mira's bitter laugh cut her off. "All the same pattern. They find something they want—minerals, dragon artifacts, ancient magic—then take it however they can."

She grabbed another bunch of herbs. "They're clever about it too. Sometimes they use threats, sometimes promises. This time they're using your boy."

The storage room door creaked. Both women froze, but it was only the kitchen cat slinking in to hunt mice.

"How long?" Ellie asked. "How long before they bring him here?"

"The formal ceremony's set for three days' time, here at Drakemere," Mira said, her voice dropping lower. "But there's whispers they might do it sooner, right there at Dragon's Fang. The changes are happening faster than they expected. Some say he's already growing scales."

"Growing scales?"

"That's what happens when they feed them dragon potions. Transformation takes hold quick—a week at most. Most don't survive it."

Ellie's hands trembled. Not just marriage—they were turning her son into some kind of monster. "This transformation . . . can it be stopped?"

"Don't know," Mira said. "Never heard of anyone trying. Most families just . . ." She swallowed hard. "Most just pretend their changed ones died. Easier that way."

"There's something else," Mira whispered. "Something my friend in the dragon caves overheard. The princess, she's—"

"Mira!" Cook Marta's voice boomed from the kitchen. "Where's them dried fish for Dragon's Fang?"

"Coming!" Mira called back. She turned to Ellie, speaking rapidly. "Listen careful. There's a gate in the lower caves, behind the old dragon sculptures. Guards change at eveningbell. That's your best chance to—"

"MIRA!"

"Just a moment more!" Mira grabbed Ellie's arm. "Find Jorr when you reach Dragon's Fang. He tends the injured dragons. Tell him Mira sent you. He'll—"

Heavy footsteps approached. Mira shoved Ellie behind a stack of barrels just as Cook Marta burst in.

"What's taking so long? And who were you talking to?"

"Just the cat," Mira said. "You know how I get, talking to animals like they're people. Here's them fish you wanted."

Ellie held her breath as Marta and Mira's footsteps retreated. She waited until the kitchen sounds grew distant before slipping out from behind the barrels.

Outside, the storm was breaking. Lightning split the sky as Ellie made her way back through the winding corridors. She had to reach Dragon's Fang Island before they forced that marriage, before the transformation took her son completely. But how? The island was likely heavily guarded, and she had no way to—

She stopped. Something Mira had said about the mining crews. They were gathering equipment, preparing for their invasion of Crystal Shores. Supply ships would be making regular runs to Dragon's Fang Island.

Thunder cracked overhead as Ellie emerged into the rain-soaked night. Dragons wheeled against the dark clouds, their shapes illuminated by lightning. Below, in the harbor, crews worked to secure ships against the growing storm. Including a supply vessel, its deck stacked with mining equipment, preparing to leave for what she hoped to be Dragon's Fang Island.

Ellie pressed herself against the wet stone as a patrol of Dragonkin passed above. The supply vessel's crew worked frantically to secure their cargo before the storm hit in full force. Mining equipment filled most of the deck—picks, shovels, and strange machines she didn't recognize.

A horn sounded from the harbor master's tower—three long notes warning of the approaching storm. The supply ship's crew moved faster, shouting to each other over the wind.

"Get those ropes secured!" A burly man—the captain, by his bearing—gestured at the mining equipment. "We leave as soon as this squall passes!"

Lightning crackled overhead. Dragons scattered for shelter, their shapes disappearing into caves high in the cliff face. Even they knew better than to challenge a storm like this.

Ellie watched the crew securing the last of the cargo. Her only hope was to follow the supply ship in the Tidedancer—if she could reach her boat before the storm hit in full force. She'd have to stay far enough behind to avoid detection, but close enough not to lose them in the darkness.

The wind drove rain like needles against her face as she made her way down toward the harbor.

Let the storm rage. Ellie had survived Sweetsnares and seadrakes to reach this place. She would find a way to reach Pryce.

Thunder shook the cliffs as she disappeared into the darkness. The real storm, she knew, was yet to come.

29. The Dark Descent

Pryce stared at his reflection in the mirror, barely recognizing himself. Scales covered most of his body now, their dark pattern spreading like frost across a window. Only a small patch on his chest remained unchanged, protected by his mother's pendant.

Trust in your blood, not their poison. Ragnarok's voice echoed in his mind.

"Too late for that," Pryce said, his transformed voice rougher than before. He touched the scales along his jaw, remembering Seren's kiss and how thoroughly he'd fallen for her deception.

The stolen documents from the war room lay scattered across his bed. Mining surveys, invasion plans, troop movements—all of it pointed to one truth: the Dragonkin never intended to protect Crystal Shores. They meant to strip it bare.

Ash watched from his velvet cushion, whiskers twitching as Pryce paced. Through the window, Skye perched on the balcony rail.

Pryce tore a crucial page from the mining survey, the one showing the vast deposits beneath Crystal Shores. His scaled fingers made the task clumsy, but he managed to fold it small enough to fit in Skye's capsule.

"Come here, girl," he called softly.

The gull hopped closer, head tilted. Pryce stroked her feathers.

"I need you to be swift," he said, securing the message in the leg capsule. "Get this to—"

The door opened. Pryce spun to find Seren. Her eyes fixed on the scattered documents.

"My love," she said. "What's this?"

"Mining surveys," Pryce said, moving between Seren and Skye. "Invasion plans. The truth about what you want from Crystal Shores."

Seren's scales flared at her temples as she stepped closer. "You don't understand what you've found, my love. These are merely contingency plans, in case the Seadrake Corsairs—"

"There are no Corsairs, are there?"

A change came over Seren's face. She moved to the window, her dress catching the dying light of Kaalm's evening sun. Below, dragons wheeled between Dragon Fang Island's volcanic peaks.

"We did what was necessary," she said. "Crystal Shores sits on the largest deposit of dragon-magic ore ever discovered. Did you think we'd let such power remain in the hands of common fishermen?"

Behind her back, Pryce gestured for Skye to take flight. The gull spread her wings silently.

"So the marriage proposal, the transformation . . ." His scaled hands curled into fists. "All of it was just to gain legal claim to my home?"

"Not all." Seren turned, and for a moment he glimpsed real emotion in her eyes. "I chose you because I saw your potential. Together, we could—"

Skye launched herself from the balcony. Seren's head snapped toward the sound, her eyes narrowing at the message capsule on the bird's leg.

"Guards!" she shouted.

The door burst open. Master Kestrel strode in flanked by warriors.

"Foolish boy." Kestrel said. "Did you think we wouldn't be watching? That we'd let you ruin everything we've worked for?"

Ash darted between legs and disappeared into the corridor as guards moved to surround Pryce. Below, Stormwing's roar shook the evening air, but the dragon remained penned in her stable.

"The transformation is too far along to stop now," Seren said. "Why couldn't you just accept your destiny?"

"Because some of us can't be bought," Pryce said, thinking of his father's empty nets. "Some things matter more than power."

"Take him to the cells," Kestrel ordered. "Perhaps some time alone will help him understand his position better."

As guards seized his arms, Pryce caught a last glimpse of Skye soaring south.

"You're wrong about one thing," Kestrel said as they dragged Pryce toward the door. "There are powers worth more than mere dragon-magic ore. Ancient powers, sleeping beneath Crystal Shores. Powers that could reshape the world, if one knew how to wake them."

Seren shot him a sharp look. "Master Kestrel."

"It doesn't matter now," Kestrel said. "By this time tomorrow, the boy will be fully transformed and married to you, my princess. Crystal Shores' resources will be ours, legally and permanently."

They led Pryce down torch-lit corridors, deep under the residence. The cells here were carved from the volcanic rock itself, their bars forged from the same metal used to chain Ragnarok.

Remember who you are, the great dragon's voice whispered in his mind as the cell door clanged shut. Remember before it's too late.

Evening shadows lengthened in Pryce's cell. His scales ached with each new growth, creeping steadily toward the last patch of Shorling skin on his chest.

Footsteps approached—lighter than the guards' usual tread. Jorr appeared at the cell bars.

"Young master," Jorr whispered, glancing down the corridor. "The princess has ordered the wedding moved to tomorrow's dawn. Once you're legally bound . . ."

"Crystal Shores will belong to them." Pryce moved closer to the bars. "Jorr, I need your help."

"Anything."

"My quiver—the one my family gave me. There's a sapphire sewn into it. A Royal Sapphire."

Jorr's eyes widened. "The rarest of gems?"

"Take it to Master Vex. Tell him I'll trade it for a cure, something to reverse what his potion did to me."

"But Master Vex never—"

"Show him the sapphire first," Pryce said. "He's a collector. He'll do it for something that valuable."

Jorr hesitated, then nodded. "I'll find your quiver and return as quickly as I can."

As the handler hurried away, Pryce sank onto the stone bench. His transformed fingers felt the scales on his arms, remembering how eagerly he'd drunk Vex's potion. How completely he'd believed Seren's lies.

The old magic stirs, Ragnarok's voice rumbled in his mind. *They seek to wake what should remain sleeping.*

"What are they really looking for under Crystal Shores?"

Power older than dragons. Older than the world you know. But such power comes with a price.

***

Jorr clutched the sapphire in his palm as he approached Master Vex's laboratory. His knuckles barely touched the door when it swung open.

"What?" The alchemist's eyes narrowed at the sight of Jorr. "Ah, the stable boy. Come to beg more healing salves for those beasts?"

"No, Master Vex." Jorr opened his palm, revealing the sapphire. "I've come to trade."

Vex's breath caught. He grabbed Jorr's wrist, pulling him inside the laboratory. The door slammed behind them.

"Where did you get that?" Vex reached for the gem.

Jorr closed his fingers around it. "It doesn't matter. What matters is what I want in exchange."

"Insolent boy." Vex's eyes never left Jorr's closed fist. "What could you possibly want that's worth a Royal Sapphire?"

"A cure. Something to reverse the transformation potion you gave Pryce, the soon to be prince."

Vex's laugh was harsh. "Impossible. The changes are permanent once they take hold. By morning, he'll be one of us completely."

"Then the sapphire goes elsewhere." Jorr turned toward the door.

"Wait." Vex moved to block his path. "There might be . . . something. Though its effects are unpredictable."

"What effects?"

Vex pulled a dusty book from his shelves, flipping through brittle pages. "Drakebane. An ancient formula. It can halt the transformation, even reverse it, but . . ." He traced spidery text with one sharp nail. "The price is high."

"How high?"

"It induces a death-like sleep. Most never wake. Those who do take at least a day to return. And there's no guarantee of survival at all."

Jorr swallowed hard. "But it would reverse the transformation?"

"Oh yes. Quite effectively." Vex closed the book. "Of course, such a rare potion would require equally rare payment."

Jorr held up the sapphire.

"I can have it ready in an hour," Vex said, snatching the sapphire. "But remember, boy—if anyone asks where you got it . . ."

"I know. I was never here."

Vex turned to his workbench, already pulling out vials and powders. "One hour," he said without looking back. "And tell your friend to choose wisely. Death, even temporary, is not a fate to be chosen lightly. He could even be buried alive."

***

Hours crept by. Pryce dozed fitfully until hurried footsteps woke him. Jorr returned, his face grave in the torchlight.

"Master Vex agreed," Jorr said, "but there's something you should know." He glanced down the corridor again. "The reversal potion—he calls it Drakebane—it will stop the transformation, but . . ."

"But what?"

"It puts the drinker into a death-like sleep. Most never wake up. Those who do, he says it takes at least a day, maybe more." Jorr gripped the cell bars. "And there's no guarantee you'll wake at all."

Pryce touched his mother's pendant. "If I seem dead, they can't force the marriage. Can't use me to claim Crystal Shores."

"But young master, the risk—"

"Would you rather I become one of them completely? Help them destroy my home?" New scales crackled across his neck. "How long until the transformation is permanent?"

"By dawn," Jorr said. "Master Vex was very clear about that."

Pryce stood. "Then we don't have much time. Did you bring it?"

Jorr withdrew a small vial filled with swirling silver liquid. "Are you certain about this?"

"No," Pryce admitted. "But sometimes the only way forward is through the dark." He reached for the vial. "Thank you, Jorr. For everything."

"What should I tell them—when they find you?"

"Tell them . . . nothing. They will assume I died from the transformation."

Pryce unstoppered the vial. "And Jorr? If I don't wake up, make sure my mother gets her pendant back."

Before doubt could stop him, Pryce lifted the vial to his lips. The Drakebane went down like liquid ice, freezing him from the inside out. He handed the vial back to Jorr before his legs buckled.

Jorr caught the vial and backed away as Pryce collapsed onto the stone floor. The cold spread through his limbs. His vision dimmed, the cell fading to gray, then black.

He sank into darkness deeper than any night, but awareness remained. Time passed strangely in his frozen state. Guards changed shifts. Torches guttered and were replaced.

"Prisoner check," a gruff voice called.

Footsteps approached his cell. A sharp intake of breath.

"By the depths—get the captain! The prisoner's down!"

More footsteps. Urgent voices. Someone rattling the cell door.

"Don't touch him," a captain ordered. "Get Princess Seren and Master Vex. Now!"

Time slipped again. How long before the princess arrived? Minutes? Hours? Pryce floated in the darkness until Seren approached.

"What happened?" Seren demanded.

"Found him like this, Your Highness," the captain said. "Not moving. Not breathing."

"Move aside." Master Vex's voice now. Cold fingers pressed against Pryce's throat. "No pulse. The transformation must have been too much for his mixed blood. I warned you this could happen with one of his heritage."

"No." Seren's voice cracked. "No, check again! He was fine at evening bell."

"The change accelerated too quickly," Vex said. "His Shorling blood rejected it entirely." The alchemist's cold fingers probed Pryce's scales. "Fascinating reaction though. I'd like to examine the body—"

"This ruins everything." Seren's dress rustled as she paced. "Captain, bring Father Blackwood here immediately. We'll perform the ceremony now, before he's completely gone."

"Your Highness," the captain shifted uncomfortably, "you can't marry a dead man."

"Now!"

The captain hurried away. Seren knelt beside Pryce's body, her fingers stroking the scales on his face. "Hold on, my love. Just a few moments more."

Master Vex cleared his throat. "Princess, I must point out that he has no pulse."

"Be silent." She stood as new footsteps approached.

Father Blackwood appeared at the cell door, clutching his ritual book. The elderly priest's eyes widened at the sight of Pryce on the floor. "Your Highness, surely you don't mean to—"

"Begin the ceremony," Seren commanded. "We'll make this quick."

"But . . ." The priest glanced at Pryce's still form. "My lady, he cannot speak his vows. Without mutual consent—"

"He consented earlier today. These witnesses can confirm it." She gestured to the guards. "Now begin."

Father Blackwood opened his book with trembling hands. "As you wish, Your Highness. Though I must note in the record that the groom appears . . . indisposed."

"Make your notes, but speak the words. The law requires a ceremony, and we will have one."

The priest's voice quavered as he began. "We gather here in this . . . unusual circumstance, to join—"

"Skip the pleasantries," Seren snapped. "Get to the binding words."

Master Vex moved closer to examine Pryce's scales. "Fascinating. They're already beginning to fade. Once death truly sets in—"

"Continue, Father!" Seren's composure cracked.

Father Blackwood spoke the ancient words. Through the darkness of his frozen state, Pryce felt Seren's hand grasp his limp one.

"Do you, Princess Seren of the Dragonkin, take this man—"

"Yes," she said. "Now pronounce it done."

"My lady," Father Blackwood's book snapped shut. "I cannot. The law requires both parties to speak their vows. Even with witnesses to his prior consent, a marriage ceremony requires the groom to be . . . well . . . alive."

"Then perhaps I should explain this differently." Seren's voice dropped to a whisper. "Either you will perform this ceremony, or I will personally introduce you to my dragons. I hear they're particularly hungry this time of year."

Father Blackwood glanced between Seren and the motionless form of Pryce, as he reopened his book. "I . . . I suppose there are some . . . alternative interpretations of the law that could apply in this . . . unique situation."

"I thought you might see it that way," Seren said.

The ceremony proceeded with unusual haste, Father Blackwood spoke the sacred words. When it came time for the groom's responses, Seren answered firmly in Pryce's stead, her voice brooking no argument from the priest.

As soon as the final blessing was pronounced, Seren turned to the small gathering of witnesses. "Lord Pryce is unfortunately feeling quite ill and will need to rest through the celebration," she said. "I trust you all understand the need for discretion regarding his absence from the festivities. We wouldn't want to worry anyone unnecessarily about his health, would we?"

The witnesses nodded.

The captain bowed deeply. "My congratulations to you and Lord Pryce on your union, my lady. I trust the arrangements we discussed for the estate's continued management are still to your satisfaction?"

"Indeed they are, Captain. Without this marriage, the mining operations have no legitimate claim. The Shorlings will resist." Seren inclined her head gracefully. "And now, if you'll excuse us, I must see to my husband's comfort." She turned to the guards. "Take him to the cold storage beneath the kitchens. Tell no one of his death until I decide how to proceed. Captain, seal off this section of the dungeon. Master Vex, you will speak of this to no one."

"But the specimens I could gather—" Vex began.

"You'll have your chance to study him later," Seren said. "For now, silence. If word reaches Crystal Shores that their precious son died during our 'training,' it will only make taking the village harder."

"And the lad's storm drake?" the captain asked. "It's been fighting the chains since he collapsed."

"Keep it restrained. Double the guards if you must. That dragon is too valuable to lose."

Footsteps retreated, leaving Pryce alone in his darkness. He tried to move, to open his eyes, but his body remained frozen. Only his mind drifted, caught between wake and sleep.

Rough hands lifted Pryce's limp body as he was carried through the corridors, ascending stone steps. The air grew warmer, filled with kitchen smells, then cold again as they descended to some lower chamber. They laid him on what felt like a stone slab.

"Poor boy," a cook whispered. "They should never have tried to change him."

"Quiet," someone said. "The princess ordered silence."

The door closed, leaving Pryce in total darkness.

30. Storm's Breaking

Lightning split the darkening sky over Drakemere's harbor as Ellie studied the supply ship from her hiding place among the cargo crates. Workers rushed to secure ropes and covers before the storm hit, their movements growing more urgent with each thunderclap.

Her burns throbbed beneath the rough servant's shirt as she adjusted her cap lower. Following in the Tidedancer would be suicide in this weather. Even if she survived the storm, the increased patrols would spot her long before she reached Dragon's Fang Island.

"You there!" A burly quartermaster's voice cut through the wind. "Stop lazing about and help with these supplies!"

Ellie kept her head down as she merged with the flow of servants loading provisions.

"Storm's coming fast," a kitchen maid said, passing Ellie a crate of dried fish. "They say it'll be a bad one."

Ellie grunted in response, keeping her voice low as she handed the crate up the gangplank. The less she spoke, the less chance of someone noticing her accent wasn't quite right for a Drakemere servant.

Thunder cracked overhead, closer now. Dragons wheeled between the fortress towers, seeking shelter in their caves.

"You!" The quartermaster appeared at Ellie's elbow, making her jump. "Kitchen staff?"

She nodded, heart pounding.

"Good. Get below and help Greta prep the evening meal. Can't feed the crew with everything rolling about in this weather."

Ellie made her way below decks. The galley would be cramped, with nowhere to hide if someone grew suspicious. But it was also the perfect place to gather information—servants always talked while they worked.

The kitchen space was warm and humid, filled with the smell of boiling vegetables. Two women worked at a scarred wooden table, peeling root vegetables.

"Another one?" The older woman—Greta, Ellie assumed—barely glanced up. "Good. Start on them potatoes. We've got forty mouths to feed before this storm hits proper."

Ellie found a knife and began peeling while she listened to the women's conversation.

"Heard anything more about that wedding up at Dragon's Fang?" the younger woman asked, reaching for another turnip.

"Hush now," Greta said. "You know we're not to gossip about the Dragonkin's business."

Above deck, someone shouted orders. The ship lurched as it pulled away from the dock. They were underway now—no turning back. Ellie sent up a silent prayer that she'd made the right choice.

The galley door burst open, letting in a blast of wet air. "Greta! Need hot food for the deck crew now. Storm's getting worse."

"Fool men," Greta said, but she began ladling soup into wooden bowls. "You there, new girl. Take these up. And mind you don't spill them—we won't waste food on this crossing."

Ellie gathered the bowls onto a tray, careful to keep her movements steady as the ship rolled beneath her feet. This was her chance to learn the vessel's layout, to find hiding places if she needed them later.

She climbed the narrow steps. Lightning flashed as she emerged onto the deck. The storm grew fiercer as they sailed toward Dragon's Fang Island.

Ellie made three more trips with food for the crew, each time gathering fragments of conversation that chilled her more than the rain.

". . . princess's chosen one . . ."

". . . transformation went wrong . . ."

". . . dead before the ceremony, they say . . ."

She nearly dropped her empty tray at that last whisper. Dead? No. She would have felt it if Pryce was gone. The pendant she'd given him, filled with their mixed blood, would have told her somehow.

"You're shivering." A kind voice startled her. One of the kitchen maids—Lena, she'd heard Greta call her—pressed a steaming mug into Ellie's hands. "Drink. It'll warm you up."

"Thank you." Ellie sipped carefully, tasting herbs and honey. She studied Lena's face, deciding to risk a question. "Is it true what they're saying? About the wedding at Dragon's Fang?"

Lena glanced around the galley before leaning closer. "Shadow drake brought word just before we sailed. Princess Seren's betrothed—that young trainer everyone's been talking about—something went wrong with his training. They say he died, but . . ." She lowered her voice further. "They performed the ceremony anyway. Over his body."

The mug trembled in Ellie's hands. "How could they? Why would they—"

"Politics," another servant said, joining their huddle. "That boy was from Crystal Shores. Without the marriage, the Dragonkin have no legal claim to the village's resources."

"Hush!" Greta's sharp voice scattered them back to their tasks. "Less gossip, more work. We've still got supplies to prepare."

Ellie returned to peeling vegetables as the ship pitched suddenly, sending root vegetables rolling across the galley floor. Ellie grabbed for the table as waves crashed against the hull. Through the porthole, she caught a glimpse of Dragon's Fang Island. Lightning illuminated its peaks, revealing dragons wheeling between the towers despite the storm.

"Depths take this weather," Greta said. "We'll never get the supplies unloaded in this."

"They say it's not natural," Lena whispered. "That the dragons are stirring it up. Ever since the boy died—"

"I said enough!" Greta's wooden spoon cracked against the table. "Get them vegetables cleaned up. And you, new girl—your cap's slipping."

Ellie's hand flew to her head. The wet fabric had indeed slipped, threatening to reveal her red hair. She ducked into the storage alcove, pretending to search for dropped potatoes while she adjusted the cap.

"Storm's holding steady on our stern," a sailor called down from above. "Should make Dragon's Fang on time!"

The storm raged as they approached Dragon's Fang Island. Lightning revealed glimpses of the fortress—a mass of dark stone and dragon-carved architecture. Ellie's arms ached from hours of kitchen work, but she forced herself to keep moving. Any sign of weakness might draw unwanted attention.

"There!" Someone shouted from above. "The signal fire!"

Through the rain-streaked porthole, Ellie saw a blue flame burning atop one of the peaks, guiding them toward a harbor on the island's lee side. The supply ship turned, using the cliffs for shelter from the worst of the storm.

"All hands to stations!" The quartermaster's voice boomed down the companionway. "Prepare for docking!"

The galley erupted into activity as servants gathered supplies and secured loose items. Ellie helped Greta tie down the cooking pots, her sailor's knots drawing an approving nod from the older woman.

"You've got some skill there," Greta said. "Worked ships before, have you?"

"My father was a fisherman," Ellie said carefully.

A massive wave struck the hull, making the timbers groan. Through the chaos, Ellie heard fragments of conversation from sailors passing the galley door.

". . . ceremony was rushed . . ."

". . . keeping the body in cold storage . . ."

". . . princess won't let anyone near him . . ."

Cold storage. They hadn't buried Pryce yet. There was still a chance to reach him.

The ship's motion changed as they entered calmer waters. Dragons perched on ledges above the harbor, their shapes barely visible through the rain.

"Right then," Greta said. "New girl, help Lena with them supply crates. Everything marked with the dragon seal goes to the main kitchens."

Ellie followed Lena up to the rain-slicked deck. The harbor was smaller than Drakemere's, but better protected. Ancient breakwaters rose from the depths like dragon teeth, sheltering the docks from the storm's fury.

"Keep your head down," Lena whispered as they approached the gangplank. "Guards are always edgy during storms. Especially now, with everything that's happened."

Ellie nodded, adjusting her cap lower. Guards in scaled armor patrolled the docks, their hands never far from their weapons.

As they waited to disembark, movement caught Ellie's eye. A gray shape darted between crates near the dock—a cat, she realized.

"That's odd," Lena said, following her gaze. "The Dragonkin hate those beasts."

The cat paused, looking directly at Ellie. Then it turned and vanished into the shadows.

"Next group!" A guard shouted. "Move quickly now!"

Ellie hefted her crate and followed Lena down the gangplank. The dock stones were slick with rain and sea spray, requiring careful steps. Above, dragons called to each other.

They joined a line of servants heading up carved steps toward the fortress.

The cat appeared again, always just at the edge of her vision.

"This way to the kitchens," Lena said, turning down a torch-lit corridor. "Mind the floor—it gets slippery when—"

"You there!" A voice made them both freeze. "The new girl."

Ellie turned slowly. A handler stood watching her.

"Sir?" She kept her eyes down.

"Those supplies go to the cold storage," he said. "Follow me."

Lena shot her a sympathetic look before hurrying away with her own crate. Ellie followed the handler deeper into the fortress.

The handler led her down steps, the air growing colder with each level they descended. Other servants passed them, carrying supplies or hurrying on errands, but none met her eyes.

They reached a heavy wooden door bound with dragon-forged iron.

"Inside," he said, pushing the door open. "Place the crate with the others."

Ellie stepped into the cold storage chamber. Shelves lined the walls, filled with supplies preserved by the cave's natural chill. But her attention fixed on something else—a shape beneath a white cloth on a stone table in the chamber's center.

The shape of a body.

The handler closed the door behind them. Ellie's hands shook as she set down her crate, trying not to stare at the covered form.

"You're here for him, aren't you?" The handler's voice quivered slightly.

Ellie's heart stopped. Had she given herself away?

"I-I saw you watching," he continued, wringing his hands. "On the docks. The way you looked when they mentioned . . ." He gestured nervously toward the covered form.

"Sir?" Ellie kept her voice carefully neutral.

The handler shifted anxiously. He was younger than she'd first thought, barely older than Pryce.

"I'm Jorr," he said softly. "I . . . I help care for the dragons. And I know who you are. You're his mother."

Ellie's hand moved to the knife hidden beneath her rough shirt. "I don't know what you mean."

"Please," Jorr whispered, stepping back. "I want to help. Mira sent word you might come. She said . . . said I could trust you."

The knife was in Ellie's hand before she consciously drew it. "How do I know I can trust you?"

"Because I've been watching over him," Jorr said. "Trying to protect him. The potion. Drakebane."

"Drakebane? Then he's not . . . ?"

"Not exactly dead," Jorr said. "The transformation was hurting him. The Drakebane reverses it, but it also . . . it makes him appear . . ." He gestured helplessly at the covered form.

Ellie lowered her knife.

"The potion induces a death-like sleep," Jorr explained. "It's temporary, but the princess . . . she thinks he's really dead. They're planning burial rites at dawn."

"Dawn?" Ellie moved to the covered form, her hand hovering over the cloth. "May I?"

Jorr nodded, fidgeting with his sleeves. "Quickly. The guards patrol every hour."

Ellie drew back the white fabric. Her breath caught at the sight of Pryce's face. Scales traced his jaw and temples. His skin was cold to the touch, but not with the finality of true death.

"The scales were worse before," Jorr said. "But we have to hurry. If we don't move him soon . . ."

A sound in the corridor made them both freeze. Jorr quickly replaced the cloth as footsteps approached.

"Hide," he said, pointing to a storage alcove.

Ellie pressed herself into the alcove's shadows as the storage room door creaked open.

"Check everything," a guard commanded. "Princess Seren wants no mistakes with the burial preparations."

"Seems wrong," another voice muttered. "Burying a man so quick, even if he is transformed."

"Orders are orders. And after that wedding ceremony . . ." The guard's voice hardened. "Well, let's just say I'm not questioning anything the princess does these days."

Ellie held her breath as the guards moved through the chamber. From her hiding place, she could see Jorr standing rigidly by the door, his hands clasped behind his back, to hide their trembling, she assumed.

"All seems secure," the first guard said finally. "Though someone, a servant, has been in here recently. These crate marks are fresh."

"Supply ship just docked," Jorr said. "I was supervising the storage."

"Hmph." The guard studied him. "Well, see that everything's properly recorded. Princess wants an inventory before dawn."

The guards' footsteps faded. Ellie waited until Jorr gave a nod before emerging.

"We have to move him," she whispered. "Now, before they come back."

"But where?" Jorr wrung his hands. "The whole fortress is on alert. And he's too heavy for me to carry alone."

Ellie studied her son's still form. "Together then. But first, tell me everything you know about this Drakebane potion. How long until he wakes?"

"Master Vex said a day at least. But . . ." Jorr glanced nervously at the door. "There's something else. The princess plans to seal him in the royal crypts at dawn. If he wakes there . . ."

"He'll suffocate. Where can we take him? Somewhere warm, where he can recover safely?"

"The old dragon caves," Jorr said after a moment's thought. "Below the training grounds. They're mostly abandoned now, except for Ragnarok, but he's kept far from the entrance. There's a chamber there with thermal vents—warm and dry."

A sound like distant thunder rolled through the fortress. But this was something else.

"The dragons are restless," Jorr explained. "They've been like this since Pryce . . . since the potion. Especially Stormwing, his storm dragon. She's been fighting the chains since he collapsed. The guards had to double her restraints."

"Can you get us to those caves?"

Jorr nodded. "But we'll need a distraction. The guards watch everything since the wedding ceremony. And you can't move through the fortress dressed as a servant—too many questions."

"What do you suggest?"

"Wait here." Jorr slipped out, returning later with a bundle of rich fabric. "Visiting nobles have been arriving for days, celebrating the wedding. No one questions them, especially if they're with a handler."

Ellie shook out an elaborate dress in deep blue, decorated with silver dragons. "Won't they notice I'm not one of them?"

"Keep your head high and no one will dare look too closely." Jorr helped her with the complicated fastenings.

"Dragonkin nobility are notoriously proud. Servants and guards know better than to stare."

The dress fit well enough, though the sleeves irritated her burns. Jorr produced a silver circlet set with dark stones.

"This won't hide your hair," he said. "But it will mark you as visiting royalty. I'll say I'm showing you the fortress."

"The supply cart," Ellie whispered, gesturing to an abandoned wheelbarrow filled with sacks of grain. "We can hide him beneath the supplies."

They quickly transferred the sacks to the ground, then carefully laid Pryce in the wheelbarrow, covered snuggly by the cloth. Ellie arranged the grain sacks around and over him, creating a convincing pile of supplies.

A roar shook the very stones, making Ellie stumble as she placed the final sack.

"Stormwing," Jorr said. "She's getting worse."

"Let's get out of here," Ellie said.

Jorr pushed the wheelbarrow forward. "The old passages—they'll lead us to the thermal caves."

They hurried through dimly lit corridors, the wheelbarrow's wheel squeaking despite their efforts to move quietly. Every few moments, another roar shook the stones, closer each time. Dust filtered down from the ceiling.

Guards shouted in the distance. Patrols mobilized, responding to the growing chaos.

"This way," Jorr whispered, guiding them down a narrower passage. "The old servants' corridors connect to maintenance tunnels that haven't been used in generations."

The passage grew darker, lit only by occasional crystal brackets casting weak blue light.

"The dragon handlers will be too busy with Stormwing to notice us," Jorr said. "But the princess's guards—they'll be searching everywhere when they notice he's missing."

They reached a junction where three corridors met. Jorr pressed his hand against a seemingly solid wall, revealing a hidden passage.

"The old ways," he explained, carefully maneuvering the wheelbarrow through the opening. "From before the Dragonkin rebuilt the fortress. They connect everything, but few remember them now."

The passage was narrow, lit only by luminous crystals set in iron brackets. The wheelbarrow's wheel squeaked despite their care.

"The caves aren't far," Jorr whispered as they navigated the corridor. "Just a bit further and—"

But before he could finish, voices echoed from the distant main corridor. Jorr froze, his hands tightening on the wheelbarrow's handles.

"The princess demands answers!" The speaker's voice carried clearly through the stone. "How could you lose track of a dead man?"

"I swear, the cold storage was secured—"

"Find him!" Princess Seren's voice cracked like a whip. "Search every chamber, every passage. He must be found."

"The guards are searching already," Jorr said. "We need to move faster."

They pushed forward through the hidden passage, no longer trying to maintain the pretense of a casual tour. The ancient corridors twisted deeper into the mountain, the air growing warmer with each turn.

Another roar shook the fortress. The dragon's cry held something beyond mere anger—there was pain in it.

"She knows," Jorr said, steadying the wheelbarrow as they navigated a particularly narrow turn. "Somehow Stormwing knows his rider is disposed. The dragons . . . they're more aware than most realize."

They emerged into a vast cavern lit by streams of molten rock flowing through channels in the walls. The heat was intense but not unbearable.

"The thermal chamber," Jorr said. "We can keep him warm here, but—"

Footsteps echoed from the passage they'd just left. Multiple sets, moving quickly.

"This way!" Jorr pulled the wheelbarrow behind a fallen column. "They're searching the old ways too."

They pressed themselves against the warm stone as guards passed the chamber's entrance. Ellie caught fragments of conversation.

". . . checking every level . . ."

". . . princess wants him found . . ."

". . . burial preparations already begun . . ."

When the sounds faded, Ash appeared on the fallen column above them, tail twitching. The gray cat meowed softly, then leaped down and padded toward a narrow opening near the floor.

"He knows the way," Jorr whispered. "Through the maintenance tunnels."

They carefully maneuvered the wheelbarrow toward the bridge spanning a deep chasm.

"Stop!" The command rang out behind them. "By order of Princess Seren!"

Ellie looked at the bridge, then at her son's concealed form. The wood looked barely strong enough to hold them all.

"We have no choice," she said.

They stepped onto the first plank. It groaned under their combined weight.

"Surrender now," the guard captain called. "There's nowhere to go."

Another dragon roar shook the cavern. Closer now. Much closer.

"Keep moving," Ellie said.

They were halfway across when the first plank snapped behind them.

The bridge swayed as another plank gave way. Behind them, guards crowded the edge of the chasm, arrows nocked but holding their fire—they needed Pryce's body intact for the princess's plans.

Ahead, through the steam rising from the thermal vents, Ellie could see the relative safety of the far side. But the bridge was failing faster now.

A massive shadow passed over them as something huge moved in the cavern above. Stormwing's roar filled the space, closer than ever.

Jorr carefully moved the wheelbarrow forward. "She knows we have Pryce."

As the next plank splintered beneath their feet, Ellie met Jorr's terrified gaze. They were out of options and out of time. The bridge began to give way.

31. The Chasm's Edge

The bridge groaned beneath their feet as another plank splintered and fell into the fiery chasm below. Ellie helped Jorr maneuver the wheelbarrow containing Pryce's seemingly lifeless body. Steam billowed up from the thermal vents, making the wooden planks slick and treacherous.

The elaborate Dragonkin dress tangled around Ellie's legs as she helped Jorr steady the wheelbarrow. The silver-threaded fabric, meant to mark her as visiting nobility, now threatened to be their undoing. She yanked at the heavy skirts, trying to free her feet as another plank gave way behind them.

"This blasted thing," she said, ripping the delicate hem to give herself more mobility.

"My lady!" Jorr's horrified whisper made her smile grimly.

"Better a torn dress than a dead son," she said, gathering the remaining fabric and knotting it at her hip. The makeshift alteration gave her the freedom to move, though the corseted bodice still restricted her breathing.

"We need to lighten the load," Jorr said. "The bridge won't hold."

Behind them, boots thundered on stone as more Dragonkin guards poured into the cavern. Ahead, through the swirling steam, Ellie caught glimpses of the far side—and their only chance of escape.

"The supplies," she said, already reaching for the grain sacks.

They worked frantically, tossing sacks into the chasm. Each loss lightened their burden, but the bridge's creaking grew more ominous. A support rope snapped with a sound like a whip crack.

"Surrender now!" An aristocratic voice carried over the sound of splintering wood. "There's nowhere to run!"

Stormwing burst through an opening in the cavern ceiling. The storm dragon's roar shook loose stones from above, forcing the guards to scatter. Wind and rain whipped through the space as Stormwing wheeled overhead, fighting to reach her unconscious rider.

"Keep moving," Ellie urged, helping Jorr steady the wheelbarrow. Her son's face remained still.

Another support rope gave way. The bridge pitched sideways, nearly sending them all into the abyss. Jorr grabbed Pryce's body as the wheelbarrow slipped, its metal frame scraping against the planks before tumbling into the chasm.

"We'll have to carry him," Jorr said, straining under Pryce's weight.

Ellie took her son's legs while Jorr supported his shoulders. Together they staggered forward, every step a battle against the failing bridge and their own exhaustion. Steam made their grip slippery, and Pryce's transformed body was heavier than she expected.

Above, Stormwing's lightning forced the guards back, but more emerged from other tunnels. Princess Seren's voice shouted: "Stop them! The burial chamber awaits its prince!"

The bridge gave a final, terrible groan. Wooden supports snapped like brittle bones. The entire structure began to collapse, starting from the far end and racing toward them like a wave of destruction.

"Jump!" Ellie screamed.

They leaped as the last planks disintegrated beneath them. For one heart-stopping moment, they hung suspended over the fiery depths. Then they crashed onto the far side, rolling away from the edge as the bridge fell away completely.

Ellie's relief lasted only seconds. Through the steam, dark shapes emerged—more Dragonkin guards, weapons drawn. They were surrounded. Ellie's knife was taken before she knew what was happening.

"A valiant effort," a commander said, stepping forward. "But ultimately futile."

Stormwing dove toward them, but a volley of arrows forced the dragon back. The storm dragon let out a cry of frustration, unable to reach them through the guards' defenses.

"Well, well." Princess Seren appeared through the steam. Her eyes narrowing as she studied Ellie's stolen finery. "You must be the famous Ellie Harper-Green.

How fitting to meet my new mother-in-law while she's wearing stolen royal garments."

Ellie lifted her chin. "Better stolen clothes than a stolen son."

"Stolen?" Seren laughed. "Your son came to us willingly. He chose power, chose me, chose to become something greater than a simple fisherman's son."

"He chose based on your lies."

"The only lie was believing a Shorling woman could raise a child of dragon blood. You're too late. Your son is gone. The prince belongs to me now."

"Take the boy," the commander ordered. Guards moved forward, tearing Pryce from their grasp despite Ellie's desperate resistance. "The burial chamber has waited long enough for its prince."

"No!" Ellie lunged for her son, but strong hands held her back. "He's not dead! The potion—"

"Silence! You've interfered with sacred rites. Perhaps a sacrifice to the volcano will teach you the price of defiance."

Ellie struggled as guards held her. She watched helplessly as they carried Pryce away, his scaled face peaceful in his death-like sleep.

They were marched through torch-lit corridors, deep into Dragon Fang's dungeons. The cell they threw her and Jorr into was carved from volcanic rock. The air stank of sulfur.

"I'm sorry," Jorr whispered once they were alone. "I thought we could save him."

Ellie pressed her forehead against the cold bars. "How long? How long did you say before they seal him in that chamber?"

"The burial rites begin at dawn," Jorr said. "But even if we could escape, the chamber is deep within the sacred vaults. The guards will be doubled now."

"Then we'll find another way." Ellie paced the narrow cell, her torn Dragonkin dress dragging in the volcanic dust. "What about the thermal vents? Could we use them to reach the burial chamber?"

Jorr shook his head. "The vents are too narrow, and the heat would kill us. Besides, they're all fitted with dragon-forged grates specifically to prevent escape."

"The guard rotation then. You said they change at dawn—there must be a moment when . . ."

"They overlap shifts," Jorr explained. "The next guards arrive before the others leave. There's never a gap."

Ellie slumped against the wall. "What about Stormwing? If we could somehow signal her . . ."

"The burial chamber is too deep underground for her to reach. The sacred vaults were built to withstand dragon attacks."

"Mira—could she help? She has access to the kitchens, maybe . . ."

"She'd never make it past the increased security. And even if she did . . ." Jorr gestured at their surroundings. "We're in the deepest part of the dungeons. The kitchen passages don't connect to this level."

"If we could just create some kind of distraction," she said, more desperate now. "We could signal someone to create a fire in the stables, or . . ."

"The stables are too far from the burial chamber. And with the wedding chaos, they've stationed extra guards at every strategic point." Jorr's shoulders slumped. "They've thought of everything."

The sound of approaching boots made them fall silent. A guard passed, torch light casting ominous shadows through the bars. When his footsteps faded, Ellie turned back to Jorr.

"There has to be a way," she whispered.

But as time passed in their volcanic prison, even her fierce hope began to fade. Every plan they discussed felt more impossible than the last. The guards were too many, the defenses too strong. And time was running out.

"The volcano sacrifice," Jorr said suddenly. "It's not just an execution—it's a ritual. They'll have to transport us through the temple passages."

Ellie looked up. "The same passages that lead to the burial chamber?"

"Yes, but—" Jorr's words cut off as boots approached their cell.

A guard appeared at the bars. He looked at Jorr. "I never thought I'd see you here. After all Master Kestrel did for you, taking you in when no one else would. Teaching you to care for the dragons." He shook his head. "And this is how you repay that kindness? By helping this Shorling woman steal our prince?"

Jorr looked away, but the guard wasn't finished.

"I remember when you first came to us—couldn't even look a drake in the eye. Now you tend the great ones without flinching." The guard's voice held a mix of disappointment and grudging respect. "You had a future here, Jorr. Could have risen high in the ranks. Instead . . ." He gestured at the cell. "Well, the volcano's flame burns traitor and enemy alike."

His expression softened slightly. "For what it's worth, I'm sorry it came to this. You were good with the dragons. But orders are orders, and the princess was quite clear about your punishment."

The guard looked at Ellie. "As for you, woman, you should have stayed in your fishing village where you belonged."

As the guard turned to walk away, he said, "Enjoy your last hours. At dawn, the volcano awaits its tribute."

32. The Awakening

Darkness. Not the gentle dark of night or even the pitch black of a moonless sky. This was a crushing, absolute darkness that pressed against him like a physical weight.

At first, there was nothing else. No sensation. No movement. Not even the comfort of his own heartbeat to remind him he lived.

Time had no meaning in this void. Had it been minutes? Hours? Days?

The first thing to return was the silence. Not ordinary silence, but deep, suffocating quiet. The kind of silence that spoke of isolation. Of abandonment. Of burial.

Next came the awareness of air—stale and thin, each shallow breath tasting of dust and age. His lungs struggled to draw in enough oxygen, though he couldn't yet feel them moving.

Gradually, a cold sensation seeped into his awareness. The eternal chill of underground chambers. Of tombs.

Panicked, he tried to rise, but his body remained frozen. He couldn't open his eyes. Couldn't move his fingers. Couldn't even quicken his breathing as the terrible reality dawned.

They had buried him. He was trapped in complete darkness, in a space barely larger than his body, with air growing thinner by the moment.

His mind screamed for movement, for escape, but his muscles refused to respond. The Drakebane's hold was still too strong, leaving him conscious but paralyzed as the horror of his situation settled over him.

Would he remain aware as the air ran out? Would his last moments be spent in this terrible stillness, unable even to cry out?

The silence, broken only by the soft whisper of his own thoughts, grew more desperate with each passing moment.

Panic surged as his mind cleared. The Drakebane potion had worked; he was alive. But he was also sealed inside a stone sarcophagus, buried in the royal crypts beneath Dragon's Fang Island.

Then sensation returned in a rush—cold stone against his back, the taste of dust in his mouth, the absolute silence of the tomb.

He tried to lift his arms, but they barely responded. The potion's effects still lingered, making his limbs feel leaden. His skin felt different—some of the scales had receded, though not entirely. The pendant his mother had given him still rested against his chest.

Pryce planted his palms against the lid, muscles trembling with effort. The stone remained unmoved by his initial push. His chest tightened—whether from fear or failing air, he couldn't tell.

They never expected anyone to wake up in here, he realized. The thought sparked anger rather than fear. They'd tried to bury him, to use his "death" to claim Crystal Shores. Seren's betrayal burned fresh in his memory.

"I will not die in this tomb."

Power surged through Pryce's body, a fusion of Shorling will and dragon strength.

He planted his feet against the stone, muscles tensing. The first push accomplished nothing. The second made the lid creak. With the third, he let out a grunt that was neither fully Shorling nor dragon, but something uniquely his own.

The stone lid shifted. A hairline crack appeared, letting in a whisper of fresh air. Pryce focused everything into one final effort, channeling his rage at Seren, his fear for Crystal Shores, and above all, his fierce determination to live.

The lid moved.

Not much—just enough to create a gap. But it was enough. Pryce twisted sideways, forcing his shoulder into the space. Sharp stone scraped against his skin and clothing as he fought to widen the opening.

With a sound like breaking ice, the lid slipped further. Pryce heaved himself up and out, tumbling onto the chamber floor as the massive stone crashed down behind him. The impact shook the chamber, sending dust cascading from above.

He lay there for a moment, gasping in the marginally fresher air. Crystals provided enough light to see his immediate surroundings—a vast chamber filled with other sarcophagi.

His burial clothes were a formal Dragonkin ensemble befitting a prince. The high-collared jacket was crafted from midnight-blue silk, embroidered with silver thread that traced patterns like dragon scales. A cloak of deeper blue hung from his shoulders, its hem weighted with small dragon-forged medallions that chimed softly as he moved.

They had dressed him as one of their own, a final attempt to claim him even in death. But the elegant garments were torn now, damaged from his desperate escape from the sarcophagus.

Pryce pushed himself to his feet, fighting off dizziness. The glow of crystals revealed towering pillars carved to resemble dragons in flight. Between them, rows of sarcophagi stretched into darkness.

A distant sound made Pryce freeze—stone grinding against stone, followed by whispers that might have been voices or merely the wind through passages.

"I'm not alone down here."

Movement flashed at the edge of his vision. Pryce spun to face it, but saw only shadows between the pillars. Yet when he turned back, the path ahead had changed. Where there had been only rows of tombs, an archway now stood.

"A test?" Pryce remembered Master Kestrel's lessons about the Dragonkin's love of trials and challenges. "The burial chamber is protected."

Pryce caught faint sounds of guards approaching, perhaps, investigating the noise.

"Which way?"

The archway's runes seemed to form words, though not in any language he recognized. Yet something in his blood responded to their pattern.

Pryce approached the archway. Though he couldn't read them directly, their meaning seemed to seep into his mind. A challenge and a warning: Only those of true blood may pass. Choose your nature or choose your grave.

Below these words were two symbols, one resembling a dragon's claw, the other a hand. A choice, then—but not the one the Dragonkin would expect.

Instead of touching either symbol, Pryce pressed his palm against the center where the two marks intersected.

For a moment, Pryce feared he'd made the wrong choice. Then the stone arch became transparent. Through it, he glimpsed a different chamber.

Behind him, the sound of boots grew louder. Guards shouting, orders being given. They would soon discover his empty sarcophagus.

Pryce stepped through the arch. As soon as he crossed, the opening solidified back into stone, sealing him off from his pursuers.

The new chamber was circular, its walls lined with dragon skulls. At the chamber's center, a figure waited—translucent, glowing, its form shifting.

"Welcome, seeker," the apparition said. "Few choose as you did. Fewer still understand why that choice matters."

"Who are you?"

"Once, I was like you—caught between two natures. Now I am guardian of the trials." The spirit gestured, and three doorways appeared in the chamber walls—red, blue, and silver. "Will you face the trial of strength? The trial of wisdom? Or the trial of spirit?"

Pryce studied each doorway carefully, remembering Old Man Finnegan's stories about the ancient Dragonkin. Their tests were rarely what they seemed.

"What happens if I choose wrong?"

The guardian's form flickered. "Those who fail remain here, joining the ranks of those who guard these halls. Choose wisely, seeker. Your mother's life may depend upon it."

"My mother? How do you know my mother?"

"Even now she faces her own trial. The volcano grows hungry, and the princess's patience grows thin."

He recalled Old Man Finnegan's words: "A Shorling's strength isn't in their muscles, lad. It's in knowing when to fight and when to think your way clear."

Pryce studied the doors again, this time with his fisherman's eye for detail. The red doorway promised raw power—tempting for someone who'd just discovered their dragon strength. The silver door beckoned with the allure of knowledge. But the blue door . . . its light rippled like the surface of Lake Dragontide on a calm morning.

"I choose the trial of spirit," he said.

The guardian's form stabilized briefly, taking on a more distinct shape. "Interesting. Most who carry dragon blood choose strength. Most Shorlings, though few have been here, choose wisdom."

The guardian gestured, and the blue door swung open. Beyond it, mist swirled. "Enter, seeker. Face what lies within your own spirit. But remember—time grows short. The volcano's hunger will not wait forever."

Pryce stepped through the doorway. The mist enveloped him, cool and thick as lake fog. When it cleared, he found himself standing on what appeared to be the surface of Lake Dragontide itself. The water was solid beneath his feet, yet it moved like liquid glass.

Reflections appeared in the surface—moments from his past. His father teaching him to tie fishing knots. His mother passing down the dragon pendant. Seren's betraying kiss. Each image flowed outward, creating overlapping memories and consequences.

Then the surface began to change, darkening. Shapes emerged—three figures that slowly took form before him.

The figures solidified, each one a version of himself. The first appeared as he'd been in Crystal Shores—a Shorling fisherman's son in worn clothes that smelled of fish. The second showed him fully transformed into Dragonkin royalty, scales gleaming, dressed in the fine clothes Seren had given him. The third was something else entirely, a perfect fusion of both natures.

"Choose," the figures spoke in unison. "Choose who you truly are."

But there was something wrong about this test. His Shorling instincts—the same ones that had helped him survive Lake Dragontide's treacherous moods—prickled in warning.

"No," Pryce said firmly.

The figures stirred. "You must choose."

"I already did. Back at the arch. I am who I am—all of it. The Shorling of Crystal Shores, the dragon blood in my veins. I won't deny either part of myself."

The water-like surface beneath his feet began to churn. The three figures wavered.

"Pretty words," the Dragonkin version sneered. "But you were eager enough to abandon your Shorling heritage when Seren offered you power."

"And you were quick to betray your new oath when things grew difficult," the Shorling version added. "Neither fish nor fowl, as Old Man Finnegan would say."

The third figure remained silent, watching.

Pryce felt anger building. A Shorling saying came to mind: The stormiest waters often hide the safest passage.

"You're right," Pryce said. "I did abandon my heritage when Seren tempted me with power. And yes, I broke faith with the Dragonkin when I discovered their true plans. I made mistakes. But a Shorling knows that every storm teaches you how to sail better."

The surface beneath his feet calmed slightly. The third figure—the merged version—nodded almost imperceptibly.

"Pretty words," the Dragonkin version said again. "But Crystal Shores will never truly accept you now. Look at yourself—scaled and changed. You're neither pure Shorling nor true Dragonkin."

Pryce touched his remaining scales. "These changes don't make me less of a Shorling."

The Shorling version stepped forward. "And what of your duty to Crystal Shores? You left them vulnerable to invasion."

"I did," Pryce admitted. "But now I understand both sides. I know the Dragonkin's strengths—and their weaknesses. Knowledge that might save Crystal Shores, if I live to use it."

The third figure finally spoke. "And if you had to choose? If saving Crystal Shores meant losing your dragon abilities? If protecting your mother meant surrendering your Shorling heart?"

"A Shorling saying tells us: 'The tide serves those who know how to read it.' I won't choose because I don't have to. My mother gave me this pendant filled with our blood mixed with dragon essence. She knew even then that being both wasn't a weakness—it was a gift."

The three figures started to blur at the edges.

"My Shorling heart gives me the wisdom to navigate troubled waters. My dragon blood gives me the strength to protect those I love. Together, they make me who I am—who I choose to be."

The third figure stepped forward as the other two faded. "And who is that, seeker?"

"I am Pryce Harper-Green of Crystal Shores. Son of Ellie and Tyler. Student of Old Man Finnegan's wisdom. Friend to dragons. I carry the blood of Lake Dragontide's people and the essence of its ancient guardians. I am exactly who I need to be."

The figure smiled—a genuine expression that carried neither mockery nor challenge. "Well spoken. But words are wind. Actions are the true test."

The water-like surface cracked like ice in spring thaw. Through the widening fissures, Pryce glimpsed the chamber below—where his mother and Jorr were being led toward the mouth of the volcano.

Pryce gasped. "What's my mom doing here? And why is she and Jorr tied up like they're about to be . . . sacrificed?"

"Time grows short," the figure said, beginning to fade. "Your trial is passed, but your greatest challenge awaits. Remember what you've learned here: true strength lies not in choosing between two natures, but in wielding both as one."

The glowing surface shattered completely. Pryce fell through the cracks, but instead of plunging into darkness, he landed softly in a new chamber. This one was carved directly from volcanic rock. Veins of crystal pulsed with light.

Distant voices echoed through the stone—guards coordinating search patterns. But beneath these sounds, Pryce heard the rhythmic chanting of a sacrificial ceremony.

The mixed blood within seemed to pull him toward one of the crystal-lined passages. Without hesitation, he began to run.

The passages twisted deeper into the mountain, growing warmer with each step.

The chanting grew louder. Pryce ran faster.

". . . by flame be purged, by fire be cleansed . . ."

He was close now. So close. Steam vented from cracks in the passage floor.

The tunnel opened onto a ledge overlooking a vast chamber. Far below, illuminated by the volcano's glow, Pryce saw the ceremonial platform where white-robed Dragonkin priests led two figures toward the edge. Even from this height, he recognized his mother's red hair and Jorr's distinctive stance.

Pryce touched his mother's pendant one last time. He was no longer the uncertain boy who'd left Crystal Shores seeking adventure, nor was he the half-transformed prisoner who'd drunk the potion. He was something new—something that bridged two worlds.

He prepared to leap.

33. The Bridge Between

Dawn painted shades of blood and shadow above the rumbling volcano. Ellie stumbled on the steep path, her bound hands unable to break her fall. Sharp rocks bit into her knees through the torn fabric of her dress.

"Up," a guard commanded, yanking her roughly to her feet.

Beside her, Jorr's face was streaked with soot and sweat as they climbed the winding path toward the volcano's mouth. Steam hissed from fissures in the ground. The ropes binding their wrists chafed with each step.

"Keep moving," another guard ordered, but Ellie noticed the slight tremor in his voice. Even the Dragonkin feared the volcano.

The rumble grew louder as they ascended. Ellie's mind drifted to Pryce—his childhood laughter, his determination to prove himself, his fierce love of dragons.

"Strange," Jorr said softly as they climbed, "how the ancient stories speak of this place."

A guard jabbed him with a spear shaft. "Silence."

"What stories?" Ellie asked, ignoring the warning.

Jorr's voice remained low. "They say dragon spirits sleep beneath the mountain. In the old tales, when sacrifices were unjust, the spirits would rise to prevent them."

"Quiet!" The guard's voice cracked slightly.

Ellie managed a grim smile. "My father used to say a stormy sea shows the sailor's mettle."

"I said silence!" The guard's scales seemed to ripple with agitation.

They reached the ceremonial platform—an outcropping of black rock jutting over the volcano. Father Blackwood stood waiting, his ritualistic robes adorned with intricate dragon motifs. He clutched a book in trembling hands.

Dragonkin nobles ringed the platform, their scaled faces illuminated by the caldera's glow. Ellie studied them, noting signs of unease in their rigid postures as they positioned them near the platform's edge.

"The sun rises," Father Blackwood announced. "The ancient rites must be observed."

He began to chant in a language Ellie did not understand. The ground trembled beneath their feet.

***

Pryce studied the impossible drop before him. It offered no safe path to the ceremonial platform where his mother and Jorr awaited their fate.

"Ragnarok," he called out mentally, reaching for the connection they'd forged. "I need your help. My mother's life depends on it."

Silence answered.

"Please," Pryce projected more forcefully. "There's no time for the tunnels, and I can't reach them alone."

Finally, Ragnarok's voice came through his mind. *Young one, I feel the tremors. My chains are doubled; the Dragonkin have strengthened my bonds. I cannot break free.*

Pryce's fists clenched in frustration. "There has to be a way."

The guard. The one with the vacant eyes. His mind is weak—perhaps . . .

Through their connection, Pryce sensed Ragnarok attempting to influence the guard's thoughts. For a moment, it seemed to work. The guard's hands moved toward the chains' locks. But then his eyes cleared, the mental suggestion gone.

Ragnarok attempted once more to influence the guard's mind, but the effort proved futile. The guard's vacant expression cleared, his hand dropping away from the chains' locks as the mental suggestion faded.

Pryce's frustration mounted. Time was running out. "There has to be another way."

The ancient dragon's mental voice carried resignation. *Young one, my powers are too weakened by these bonds. I cannot—*

A familiar screech cut was heard. Pryce could see through Ragnarok's eyes Stormwing bursting into view.

"Yes!" Pryce exclaimed as his dragon channeled lightning through her body. The massive surge struck Ragnarok's restraints, overloading the dragon-forged metal. With a sound like thunder, the chains shattered.

The dragons soared from the cave, searching for Pryce.

When they found him, Pryce didn't hesitate. He leaped through the opening in the floor and onto Ragnarok. Stormwing fell into formation behind them as they descended toward Ellie and Jorr.

On the platform, Father Blackwood's chanting reached a fever pitch. The first rays of sunlight pierced the horizon.

"Now!" he commanded. "The sacrifice must be completed!"

Ellie and Jorr were forced toward the edge.

Ragnarok emerged from the volcanic mist, Pryce astride his back. Stormwing flanked them. The assembled nobles scattered in panic.

"Mom!"

Father Blackwood shouted, "Complete the sacrifice! Now!"

The guards shoved hard. Ellie felt the ground disappear beneath her feet as she and Jorr plunged toward the waiting lava below.

34. Blood on the Mountain

As Stormwing swooped down to catch them, Ellie and Jorr grappled to secure themselves on the dragon's back. With her wrists bound tightly, Ellie clung desperately to the rough scales, the wind tearing at her hair and whipping it across her face. For a terrifying moment, she felt her restrained hands slipping, her grip loosening.

"Hold on!" Jorr shouted.

"I'm trying!" Ellie screamed back. The ropes binding her wrists dug into her flesh, but the fear of plummeting into the molten lava below overrode any discomfort.

Stormwing banked sharply to the left, dodging a gust of turbulent air spiraling off Ragnarok's colossal wings. Ellie glanced over to see Pryce astride the massive dragon.

"Ellie, if you could possibly scream less and hold on more, that would be tremendously helpful!" Jorr called out.

Ash's terrified yowls emanated from the carrier strapped securely to the saddle.

Pryce leaned forward, shouting instructions to Ragnarok. But the dragon seemed sluggish, his responses delayed, his movements hampered by his injuries. Stormwing, though better trained, more agile, was struggling with her two passengers.

Another violent gust hit them, a force that threatened to rip them from Stormwing's back. Jorr's grip slipped. His hand clawed at empty air, before he began to slide off Stormwing's side, his body dangling.

"Jorr!" Ellie lunged, wrapping her bound hands around his tunic just as he lost his hold completely.

Jorr's weight pulled at Ellie's arms as he shouted, "This wasn't part of the plan!"

"Hang on, I've got you!" Ellie's muscles strained as she fought to pull him back up.

Stormwing dipped, adjusting to the sudden shift in weight, her wings beating furiously. With a mighty effort, Ellie hauled Jorr back onto the saddle. They collapsed against each other, panting.

Pryce maneuvered Ragnarok closer. "We need to land! There's a mountaintop on the far side of the island—we can regroup there!"

The dragons, responding to Pryce's command, angled toward the distant peak, a small, rocky plateau that offered a temporary refuge. As they descended, the winds grew more erratic.

"Get ready for a rough landing!" Jorr said, bracing himself.

Ellie tightened her grip on Stormwing's saddle horn as the dragon began her approach. The dragon flapped her wings furiously, kicking up clouds of dust and pebbles that pelted them like tiny, stinging missiles. They hit the ground with a bone-jarring jolt, bouncing along the uneven terrain before coming to a halt.

"That was smoother than expected," Jorr said, attempting a grin.

Ellie shot him a look. "Speak for yourself. '

Above them, Ragnarok struggled to control his descent. His massive body buckled as he touched down, and he crashed onto his side with a pained roar.

"Ragnarok!" Pryce leaped from the dragon's back.

Ellie and Jorr scrambled to their feet, struggling with the ropes still binding their wrists. Pryce hurried over, his hands reaching for the knots.

"Hold still," he said. His fingers worked frantically, but the ropes refused to give. "These are tighter than I thought."

"Can you get them off?" Ellie asked, wincing as the cords dug into her skin, cutting off her circulation.

"I'm trying." After several moments, he managed to loosen the bindings. The ropes fell away, and they both flexed their sore wrists.

"Are you both okay?" Pryce asked.

"We're alive, thanks to you," Ellie said. She pulled him into a fierce hug.

"I wasn't sure I'd make it . . ." Pryce's voice trailed off, his words choked with emotion.

Ellie pulled back slightly, her hands framing his face. "What have they done to you?"

He looked away, his gaze shifting towards the ground. "It's a long story."

Jorr cleared his throat, drawing their attention. "You should have seen him before, Ellie. Scales everywhere. All over his body. You wouldn't have recognized him."

"Why are you here?" Pryce asked, turning to his mother.

She sighed. "To save you. To bring you home."

Ash burst out from the carrier with an indignant yowl. The cat's mottled fur was standing on end.

"Ash!" Pryce knelt as the cat bounded toward him, rubbing against his legs. "I missed you too, you troublemaker."

Ellie glanced around, her eyes scanning the rocky, desolate landscape. "Why aren't they pursuing us?"

As if in response, a deep, ominous horn blasted.

"That's a Dragonkin war horn," Jorr said.

They rushed to the edge of the plateau, looking out over the island's far side.

The horizon was dotted with ships—dozens, no, hundreds—advancing in tight formation, a vast armada that stretched as far as the eye could see. Sleek warships, bristling with weaponry, sailed alongside bulky, ungainly barges laden with mining equipment, their purpose clear. Above them, a swarm of dragons filled the sky.

"By the stars," Ellie said. "They're heading for Crystal Shores."

"This isn't just an attack. It's an invasion. A full-scale invasion," Pryce said.

"We have to warn them. We have to get back to Crystal Shores and warn them," Ellie said.

Ragnarok let out a low, pained growl, a sound of distress that drew their attention. Pryce turned to see the dragon attempting to stand, favoring his injured leg, his movements hampered by the deep gash that ran along his hindquarters.

"Ragnarok's hurt," Pryce said. "He can't fly like this. He's in no condition to fly."

Jorr knelt beside the dragon, examining the deep gash "This is bad. Really bad. He needs rest and treatment. He needs time to heal."

"We don't have time," Ellie said. "Crystal Shores is in danger. We have to warn them."

Pryce's eyes moved to Stormwing. "You can take Stormwing back. Warn the village. You and Jorr can fly back on Stormwing."

Jorr shook his head. "You should go. You can ride Stormwing better than we can. I doubt we'd be able to outrun the Dragonkin."

Pryce thought a moment, then said, "I can't abandon Ragnarok. And If I leave, the Dragonkin will find you. They'll kill you."

"We'll be fine, we'll find a place to hide," Ellie said. "The village needs to know what's coming. They need time to prepare."

Before they could argue further, a distant roar drew their attention skyward. A single dragon broke away from the main fleet, banking sharply towards the mountain.

"They've spotted us," Jorr said.

Ellie scanned the rocky terrain for any sign of cover. "There's nowhere to hide up here. We're completely exposed."

"Then we fight," Pryce said.

Jorr gave a short, humorless laugh. "With what weapons? We have nothing."

"We have dragons," Ellie said.

"Get Ragnarok behind those rocks," Pryce said. "You two stay with him, Stormwing and I will take on this Dragonkin."

Jorr moved to help the injured dragon towards a cluster of boulders that offered some semblance of cover.

Pryce sprinted towards Stormwing. He vaulted onto her back, the dragon shifting beneath him, and taking flight, soaring into the air to meet the approaching threat.

From atop Stormwing, Pryce assessed the incoming threat. Only one dragon had left the fleet. He recognized Raven's familiar silhouette atop her copper drake.

"It's Raven," he called down to the others. "She's a friend. She might be able to help us."

Raven guided her drake to a graceful landing beside Stormwing, now back on the ground.

"You're in terrible danger," she said. "The entire fleet is mobilizing. Queen Nymeria plans to strip mine Crystal Shores for dragon-magic ore."

"We saw the ships," Pryce said. "But why help us? You're risking yourself."

"Because what they're doing is wrong, all of it. It's not right." She unstrapped a second sword from her saddle and tossed it to Pryce. "Here. You'll need this. They want all of you . . . dead."

"Incoming!" Jorr said with alarm. "Dragon approaching from the west!"

"It's Thane," Raven said. "Quick—play dead, all of you. Dragons too. I'll tell him I killed you. It's our only chance."

They scrambled to arrange themselves convincingly. Ragnarok and Stormwing settled into lifeless poses. Pryce lay sprawled near his mother, trying to still even his breathing, to mimic the stillness of death.

"There's no blood," Jorr said suddenly. "He'll see there's no blood. He'll know we're not dead."

Pryce rushed to Ragnarok. "I'm sorry, old friend." He pressed his hand against Ragnarok's wounded leg, smearing his fingers with the blood. He quickly spread the blood on his face and clothes, and then on Ellie and Jorr, creating a gruesome, convincing illusion of a bloody battle. He resumed his 'dead' position.

Through barely opened eyes, he watched Raven soar to meet Thane's approaching shadow drake. Their dragons circled each other in an aerial dance.

"It's done," Raven could be heard saying. "The traitors are dead. They won't be causing any more trouble."

Thane's cultured accent held a note of suspicion. "All of them? That one looks like Pryce. I thought he was dead in the tomb. I thought he was buried."

"Trust me, they're dead. I made sure of it."

"I need to verify this personally," Thane said. "The Queen will want proof."

35. Rebellion Rising

Pryce held his breath, keeping absolutely still as Thane's shadow drake circled overhead. The blood from Ragnarok's wound felt sticky on his face, but he didn't dare move to wipe it away.

"I need to verify this myself," Thane said.

Another blast from the war horn echoed across the mountaintop.

"There's no time," Raven called back, her copper drake maintaining position between Thane and the bodies below. "The fleet needs us. The attack begins soon."

Thane's drake swooped lower, and Pryce could smell the creature's distinctive shadow-mist scent.

"Do you really believe these simpletons could survive that fall?" Raven asked. "Even their dragons are dead. Look at them."

The shadow drake landed with a heavy thud. Pryce heard Thane's boots hit the ground, followed by the metallic scrape of his sword being drawn.

"These Shorlings are surprisingly resilient," Thane said. "Like cockroaches. I want to be certain."

The war horn sounded again, longer and more insistent this time.

"Thane, the Queen commanded all riders to join the fleet before the attack. Do you want to explain why you disobeyed a direct order?"

Pryce felt Thane's presence moving closer. Through barely-open eyes, he saw the Dragonkin's boots stop mere feet away.

The horn blast came again, followed by distant roars of dragons.

"By dragon's blood," Thane cursed. He strode forward and ripped the dragon pendant from Pryce's neck. "If they somehow survived . . ." His eyes narrowed at Pryce's torn burial garments—the midnight-blue silk and silver embroidery now stained with blood and dirt. "These clothes . . . these are from the burial chamber. The same chamber where you were supposedly entombed, Shorling."

Raven's copper drake shifted uneasily. "The clothes mean nothing. We found him wandering, delirious from the transformation potion. I ended his suffering myself."

"Did you now?" Thane circled Pryce's motionless form, his boots crunching on loose rocks. "Are you suggesting he was the walking dead, escaping his tomb?"

"What does it matter?" Raven's voice carried a hint of strain. "They're dead. All of them. Isn't that what the queen wanted?"

Thane held up the dragon pendant. "This pendant. . . I've seen it before. It contains mixed blood—Shorling and dragon." He turned to study Ragnarok's seemingly lifeless form. "And this dragon . . . how exactly did you manage to subdue Ragnarok alone, Shorling?"

The war horn sounded again.

"Now come, Thane. We're already late."

The shadow drake's wings created gusts of wind as it took flight. Pryce waited until the sound of wing beats faded completely. He sat up, wiping blood from his face with his sleeve.

Ellie stood, helping Jorr to his feet. "How much time do we have?"

"Hours at most," Pryce said. "The Queen probably wants to attack at dusk, when the shadow drakes are strongest."

"Someone needs to get to Crystal Shores," Ellie said. "But Ragnarok can't fly in this condition."

The massive dragon growled softly, trying to stand despite his injuries. Blood still seeped from the deep gash along his hindquarters.

"I won't leave him," Pryce said firmly.

"Then we split up," Jorr said. "Pryce, you take Stormwing, warn the village. We'll tend to Ragnarok's wounds and follow when we can."

Pryce shook his head. "The Dragonkin will find you. They'll kill you both."

"We don't have time to argue," Ellie said. "Crystal Shores needs to be warned. They need time to prepare."

Stormwing nudged Pryce's shoulder, as if understanding the urgency of their situation.

**

Old Man Finnegan sat on his porch, sipping his morning Seaweed Brew and watching Tidewing gulls circle overhead. The familiar routine felt hollow today—his thoughts kept drifting to Pryce, wondering if the boy was still alive.

A flash of movement caught his eye. A bird approached from the great lake, flying erratically.

The messenger bird's flight was labored, her wings beating desperately against exhaustion. She barely managed to land on his porch railing, letting out a weak caw.

"Easy there, lass," Finnegan said softly, noticing the brass message capsule attached to her leg. He squinted at the exhausted bird, wondering if this was Pryce's messenger—what was her name? Skye?

His gnarled fingers worked carefully to remove the water-damaged paper from the message capsule. Most of the text was smeared and illegible, but a few key phrases remained clear: ". . . forces converge at . . . fleet deployment . . . mining operations commence . . . Crystal Shores sector . . . ore extraction . . . resistance expected minimal . . ."

Finnegan frowned as he pieced together the message's meaning. Were the Dragonkin planning to strip mine Crystal Shores?

"Sweet mercy." Grabbing his walking stick, he hurried down Chantey Street as quickly as his old legs would carry him, passing startled villagers.

He found Tyler at the docks with Tobias and Ana, the three of them repairing fishing nets.

"Tyler!" Finnegan called, slightly out of breath. "We have trouble."

Tyler looked up. "What is it?"

Finnegan handed over the damaged parchment. "From a messenger bird—Pryce's bird."

Tyler and the others huddled around the message, working to decipher its full meaning.

"They're planning an invasion," Ana said, looking out over the water.

"This isn't just another raid," Tyler said, running his fingers through his blonde hair. "They're probably bringing their entire fleet with mining equipment. This is a full-scale invasion force."

Tobias adjusted his cap. "We need to warn everyone."

"Get everyone to the town Hall," Tyler said, quickly coiling the fishing net. "And get Mayor Wright and anyone else you can find. We don't have much time."

Within the hour, the Town Hall was packed with concerned villagers. Mayor Helen Wright stood at her podium, her usual patronizing demeanor replaced by genuine worry as Tyler explained the situation.

"Nonsense," Gavin Brooks called out from the crowd. "Why would the Dragonkin waste time on our little fishing village?"

"When the tide rolls back too far, a storm is sure to follow," Finnegan said. "The signs are there for those willing to see them."

"We can't just ignore this warning," Tyler said, standing beside the mayor. "If we're wrong, we waste a day of fishing. "

"But a Dragonkin invasion?" Doyle scoffed. "Gavin is right. What would they want with our humble fishing village?"

"Our fish aren't worth the trouble," another villager added.

Ana stepped forward "You're thinking like fishermen, not warriors. Crystal Shores has strategic value—deep harbor, clear view of shipping lanes."

"And something more valuable than fish," Tyler said. "Dragon-magic ore deposits could be beneath our feet."

Mayor Wright adjusted her glasses. "That's just an old legend—"

"I've seen their mining operations on other islands," Tobias said. "They strip everything, leave nothing but ruins."

Gavin smoothed his tie. "Perhaps we could negotiate—"

"With Dragonkin?" Ana's laugh was harsh. "You might as well negotiate with a storm drake."

"We should abandon Crystal Shores while we still can," Doyle said. "Take what we can carry and head inland before the Dragonkin arrive. No sense dying for empty nets and wooden houses."

Tyler shook his head. "This isn't just about houses and nets, Doyle. This is our home—generations of Shorlings have lived and died here. If we run now, we'll have nowhere left to call our own."

"Better homeless than dead," Doyle said.

"We can't abandon Crystal Shores," Tyler said firmly.

"Then we fight." Ana drew the knife from her belt.

Mayor Wright raised her hands. "With what? Fishing nets against dragon fire?"

"You'd be surprised what a well-placed net can do," Tobias said. "Especially if we reinforce them with steel wire from the shipyard."

"The old watchtower," Ana suggested. "We can use it as a lookout point."

Tyler nodded. "And the fishing boats—we can position them as a first line of defense."

"I want to help!" Faye said, moving next to her father.

"Okay," Tyler said. "I need you to help evacuate the young and elderly inland. Take them to the caves beyond Eldengrove."

"But—"

"This isn't up for debate, Faye."

Gavin cleared his throat. "I have access to certain resources—"

"That you'll be sharing freely," Ana interrupted, her knife still in hand.

"Of course," Gavin said quickly. "For the good of the village."

The crowd began to shift, fear giving way to determination. They broke into groups, each focusing on different aspects of the defense. Some gathered fishing harpoons and began sharpening them into weapons. Others dragged carts and barrels to create barriers along the shoreline.

As the village buzzed with urgent activity, Finnegan took a moment to look out over Lake Dragontide. A dark shape appeared on the horizon—a dragon approaching fast.

36. The First Wave

Ellie knelt beside Ragnarok's massive form. The dragon's scales radiated heat like sun-warmed stones, but she could feel him trembling beneath her touch. The wound along his hindquarters still bled, dark fluid seeping between scales.

"He's getting worse," she said, glancing at Jorr.

The young handler paced nearby. "There might be a way," he said. "An old Dragonkin method called the Heartfire Confluence. But . . ." He wrung his hands. "I've only ever watched Master Kestrel perform it."

"What do you need?"

"Dragonscale Moss, volcanic ash, and . . ." Jorr swallowed hard. "Dragon blood freely given."

Ragnarok's massive head swung around, eyes fixing on Jorr with sudden intensity. A low growl rumbled through the ground.

"He doesn't trust Dragonkin healing," Jorr explained. "After what they did to him—"

"Then we do it differently," Ellie said. "My blood carries dragon essence. Will that work?"

Jorr studied her thoughtfully. "Maybe. If your heritage is strong enough."

"Dragonscale Moss? I thought that was only found in Thornveil Wilds." Ellie remembered her treacherous journey through the forbidden forest to find it to make an elixir to heal her Grandpa Joe.

"They grow it here on the volcanic slopes. But the ash must come from the sacred caves. Getting there without being seen . . ."

"We don't have a choice." Ellie stood, brushing dust from her knees.

The next hour passed in tense silence as they worked. Jorr harvested Dragonscale Moss while Ellie crept into a cave entrance, scraping volcanic ash from ancient ceremonial bowls. Twice they had to hide as patrol dragons passed overhead, their shadows sweeping the mountainside, while Ragnarok played dead.

Back at Ragnarok's side, Jorr mixed the ingredients in a crude bowl fashioned from curved bark.

"The blood," he said. "Just a few drops."

Ellie's burns from the Sweetsnare still hadn't fully healed. She pressed her thumb against one of the cracked blisters, letting the blood well up.

Jorr began to chant in an ancient tongue. The mixture in the bowl turned darker, like storm clouds gathering before rain.

"Now we apply it to his wounds," he said. "But be careful. If he resists—"

Ragnarok's growl cut him off. The dragon's muscles tensed as Ellie approached with the salve.

"Easy," she said, remembering how she used to calm injured fishing boats' guard dogs back home. "We're trying to help."

She reached out slowly, letting her hand rest on his scales near the wound. After a long moment, the dragon relaxed slightly.

As they worked the salve into his injuries, a soft blue glow began to emanate from beneath his scales. Ragnarok's breathing steadied, the trembling in his muscles easing.

"It's working," Jorr said. "The Heartfire Confluence is actually—"

A horn blast echoed across the mountain, making them all freeze.

"Search parties," Jorr said. "They'll sweep the mountain in sections, working their way up from the base. That's how Master Kestrel trained us to hunt escaped dragons." He glanced at the steep paths below. "They'll have shadow drakes with them—they can smell blood, and Ragnarok's leaving a trail."

"Can he fly?" Ellie asked, watching Ragnarok test his wounded leg.

"He'll have to."

They climbed carefully onto his broad back. Ellie gripped the spinal ridges as Ragnarok spread his wings.

"The healing isn't complete," Jorr warned. "He won't be able to fight."

"Then we'll have to be clever."

***

Pryce guided Stormwing toward Crystal Shores. The village looked different now. Fishing nets hung between buildings like massive spider webs. Overturned carts blocked the streets. From above, he spotted villagers carrying makeshift weapons and rolling barrels into position.

Ash peered from his carrier, fur bristling at their rapid descent. Below, a sentry's horn sounded—two short blasts followed by a long note. The village's warning system.

Old Man Finnegan stood on the dock, leaning on his walking stick. He squinted upward as Stormwing landed.

"By the lake's depths," Finnegan said, taking in Pryce's changed appearance—the remaining scales, the torn burial clothes. "You look like you've been through the Dragon's Maws and back."

"Worse," Pryce said, sliding from Stormwing's back. "The Dragonkin fleet is coming. They're planning to strip mine Crystal Shores for dragon-magic ore."

"We know." Finnegan gestured toward the town hall. "Your bird brought word. Your father's gathering everyone now."

They hurried through the fortified streets. Ana supervised a group stringing wire between posts. Tobias directed others in positioning oil barrels. Even Gavin had shed his fine clothes for practical work gear as he helped stack sandbags.

Inside the town hall, Tyler stood before a gathering of villagers. He turned as Pryce entered.

"Pryce." His father's voice cracked. Then his eyes narrowed, noting the scales. "What did they do to you?"

"It doesn't matter now," Pryce said. "What matters is I know their tactics. I know how they'll attack."

Mayor Wright stepped forward, adjusting her glasses. "Then tell us everything."

Pryce moved to the large table where maps of Crystal Shores lay spread out. "They'll come in three waves. Shadow drakes first, striking as the sun sets—that's when their magic is strongest. Then the fire drakes will burn our defenses. The storm drakes will follow, their lightning targeting anything that survives."

"And the ships?" Ana asked.

"They'll hold back until the dragons soften our defenses. But they're bringing mining equipment, massive drills and excavation gear. Once they establish a beachhead . . ." He couldn't finish the sentence.

"Then we stop them at the shore," Tyler said firmly.

"The nets won't hold dragons," Mayor Wright said.

"No," Pryce agreed. "But I know something that might." He turned to Gavin. "Your fireworks powder—how much do you have?"

Gavin straightened. "Three barrels in my warehouse. Was saving it for the summer festival, but . . ."

"Take me there," Pryce said. "And I'll show you how to turn it into something that even dragons will fear."

Tyler rolled up the maps. "How long until they arrive?"

"Hours," Pryce said. "They'll wait for dusk when the shadow drakes are strongest."

"Then we have work to do." Tyler turned to the gathered villagers. "Ana, take your group to the watchtower. I want eyes on that horizon."

Ana nodded, already heading for the door.

"Mom and Jorr should arrive soon." Pryce said.

"You've seen your mother?" Tyler's voice caught.

"She's helping Jorr heal Ragnarok. A great black dragon. If they can get him here in time, he might turn the tide."

Shouts erupted from outside. Everyone rushed to the windows. Faye stood in the street, pointing at the sky. A dozen Tidewing gulls circled overhead.

Tyler pushed through the town hall doors. Faye stood in the street, her red hair tangled.

"You're supposed to be evacuating with the others," Tyler said.

"Somebody needs to manage the messages." Faye reached up to catch a descending gull. "Look at this system—each bird knows its route. We can warn the whole countryside in minutes if the Dragonkin attack from an unexpected direction."

Gordan Flintjaw stood at the edge of the crowd, his arms crossed. He watched the preparations with a sneer.

"You expect us to follow him?" Gordan called out, pointing at Pryce. "Look at him—he's not even Shorling anymore. He's one of them."

"Quiet, Flintjaw," Tyler said sharply. "Unless you've got a better plan?"

Gordan spat on the ground but said nothing more.

A shout came from the watchtower. Everyone turned toward Ana's voice: "Ships on the horizon! Dozens!"

"Get to your positions," Tyler commanded. "And may the lake's depths protect us all."

Villagers scattered to their posts. Pryce walked to where Stormwing paced near the dock, her scales crackling with nervous energy. Ash peered from his carrier at all the activity.

"Let's get that firework powder," Pryce said to Gavin. "I'll show you how to make something special."

"The powder's this way," Gavin said, leading Pryce toward his warehouse near the docks.

Inside, the air smelled of sulfur and salt. Gavin lit a lantern, illuminating rows of barrels. He pointed to three marked with red symbols. "That's all of it."

"We'll need copper bowls," Pryce said, remembering Kestrel's lessons about explosives. "And salt—lots of it."

"What exactly are we making?"

"Something I learned from the Dragonkin. When it explodes, it'll create a cloud that blinds dragons. Disrupts their sense of direction."

Stormwing stuck her head through the warehouse door, sniffing curiously at the barrels.

"Not too close," Pryce warned her. "This stuff is dangerous until we mix it properly."

They worked quickly, measuring powder into copper bowls as Pryce explained the process. Other villagers joined them, forming a line to pack the mixtures into small clay pots.

"These go on the ends of spears," Pryce demonstrated. "When they hit something solid, they'll burst."

"Like that time we rigged Doyle's fishing nets with seaweed pods?" Kai's voice came from the doorway. The white-haired youth stepped into the warehouse, a quiver of arrows slung across his back.

Pryce looked up, surprised to see his friend. "Kai? I thought you'd evacuated with the others."

"And miss all the excitement?" Kai picked up one of the clay pots, examining it carefully. "Besides, someone needs to keep you from doing anything too reckless." He gestured to the powder. "Think we could modify these for arrows? Give us some range?"

"That . . . could actually work," Pryce said. "We'd need smaller pots, though. And a way to secure them to the arrowheads."

"You know," Kai said as they worked, "those scales actually make you look somewhat intimidating. Might help scare off the Dragonkin."

Pryce chuckled. "Good to know my partial transformation is good for something."

A villager appeared in the doorway. "Tyler wants you at the town hall. Says it's urgent."

"Keep mixing," Pryce told Gavin. "Remember, equal parts powder and salt. Kai, can you supervise the arrow modifications?"

"Already on it." Kai began organizing villagers into an assembly line. "Just like fletching fishing arrows, folks, but try not to drop these ones."

He followed the villager through the crowded streets. Shorlings rushed past carrying weapons, nets, and makeshift bombs. The town hall had become a command center, with Tyler and Mayor Wright bent over maps.

"Look at this," Tyler said as Pryce entered. He pointed to a message scroll. "From the eastern lookout post. They've spotted something strange about the Dragonkin ships."

"What kind of strange?"

"They're carrying huge metal frames. Like nothing we've seen before."

"The mining equipment. They'll try to set it up as soon as they secure the beach." He studied the maps. "We need to keep them off this stretch of shore. It's the only place deep enough for their larger ships."

"That's where we've set most of the traps," Tyler said. "Oil barrels beneath the water, nets weighted with hooks . . ."

A horn blast from the watchtower cut through their discussion—three long notes.

"They're launching the first wave," Pryce said. "The shadow drakes will come in low, using the evening sun to hide their approach."

"How do we fight what we can't see?" Mayor Wright asked.

"Listen for their wings," Pryce said. "Shadow drakes sound different than other dragons—more like wind through silk. And watch for disturbances in the air, like heat waves on a hot day."

"There!" A sentry shouted from the watchtower. "Movement over the water!"

Pryce squinted at the horizon. The air seemed to ripple and twist, as if the sunset itself was being pulled apart.

"Get those spears ready," Tyler called out. "Wait for my signal!"

Villagers took positions along the shoreline. Kai appeared at Pryce's side, his bow ready with one of their modified arrows. "Just like hunting lake birds."

"Except these birds breathe fire and want to kill us."

"Details, details." Kai nocked an arrow. "At least the targets are bigger."

"Steady," Tyler said as the rippling air drew closer. "Steady . . ."

The rippling air solidified into dark shapes. Shadow drakes, at least twenty of them, their scales bending light around them like smoke. Their riders wore black armor that seemed to absorb the fading sunlight.

"Now!" Tyler shouted.

Spears and arrows arced through the air, trailing smoke. Kai's first shot struck true, the modified arrow exploding against a drake's chest in a cloud of white powder. The clay pots shattered, forcing the shadow drakes to become fully visible as they lost concentration.

"It's working!" Mayor Wright said.

"Thank the lake's depths for your crazy ideas," Kai called to Pryce, already drawing another arrow.

But three drakes broke through, diving toward the shoreline. Their riders hurled hooks attached to ropes, trying to create anchor points for the ships that would follow.

"Cover me!" Pryce shouted to Kai as Stormwing launched herself from behind the town hall. They slammed into the nearest shadow drake, lightning crackling from Stormwing's scales. Below, Kai's arrows kept the other drakes at bay, each shot creating clouds of disruptive powder.

"Look!" Ana's voice carried from the watchtower. "Something's coming from the north!"

Pryce turned Stormwing in time to see a massive shape approaching. For a moment, his heart sank—until he recognized Ragnarok's distinctive silhouette, with his mother and Jorr clinging to the great dragon's back.

"Friend or foe?" Kai shouted up at him.

"Friend," Pryce called back. "But what's behind them isn't."

The Dragonkin fleet emerged from the horizon, their ships dark against the dimming sky.

The battle for Crystal Shores was about to begin.

37. Battle for Crystal Shores

Pryce watched from Stormwing's back as Ragnarok landed heavily on Crystal Shores' beach, his massive form sending tremors through the sand. Ellie and Jorr clung to the great dragon's scales, appearing exhausted. The makeshift bandages along Ragnarok's hindquarters were stained dark with blood.

"Mom!" Pryce guided Stormwing down beside them. "You made it."

"Barely," Ellie said, sliding from Ragnarok's back. She stumbled slightly, and Pryce caught her arm. "The Dragonkin patrols were everywhere."

Ash poked his head out of his carrier, meowing a greeting to Ellie. Above them, Skye circled watchfully.

"Ragnarok's wounds have reopened," Jorr said, checking the bandages. "He won't be able to fight for long in this condition."

Tyler appeared from the hastily constructed barricades. His eyes widened at the sight of Ellie, and he rushed forward to sweep her into his arms.

"El," Tyler said, voice rough with emotion. He kissed her deeply, then pressed his forehead against hers. "Thank the depths you're safe." Only then did his gaze shift to Ragnarok, and he instinctively pulled Ellie closer.

Tyler looked at Pryce with concern. "Is that beast safe to have around? I've never seen a dragon that size."

The great dragon's head swung around, regarding Tyler with curious eyes. Pryce felt Ragnarok's voice in his mind: Your father has a warrior's heart, young one. Like you.

Before Pryce could respond, a horn blast cut through the evening air. Ana's voice carried from the watchtower: "They're coming!"

The shadow drakes retreated into the gathering darkness, but Pryce knew the battle was far from over. Through gaps in the smoke, he spotted the second wave approaching—fire drakes, their scales glowing like embers against the darkening sky.

"Fire drakes incoming!" he shouted from Stormwing's back. "Get those water barrels ready!"

Below, Kai directed a group of villagers positioning barrels along the shoreline.

The first fire drake opened its mouth, unleashing a stream of flame that turned night to day. Villagers scattered as fire rained down, but the specially prepared barrels exploded from the heat, sending plumes of water and steam into the air.

"It's working!" Kai shouted. "The steam is disrupting their aim!"

But more fire drakes followed, their combined assault turning the beach into an inferno.

"We need height!" Pryce called to Stormwing. They soared above the chaos, where he could better direct the defense. Storm dragons and fire drakes were natural enemies.

A familiar roar shook the air as Ragnarok joined them, Jorr clinging to his back. The massive black dragon's presence seemed to give the fire drakes pause.

"The third wave is coming," Jorr shouted to Pryce. "Storm drakes—dozens of them!"

Lightning split the sky as the storm drakes descended, their scales crackling with electricity. Leading them was Thane.

Near the docks, the watchtower snapped as dragon fire ate through its supports. The structure began to collapse, and Pryce glimpsed someone trapped beneath falling debris.

"Help!" Gordan's voice carried over the battle noise.

"Hold on!" Pryce banked Stormwing toward the burning tower. Through the smoke, he saw the bully pinned beneath a fallen beam, flames approaching rapidly.

Stormwing landed beside the debris, her wings creating gusts that helped hold back the fire. Above them, storm drakes and fire drakes clashed in spectacular explosions of lightning and flame.

They barely made it back to Stormwing before the tower collapsed completely. As they took flight, Gordan's arms tight around Pryce's waist, a wall of lightning cut through the air before them.

Thane's drake emerged from the electrical storm. "Still playing hero?"

"Get to safety," Pryce told Gordan, letting him slide from Stormwing's back onto a nearby roof that hadn't caught fire yet.

The air crackled with energy as storm drakes filled the sky. Below, Kai's arrows found their marks with deadly accuracy, but for every dragon that fell back, two more seemed to take its place.

"Crystal Shores ends tonight," Thane said, drawing his sword.

Their dragons clashed above the burning village. Stormwing's natural storm abilities matched the enemy drakes, while Ragnarok's massive bulk scattered their formations. But the Dragonkin ships drew closer.

"The ships are almost in range!" Kai shouted from below. "We need to stop them before they land!"

Pryce broke away from his duel with Thane, diving toward the lead ship. There, on the deck, stood Princess Seren. His mother's pendant gleamed at her throat.

"Now!" Tyler's voice carried across the water. Oil slicks ignited, creating a wall of flame between the ships and shore. But the Dragonkin vessels pushed through, their hulls protected by dragon-forged metal.

Thane pursued Pryce, their aerial battle carrying them over the lead ship. "You're no Dragonkin. Just a Shorling who forgot his place!"

Pryce felt Stormwing's exhaustion—she had never fought this long or hard before.

"My place," Pryce said, parrying Thane's strike, "is wherever I choose it to be!"

A blast of lightning from Thane's drake caught Stormwing's wing. They tumbled, landing hard on the ship's deck. Crew members scattered as Thane landed behind them.

"So the rumors were true." Seren's violet eyes widened at the sight of him. "You survived the tomb."

"Disappointed your dead husband came back to life?" Pryce asked, struggling to his feet.

"Never that." There was a sadness in her expression. "Though it would have been simpler if you'd stayed dead. Crystal Shores will be mine, just as you should have been."

"That ceremony over my body wasn't real."

"We could have ruled together." She stepped closer, the pendant Thane had taken from him at her throat. "We still could. Join me now, and I'll spare your village."

"More lies? Like the Seadrake Corsairs? Like the marriage you performed while I lay dead?"

"Not everything was a lie." Her voice softened. "What I felt for you—what I still feel—that was real."

"Then stop this."

"I can't." Seren's scales flared with emotion. "Crystal Shores' resources will strengthen the Dragonkin."

"I won't help you destroy my home."

Thane moved forward, blade raised. "Enough talk. Let me end this, Princess. Your feelings for this Shorling make you weak."

Seren ignored him, her eyes locked on Pryce. "Then you leave me no choice."

She raised her hand, signaling the fleet. More dragons appeared through the smoke, their riders ready to rain destruction on Crystal Shores.

"There's always a choice," Pryce said softly. He stepped closer to Seren. "You taught me that."

Before she could respond, he kissed her. For a moment, she melted against him, her guard dropping. His fingers found the pendant's chain, unfastening it as their lips met.

Suddenly, Ragnarok roared. The massive dragon burst through the clouds, breathing fire that scattered the approaching drakes. In the confusion, Seren felt the pendant's absence.

"No!" She reached for her throat as Pryce backed away, the pendant clutched in his hand.

A messenger drake swooped down, landing hard on the deck. "Princess! Queen Nymeria's ship is under attack! Seadrake Corsairs—real ones—have been spotted near Drakemere!"

"Sound the retreat," she commanded. "All ships, return to Drakemere. The Queen needs us."

"But Crystal Shores—" Thane protested.

"Will have to wait."

As Pryce mounted Stormwing, Seren called out: "This isn't over, Pryce Harper-Green. I will return."

"I know," he said, the pendant now back around his neck. "And I'll be waiting."

They took to the sky as horns sounded the Dragonkin retreat. Below, Crystal Shores erupted in cheers of victory. Fire drakes pulled back, storm drakes scattered, and the great ships turned away from shore.

Stormwing banked toward the shoreline where Pryce's parents waited. Kai stood with them, bow still ready, while Ragnarok landed nearby with Jorr. Ash peered from his carrier, still flustered from battle, while Skye circled overhead, letting out triumphant screeches.

"Not bad for a fisherman's son," Kai said, shouldering his bow. "Though next time you want to start a war, maybe give us more warning?"

"Next time?" Pryce laughed, sliding from Stormwing's back. "I think one invasion is enough."

His mother pulled him into a fierce hug. "Don't be too sure. Seren isn't the type to give up easily."

"Neither am I," Pryce said, returning her embrace.

The sun had long since set over Lake Dragontide, but the fires from battle still colored the sky in shades of orange and gold. Crystal Shores had survived, though many buildings smoldered and the docks would need rebuilding.

Tyler stepped forward, surveying the damage. "We've got a lot of work ahead of us."

As Pryce turned to respond, a small, leather-bound book slipped from his back pocket, landing on the ground with a soft thud. "Legends of Dragontide" was barely legible on its worn cover—the same book Gordan and Dirk had tried to destroy that day that felt like a lifetime ago.

Kai picked it up, brushing ash from its cover. "Still carrying this around? After living through your own dragon legend?"

"Maybe it's time to write some new stories," Pryce said, taking the battered volume.

38. A New Dawn

Morning sunlight streamed through breaks in Crystal Shores' damaged buildings. Pryce sat on the repaired dock, "Legends of Dragontide" open in his lap. He'd found a few blank pages at the back, where he'd begun writing his own story in careful script.

"Still scribbling in that old thing?" Gordan asked, approaching with a bundle of fresh timber over his shoulder. The morning work crews were already busy rebuilding.

"Someone should record what happened here," Pryce said, closing the book. "So others know the truth about the Dragonkin."

"And about you." Gordan set down his load. "Listen, about all those times I tormented you—"

"Water under the dock," Pryce said, standing.

"No, let me finish." Gordan's usual bravado was gone. "You could have let me burn in that tower. Nobody would have blamed you. But you didn't."

Before Pryce could respond, Kai appeared with his father's latest delivery of metalwork for repairs. "If you two are done with the touching reunion, Mayor Wright wants everyone at the town hall."

Inside the crowded hall, the mayor stood at her podium, glasses perched on her nose. The room had been cleaned of battle plans and weapon racks, though scorch marks still darkened one wall.

"Crystal Shores owes its survival to many," she began, "but none more than Pryce Harper-Green. His courage, and his unique connection to both our world and that of the dragons, saved us all."

Gavin stepped forward. "Which is why I'm forgiving his loan entirely. Consider it payment for saving not just our lives, but our future."

"And that's not all," the mayor said. "The council has decided to officially recognize Stormwing and Ragnarok as protectors of Crystal Shores. They'll always have sanctuary here."

Finnegan hobbled forward, leaning on his walking stick. "Speaking of sanctuary," he said, "what will you do now, lad? Crystal Shores would welcome its hero home."

Pryce touched the scales along his jaw. "I've been thinking about that. The Island of Emberfall—it needs someone to rebuild it properly."

Finnegan tapped his stick on the floor. "Though you might want to check under the floorboards in the barracks before you start renovating."

Pryce grinned, remembering the coins he'd hidden there. "That's the first step. But I have bigger plans. A refuge, maybe. Somewhere dragons and Shorlings can coexist."

The celebration continued through the day. During a quiet moment, Pryce gave his mother the jewelry box he'd wanted to buy her since before everything began.

As evening approached, Pryce stood on the docks. Stormwing and Ragnarok waited nearby.

Pryce soared toward Emberfall as the sun set over Lake Dragontide. At the barracks, Pryce found the hidden coins exactly where he'd left them.

Standing on the mountain ledge, Stormwing and Ragnarok beside him, he watched stars emerge above the lake. Ash wound between his legs, purring, as Skye circled lazily overhead, waiting for the opportune moment to drop a pebble on the feline's head.

Together, they made an unlikely family—dragons, cat, bird, and the boy who bridged two worlds.

He was neither fully Shorling nor Dragonkin. He was something new—a bridge between worlds. And his story was just beginning.

Opening the book to a fresh page, Pryce began to write.

The End

***

Thank you for reading!

You might be interested in Book 3:
Dragontide's Revenge

ConnieMyres.com

Connie S. Myres

ALSO BY CONNIE

STANDALONE BOOKS

Twisted Intentions, Beneath the White Veil, Ring,
Haunting of Ender House, Rest Stop Terror, Solus,
Who Killed Sweet Violet?, Lucifer's Island, Raven's
Ridge

DRAGONTIDE

Dragontide's Daughter, Dragontide's Son (Upcoming:
Dragontide's Revenge)

PACIE ROSE MYSTERIES

Pacie Rose Mysteries (Books 1–3)
Slenderman, Hornet, Wolf
Jezebel, My Name is Mr. Dibble

RANCOR

Rancor: A Paranormal Psychological Thriller (Books 1
& 2)
Sinister Attachments, Unrestrained

SEVEN SEALS REDUX

Seven Seals Redux: The Complete Apocalyptic Novel
Series (Books 1–7)
White Horse, Red Horse, Black Horse, Pale Horse,
Tribulation, Signs, Trumpets

SUSPENSE STORIES

Suspense Stories #1: Raven's Ridge, Lucifer's Island, Sinister Attachments

WATCH FOR SPOOKY SHORTS

Spooky Shorts A-G: A Collection of Creepy Short Stories
Apple Pie, Black-Eyed Kids, Creature, Dungeon, Electric, Fairy, Genie, House, Ice, Joker, Kiss, Lucid (Upcoming: Minion, Neighbor, Obelisk, Pattern, Quest, Rumor, Squatch, Time, Underworld, Visitor, Wolf, X-axis, Yellow, ZoZo)

The complete list of books can be found at ConnieMyres.com

.

VISIT CONNIE'S WEBSITE

Visit Connie's website and find her books, writer's tool-box, blog, sales, videos, and more.

https://www.ConnieMyres.com

Connie S. Myres

LEXICON

Characters

Ana: (supporting character)

She faces danger head-on. Tyler and Ellie's friend from Book 1. Ana is a fighter. Helped Ellie rescue Tyler in Book 1. "Next was Ana, a fierce-looking woman with sun-bronzed skin and a scar running down her cheek. She had a reputation as a skilled fighter and had no qualms about facing danger head-on."

Aurix (supporting character):

A young Dragonkin attendant at Drakemere Island, distinguished by luminous copper-colored scales that catch the light like burnished metal. Third-year apprentice to Master Kestrel. Serves as an escort to new arrivals and messenger for Master Kestrel. Aurix represents a younger generation of Dragonkin, born into their culture rather than transformed by it. Their scales are notably more prominent than those of converted Dragonkin, suggesting a deeper connection to their draconic heritage. Despite their youth, they move with the fluid grace characteristic of their kind.

Captain Draven: (minor character)

Deceased. Finest sailor from the past. Pryce asks Finnegan about a picture. "That's 'The Last Voyage of Captain Draven.' He was one of the finest sailors to ever navigate Lake Dragontide,"

Finnegan said. "But even he couldn't escape the wrath of the seadrakes."

Captain Zharan: (deceased antagonist)

Was a Dragonkin Marauder in Book 1. Known for his ruthless efficiency in combat and a cold, tactical mind. Captain Zharan is a towering figure, easily distinguished by his scarlet war paint that slashes across his eyes like war stripes, giving him a fearsome appearance. His armor is less ornate than his peers', favoring function over form, but it is reinforced with black dragon scales that glint menacingly in the light.

Commander Shadowspear: (antagonist)

A Dragonkin commander distinguished by deep indigo scales that seem to absorb light. Wears armor reinforced with shadow drake scales. Has a distinctive scar from temple to jaw. Known for tactical brilliance and ruthless efficiency. Young for a commander but earned his position through ruthless competence. Rides a shadow drake named Nightshade. His aristocratic voice carries deadly authority. Leads the pursuit of Ellie as she searches for Pryce.

Cook Marta: (supporting character)

The head cook at Drakemere Palace. Round-faced woman with flour-dusted arms. Known for running a tight kitchen and having little patience for gossip or laziness. Efficient and sharp-eyed.

Declan: (supporting character)

Declan is a quiet, unassuming man with a gentle demeanor. Declan is a cook. Helped Ellie rescue Tyler in Book 1. Finally, there was Declan, a quiet, unassuming man with a gentle demeanor. He was the ship's cook and had a way with herbs and medicines that would undoubtedly come in handy on their journey.

Eloise Harper-Green: (supporting character)

Strong willed. Protects Pryce. The hero of book 1. Married to Tyler. Has two children, Pryce and Faye. Age 30s. Long wavy, red hair. Ellie Harper-Green, now in her 30s, once a hero who saved Crystal Shores, now faces her greatest challenge as her son Pryce joins the Dragonkin Marauders. Torn between her maternal instinct to protect Pryce and her duty to defend the village, Ellie struggles to find a way to bring her son home without compromising the safety of Crystal Shores. As the marauders' attack looms, Ellie must confront her own past, trust in Pryce's ability to make the right choice, and find a way to unite the village against the coming threat.

Father Blackwood (supporting character):

The elderly priest at Dragon's Fang Island who serves the Dragonkin nobility. Performs official ceremonies including marriages and transformations. Distinguished by his trembling hands and nervous demeanor, especially when confronted by Princess Seren. Despite his position, he shows reluctance to break religious laws and traditions, though ultimately caves to pressure from the Dragonkin leadership. Carries a ritual book containing ceremonial texts and keeps careful records of all official proceedings, even when coerced into performing questionable rites.

Faye Harper-Green: (supporting character)

Curious. Pryce's younger sister, 13 yrs. old. Long curly red hair. Freckles.

Faye's Messenger Gull Network

A sophisticated communication system developed by Faye, utilizing trained Tidewing gulls to rapidly transmit messages across vast distances. Each bird is uniquely trained to follow specific routes and deliver messages with remarkable precision. The network allows for near-instantaneous communication across the countryside, providing critical intelligence about potential threats or coordinating defensive strategies. The system's efficiency lies in the birds' innate navigation skills and Faye's meticulous training methods.

Gavin Brooks (supporting character)

Greedy entrepreneur. Wears a suit and tie. A local entrepreneur looking to capitalize on the artifact.

Grandpa Joe Harper: (minor character)

Deceased elderly great grandparent of Pryce. Ellie got Elixiron to save Grandpa Joe's life. Sailor. Told tales of Lake Dragontide and its mysteries. Used a lot of Shorling wise sayings or proverbs.

Greta (minor character):

Head cook on the supply ship to Dragon's Fang Island. A no-nonsense woman who runs her galley with strict efficiency. Dislikes gossip but maintains order among her kitchen staff. Distinguished by her sharp commands and practical nature. Demonstrates knowledge of proper food storage and preparation for long sea voyages.

Jack: (supporting character)

Helped Ellie rescue Tyler in Book 1. The motley crew consisted of Jack, a lanky man with a mop of unruly red hair. He claimed to have sailed the Dragonspine Reaches before and knew the waters like the back of his hand.

Jorr (dragonkin helper)

A young dragonkin who helps care for the dragons. Has scales of a deep, earthy brown. He wore a mix of leathers and hides.

Kai Frostborne: (supporting character)

Pryce's loyal best friend. White, blonde hair. Tall, lean. Casual. Sometimes says a Shorling wise saying or proverb.

Lena (minor character):

A kitchen maid on the supply ship to Dragon's Fang Island. Shows kindness to Ellie (disguised as "the new girl") by offering her warm drinks and guidance. More willing to share gossip about the Dragonkin than other servants. Helps transport supplies and works under Greta in the galley.

Master Kestrel (mentor, supporting character):

The Dragonkin's preeminent dragon trainer, known for his unorthodox but effective methods. A tall, lean man in his late forties with sharp features and calculating gray eyes. Has subtle gray scales that looked like polished steel. Intricate dragon-scale tattoos wound up his arms. Despite his intimidating reputation, he carries himself with an aristocratic air and speaks with careful precision. Wears traditional Dragonkin training leathers in deep burgundy. His own dragon is a rare Shadow Drake named Nightweaver. Master Kestrel serves as Pryce's mentor but may have ulterior motives for training the young Shorling.

Master Vex (Dragonkin, antagonist)

An elderly Dragonkin alchemist who specializes in dragon-shorling transformation. His scales are dull with age, but his eyes burn with intensity. Most notable for his filed, pointed teeth and his work with transformation potions. Serves the Dragonkin leadership by helping transform shorlings into Dragonkin through magical means. Based on Dragon's Fang Island, where he maintains a laboratory filled with ancient scrolls and mysterious potions. His most significant creation is a dark, swirling potion that can awaken dormant dragon blood in those who possess it. Despite his aged appearance, Master Vex represents one of the most dangerous aspects of Dragonkin society—their ability to corrupt and transform others to their cause.

Mayor Helen Wright: (supporting character)

Age 50s. Mayor of Crystal Shores for many years. Short curly gray hair. Wears glasses. Patronizing.

Mira: (supporting character)

A servant at Drakemere Palace who helps Ellie. Lost her own son to Dragonkin transformation experiments. Works in the kitchens under Cook Marta. Has knowledge of herbs and healing. Her son's loss motivates her to help other families affected by Dragonkin magic.

Old Man Doyle (minor character)

An old man who raises goats in Crystal Shores. "Pryce saw Old Man Doyle's prized goats running loose, bleating in terror as they darted between houses."

Old Man Finnegan: (supporting character)

75 yrs. old. Wrinkles, thin white hair. Uses a gnarled walking stick. Wears well-worn cap. Was a dragon hunter in his youth. Has knowledge of dragons. Loyal, willing to help Pryce. Lives in cottage by the fishing dock. Casual, occasionally uses Shorling wise sayings, proverbs.

Princess Seren: (Dragonkin Marauder)

Less evil than her mother, Queen Nymeria. Addressed as Your Highness . Assigned to seduce Pryce into becoming a Dragonkin Marauder, ends up falling in love. Seren has long blond hair and her skin has a few subtle dragon scales. Violet eyes. Wears a white dress adorned with intricate dragon motifs in silver thread.

Pryce Harper-Green: (protagonist)

17-year-old male with dark wavy hair from Crystal Shores. Discovers a talent for training dragons and joins the Dragonkin Marauders before realizing he must save his village. Is the son of Ellie and Tyler and helps in their fishing business.

Pipwhistle (ally, creature)

A Quibnocket, similar to leprechauns. Ellie calls him Pip, and he sometimes calls her Ellie-belly. Quibnockets are mischievous. They can blend into shadows despite their vibrant, patchwork. A cloak stitched from the remnants of travelers' garments. They are skilled pickpockets and can create illusions that dance in the air. They are jovial and have a mop of wiry hair. Speaks in riddles and rhymes. Despite their penchant for petty thievery, Quibnockets have a heart of gold, hidden beneath layers of cunning and playfulness. They have a deep, resonant laugh, reminiscent of the tinkling of bells, often giving away their hiding spots, yet they somehow manage to stay one step ahead. Though initially a thorn in the side of many, Quibnockets true nature is that of a guardian of forgotten lore and lost paths. They become unlikely allies, whose tricks and illusions serve to protect, guide, and occasionally confound. In the end, a Quibnocket's role transcends that of a mere pickpocket; he is a catalyst for change, a bringer of light cloaked in the guise of a trickster, whose deepest joy comes from seeing the seeds of greatness unfold in those he deems worthy of his peculiar brand of meddling.

Raven (supporting character):

A female trainee at Dragon's Fang Island with short dark hair. Shows kindness to Pryce. Experienced dragon rider who helps teach him basic maneuvers. Rides copper-scaled drake.

Roan: (supporting character)

An elderly fishing boat captain who brings catches to Drakemere Palace. Hires Ellie (disguised as "Sara") when she volunteers to help with his understaffed crew. Responsible for delivering silver trout for the storm drakes.

Stormwing (nickname: Storm):

Pryce's dragon. A Lake Dragontide Storm Dragon with deep blue and silver scales, and electric blue eyes. Friendly to Pryce. Stormwing has a particular fondness for fish, especially silver trout from Lake Dragontide. He has a habit of shaking himself like a dog after flying through clouds, much to Pryce's amusement (and occasional annoyance when he gets soaked). Stormwing also enjoys the sound of Pryce's laughter, often purposely doing silly things to elicit it.

Thane Zharan

A young Dragonkin stood there, perhaps a few years older than Pryce, with features that seemed carved from stone. Dark scales traced patterns across his temples. Thane rides a shadow drake. Has a cultured accent that seemed common among the Dragonkin nobility. His scales weren't just dark—they were scarlet, like war paint slashed across his skin. Thane calls Pryce, dragon prodigy. Pryce's dad, Tyler, had defeated his father, Captain Zharan, in Book 1.

Tobias Underhill: (supporting character)

Longtime friend of Ellie and Tyler. Casual. Sometimes says a Shorling wise saying or proverb. Tobias Underhill has black hair, wears a cap. Tobias is taller than Jack and Ana.

Torren: (minor character)

A fishing crew leader mentioned by Ellie when creating her cover story as "Sara." Used as part of her deception to infiltrate Drakemere Palace.

Tyler Green: (supporting character)

Pryce's father. Tyler Green, now in his 30s, blonde hair, once an Oceanrider and now a respected leader in Crystal Shores, faces his greatest challenge when his son Pryce is lured away by the Dragonkin Marauders.

Queen Nymeria: (antagonist)

A Dragonkin Marauders. Has silver eyes and recruits Pryce with promises of wealth and power. Wears a flowing cloak of midnight blue that blends seamlessly with the shadows. Her face is often obscured by a hood, leaving only her piercing silver eyes visible. Dark hair with gray streaks. A queen who wants to conquer Crystal Shores. Nymeria seeks to expand her empire by conquering Crystal Shores. She strategically uses her daughter to entice Pryce, recognizing his dragon-training abilities as a valuable asset. Mother of Princess Seren. Conniving.

Creatures & Animals

Ash (pet):

Pryce's pet cat left on the island by the Oceanriders. House cat with mottled gray fur. Left on the island by the Oceanriders. Male.

Aurathorn (dragon):

A great dragon with Dragonscale Moss in its lair. Lives in cave in Thornveil Wilds. Draco nobilis (Dragon).

Copper Drake (dragon):

Raven's dragon mount, distinguished by copper-colored scales.

Crystal Dwellers (creature)

Indigenous inhabitants of Aetheria Island, these beings stand about the height of a shorling child. They have semi-transparent skin, which shifts between flesh and crystal, reflecting light like water's surface. They possess eyes resembling polished moonstones and move with grace. Highly secretive, Crystal Dwellers prefer to observe from hiding, rarely interacting directly with visitors. They appear to be the last remnants of an ancient civilization that once lived in harmony with seadrakes, as evidenced by the carvings in their ruined city. Their true nature—whether they are transformed shorlings, magical beings, or something else entirely—remains unknown. Also called Watching Creatures.

Dragon spirits (creature):

Ancient beings said to slumber beneath Lake Dragontide, awakened by Pryce to defend Crystal Shores.

Dryad: (antagonist creature)

Viscous forest protectors. Live in Thornveil Wilds. Twisted shorling-like figures, their bodies composed of gnarled bark and reaching branches, Lumbering. Twisted shorling-like figures, their bodies composed of gnarled bark and reaching branches, lumbered into the clearing. Empty sockets burned with pinpricks of smoldering light.Its arm—if it could be called such—composed of interwoven vines and branches as thick as a man's torso, lashed out with startling quickness.

Fire Drake (dragon)

Fire drakes are massive. Their wings trail ember-bright sparks.

Moonshark: (animal)

A large fish in Lake Dragontide. Dragons like to eat them.

Nightclaw: (dragon):

A dragon from the past. Pryce asks Finnegan about a picture. "Ah, that's the tale of Aurathorn and Nightclaw," Finnegan explained as he adjusted the kettle over the fire. "Aurathorn was a guardian dragon, protector of an ancient elixir. Nightclaw sought to steal it for his own gain. Their battle lasted for days, shaking mountains and boiling rivers."

Nightweaver (dragon):

A Shadow Drake dragon. Master Kestrel's dragon.

Ragnarok (creature)

A colossal dragon of immense power, with scales the color of polished night and eyes that burn with a fierce, internal blaze. Ragnarok is a creature of raw, untamed might, chained within the depths of Dragon's Fang Island, and his roars carry an aura of menace. The name itself echoes a cataclysmic end, reflecting both his destructive potential and his role as a harbinger of change. He is a being that inspires dread and awe, refusing to be broken or controlled, with a hidden capacity for either destruction or a new beginning. The Dragonkin seek to control Ragnarok, but the beast harbors a deep hatred for them. Ragnarok's presence is a threat to the established order and a key factor in the conflict of the Dragonspine Reaches. The dragonkin believe Pryce will be able to tame the dragon. Can speak to Pryce with his mind. Calls Pryce 'young one.'

Seadrake (creature):

A massive, serpentine creature with obsidian-like scales and sharp fangs. Monsters said to drag ships to the depths. Worshipped by Dragonkin marauders.

Shadow Cats (creature)

Look vicious but are gentle unless provoked. Travel in packs. Eyes glow like embers in the dark.

Shadow Drake (dragon)

Shadow Drake (dragon):
> A rare and enigmatic species of dragon known for its ability to blend with darkness. Their scales shift between deep

obsidian and twilight purple, seeming to absorb light rather than reflect it. Slightly smaller than Storm Dragons but more agile, Shadow Drakes possess extraordinary stealth capabilities. Their eyes glow with an ethereal amber light, and they can produce a unique dark mist that cloaks their movements. These dragons are highly intelligent and selective about their riders, forming deep psychological bonds with those they choose. Most famous example is Nightweaver, the mount of Master Kestrel. Shadow Drakes are particularly active during dusk and dawn, using their natural camouflage to hunt. They prefer caves and shadowy grottos as lairs, and their presence is often marked by an unusual stillness in the air.

Shadow Wolves (creature):

Creatures whose howls can freeze blood.

Skye (pet):

Pryce's female pet bird, a messenger bird. The bird's plumage was a mix of soft grays and whites, with distinctive black markings on its wingtips. Around its leg was a small brass cylinder - a message capsule.

Storm Dragon (dragon):

A species of dragon native to the area, known for their ability to sense and navigate through storms. Intelligent. Controls storms. Encased in scales that shimmer like dark storm clouds, its body crackles with electric blue energy. Massive wings span. Its eyes glow with a fierce, lightning-like intensity, and its fearsome maw sparks with electric arcs. sparks with electric arcs. Known for its mastery over the elements, the Storm Dragon can summon fierce thunderstorms, unleash bolts of lightning, and generate powerful wind gusts. Its presence often heralds incoming storms.

Thornveil Wolf: (creature)

Large wolf, with large footprints. Smells of musk. Amber eyes.

Tidewing gulls (animal):

Trained birds used to carry messages between ships and the shore.

Places and Locations

Aetheria (unknown island)

Aetheria." Pipwhistle explains that it is an island where the veil between worlds is thin, making it a place where the past, present, and future often meet, hinting at its unique properties and the dangers it holds. He explains the origin of the name and hints at its connection to both the dragons and the seadrakes. He mentions that it has been called many different names, and that Aetheria is just what he calls it.

Azure Suite (palace room)

The Azure Suite, located in the palace on Drakemere Island, took Pryce's breath away. The ceiling soared overhead, and one entire wall opened onto a private balcony overlooking the dragon aeries below. The furniture was elegant yet sturdy, crafted from deep blue wood he'd never seen before. A massive bed dominated one corner, its covers embroidered with silver thread that mimicked dragon scales. Expensive blue vase by the window. Pryce's room at the palace.

Chantey Street (street):

A street in Crystal Shores, known for the aroma of fresh fish.

Crystal Shores: (village)

Poor fishing village on Lake Dragontide, Pryce's home.

Dragon's Fang Island (island):

A remote training ground for elite Dragonkin dragon riders, located even further from Crystal Shores than Drakemere Island. Dragon's Fang Island is where Master Krestel works with the most promising riders. Named for its distinctive spire of black rock that resembles a dragon's tooth piercing the sky. The island features treacherous terrain ideal for advanced flight training, including narrow canyons, steep cliffs, and thermal vents. Ancient training grounds and dragon caves honeycomb the island's interior.

Dragon's Maws (location):

Massive whirlpools that dot the waters between the Dragonspine Reaches. These treacherous formations are marked by patches of eerie blue light from deep trenches where ancient creatures dwell. 5 sets of whirlpools to navigate?

Dragonclaw Island (island):

Where Tyler was left for medical attention.

Dragonkin Palace (palace):

Located on Drakemere Island. The entire palace had been carved into the rock, its windows and balconies adorned with dragon motifs. Dragon-sized openings dotted the cliff face like honeycomb. The corridors were vast enough for dragons to pass through comfortably, their walls adorned with luminous crystals that cast a warm glow. Elaborate tapestries depicted dragons and Dragonkin working together in harmony. Princess Seren lives there.

Dragonspine Reaches (region):

A vast, uncharted chain of islands, rumored ancestral home of dragonkin. The Dragonspine War begins at the Dragonspine Reaches, that treacherous expanse of jagged volcanic islands beyond the churning Undertow Sea, had long been a tenuous borderland between the seafaring Oceanrider clans and the raiding parties of seadrake-worshipping marauders from the east.

Drakemere Island (island):

The primary stronghold of the Dragonkin Marauders, located far across Lake Dragontide. Built into towering cliffs, featuring a grand palace carved directly into the rock face. Known for its extensive dragon aeries and training grounds. The island maintains a surprisingly refined atmosphere despite its fearsome reputation. Multiple levels of stone terraces cascade down the cliffside, each hosting dragon perches and elaborate gardens. The palace itself showcases intricate dragon-inspired architecture with high, arched ceilings to accommodate dragons moving freely between indoor and outdoor spaces.

Eldengrove (place):

This ancient woodland is a sanctuary of tranquility.

Heartwood Tree (plant):

Located at the center of Nighthollow Grove, said to be a place of great magic and power.

Injured Dragons' Cave (location):

A hidden cave on Dragon's Fang Island where injured and broken dragons are kept chained to the walls. Evidence of the Dragonkin's harsh training methods.

Island of Emberfall: (island):

An isolated, volcanic island a few hours sail from Crystal Shores. Once used as an Oceanrider outpost, now abandoned. Cloaked in dense jungle foliage. Occasional plumes of smoke from towering volcanic peaks. The air is thick with the scent of damp earth, punctuated by the occasional tang of sulfur from the still-active geothermal vents.

Lake Dragontide (lake):

A fresh water great lake similar to Lake Superior. Has seasonal icebergs.

Mariner's Table (eatery):

A seaside eatery in Crystal Shores.

Rusty Anchor Inn: (inn):

An inn down by the docks in Crystal Shores. Gavin Brooks stays there.

Scholaring Building (building):

An educational institution in Crystal Shores.

Siren's Pass (place):

A dangerous but quick route through the Reaches. Crawling with Dragonkin Marauders.

Thornveil Wilds (place):

A forbidden and dangerous forest.

Tidelore Hall (building):

A museum dedicated to Crystal Shores' history and lore.

Town Hall (building):

Located in Crystal Shores. Has an imposing facade of the town hall came into view, its clock tower. Front door creaks. Corridor has carpet. The mayor's office is located here.

Undertow Sea (sea):

The sea beyond Lake Dragontide.

Wildsedge River (river):

A swift, dark river separating the village from Thornveil Wilds.

Wildsedge Bridge (bridge):

Connects Crystal Shores to Thornveil Wilds. C crosses Wildsedge River. Has guard tower.

Ships

Blue Horizon (boat):

Tyler's fishing ship. The Blue Horizon is a sturdy fishing vessel, its weathered hull painted a deep azure that echoes the color of the lake it tirelessly navigates. Measuring just over forty feet in length, the ship boasts a sleek, time-tested design that cuts through the waves with ease. Its mast is tall and resilient, topped with a vibrant blue sail that can be spotted from miles away. The deck is practical and well-maintained, equipped with sturdy nets, fishing gear, and ample storage for the day's catch. Below deck, a cozy cabin provides shelter against the elements, where the faint scent of old wood.

Dread Wyrm (ship):

Nymeria's ship, used to transport Pryce away from Crystal Shores.

Swiftwind (boat):

A smaller, faster ship. Pryce wants to fix the old, abandoned Swiftwind so he can use it. Ellie chartered it for the rescue of Tyler in Book 1.

Tidedancer (boat):

An abandoned fishing vessel found on Aetheria Island. Has two masts with weathered but intact rigging. Features a small cabin with a bunk, storage compartments, and mounting table. Despite its age, the curved bow and deep hull were built for both speed and hauling heavy catches.

Wavecrest (ship):

The ship Tyler was assigned to as an Oceanrider during war with the Dragonkin Marauders.

Wavecutter (ship)

Ellie's deceased father's fishing vessel. "Keep the Wave-cutter's crow's nest to port," she said, recalling her father's tales. "Then three lengths past the merchant galley's bones."

Things

Auron Herb (plant):

Ingredient for Elixiron.

Brass Key (key):

Ellie got this heavy, brass key from a bird's nest while with Pipwhistle. Pipwhistle's fingers closed around the key. "Ah, this is no ordinary key, my dear Ellie," he said, holding it up for her to see. "This is the key to unlocking a most wondrous discovery.

Combat Saddle (item):

Special dragon riding equipment used in battle training, featuring reinforced grips and weapon holders.

Dragon pendant necklace (necklace):

Ellie's family heirloom. Ellie's necklace with the dragon pendant, designed to reflect her connection to her family's seafaring heritage and the mystical elements of "Dragontide's Daughter." The pendant is intricately designed to capture the ancient mystique and magic associated with dragons, making it a meaningful and elegant heirloom for Ellie and Pryce. The red fluid in the glass bubble contains draconic essence—Ellie and Pryce's bloodline mixed with dragon blood. The bog dweller call it "dragon's tear"

Dragon's tear (pendant):

What the bog dwellers initially want in exchange for helping Ellie. It's revealed to be Ellie's pendant.

Dragonscale Moss (plant):

A key ingredient for Elixiron, found in Thornveil Wilds. A rare botanical species found growing on volcanic slopes, characterized by its ability to absorb and retain magical essences. Typically used in advanced healing practices among Dragonkin, the moss has a distinctive scale-like texture that allows it to adhere to dragon scales and extract latent healing energies. Its coloration ranges from deep emerald to ashen gray, often blending seamlessly with volcanic rock formations.

Drakebane (potion):

A rare and dangerous alchemical potion created by Master Vex that can halt and potentially reverse dragon transformation magic. Silver in color with a swirling, liquid ice appearance. When consumed, induces a death-like state where the drinker appears completely lifeless - no pulse, no breathing. Most who take it never wake up. Those who do require at least a day in this suspended state. The potion acts by suppressing dragon magic in the blood, essentially "killing" the transformation process. Its recipe is ancient and requires rare ingredients, making it extremely valuable and difficult to obtain.

Elixiron (medicine):

A rare and expensive medicine with healing properties.

Ellie's ring (ring):

A simple silver ring given to Ellie by Tyler as a promise.

Glimmerpetal Powder (ingredient):

Ingredient for Elixiron.

Heartfire Confluence

An ancient Dragonkin healing ritual that combines sacred ingredients—typically including dragon blood, volcanic ash, and Dragonscale Moss—to mend severe injuries. The technique relies on a delicate magical transfer of life essence, requiring precise chanting and a deep understanding of draconic physiology. When performed correctly, the ritual manifests as a soft blue glow that emanates from beneath a dragon's scales, knitting wounds and restoring strength.

Heartwood Bark (ingredient):
Ingredient for Elixiron.

Hunting knife (knife):
Given to Ellie by Bram.

Moon Flower (plant):
A magical flower native to Thornveil Wilds.

Razorclaw's wine (wine):
Razorclaw's wine is a strong wine.

Royal Sapphire (stone):
A rare and valuable stone with magical properties. It is a deep, swirling blue, with flecks of gold that seemed to dance in the light. Ellie got the royal sapphire as a wedding gift from Pipwhistle several years ago. Tobias leaned in for a closer look. "That's a Royal Sapphire," he said in awe. "They're incredibly rare and valuable. It's said they hold ancient magic and can grant their bearer great wisdom and insight." Ana jumped in. "It's also a symbol of royalty. Whoever possesses it is said to have the favor of the old kings."

Seafarer's Sigil (compass):
A compass-like device that guides Ellie, she found it in an iceberg years ago. A mystical compass intertwined with dragon elements, resonating with the themes of navigation, magic, and the deep connection to the sea and dragons. Has a capsule of [dragon blood or essence]

at its center. Originally, in Book 1, Ellie found the compass in an iceberg. The Seafarer's Sigil is a creation of the ancient Drakken Lords—a powerful, mystical race with a deep connection to the primordial forces. They were dragonkin, you see, with mastery over the elements and arcane magics. Requires a connection with the user to function. Has a coiled dragon's tail etching that acts as a direction-of-travel arrow. Features a rotating bezel with symbols indicating dangers or safe havens. Has an inner dial that acts as a celestial map. Requires a sample or essence of the target to guide the user effectively.

Seaweed Brew: (tea):

A tea with a briny taste. Is comforting. Old Man Finnegan made this tea.

Silvermist Essence (ingredient):

Ingredient for Elixiron.

Starlight Dew (ingredient):

Ingredient for Elixiron.

Triton's Trumpet (horn):

A conical shell used as an amplifier by the bearded judge.

Wooden token: (item)

A wooden pass stamped with a dragon's head design. Given to servants cleared for delivery duty at Drakemere Palace. Required for movement through certain areas of the palace. Losing it results in severe punishment.

Organizations & Groups

Dragonkin (antagonist):

Part shorling and part dragon. Mentioned as having a warship approaching the battle scene. They have dragon blood and a complex political situation.

Dragonkin Marauders (antagonist group):

Part shorling, part dragon. Skin has varying degree of dragon scales. Group that Nymeria belongs to and recruits Pryce into. Later revealed to be planning an invasion of Crystal Shores. Enemies present in the Dragonspine Reaches. In the context of the dragonkin marauders, raising a "fell banner" signals their savage, destructive intentions as they unite the tribes under one dreadful symbol before marching to war against the Oceanriders. It's an ominous, foreboding flag representing their fierce, merciless nature.

Drakken Lords (antagonist):

Oceanriders (navy):

The navy of the Shorelings.

Shorlings (group):

What the people of Crystal Shores call themselves. Fisherman. Occasionally they speak using proverbs and wise sayings.

Events

Dragonspine War (war):

Described as a conflict between Oceanriders and seadrake-worshipping marauders from the eastern shores.

Religion

Seadrake Worshipping (religion):

Certain raiding tribes or marauder groups (Dragonkin Marauders) in the Dragonspine region are described as "seadrake-worshipping." This suggests they revere the seadrakes as sacred, powerful entities worthy of devotion and worship. The seadrakes may be seen as patron deities, bringers of fortune/destruction, or embodiments of primal forces of the sea. Seadrake-worshipping tribes likely incorporate rituals, totems, and other practices to honor and appease these draconic beings.

Currency

Embercrest Coin (money):
An ancient coin with magical properties.

Gilded Gryphons (money):
Gold coins, worth about 5 Thornveil Pieces each.

Thornveil pieces (money):
Silver coins used as standard currency.
>   1 Dragonshard = 10 Pieces
>   1 Tidecrest = 100 Pieces

Concepts

Dragon sickness (illness):
A term used to describe greed or obsession with treasure.

Dragonfire (power):
Associated with power and the essence of dragons.

Dragon training (skill):
Pryce's special talent, allowing him to communicate with and calm dragons.

Flora:

Various unique plants and fungi described in the Thornveil Wilds, including glowing moss, iridescent blue ferns, and mushrooms of various colors and sizes.

Sweetsnare (plant):

A massive carnivorous flower native to Aetheria Island, known for its deceptive honey scent. Its petals deep crimson with veins of purple running through them like river tributaries. The bloom is large enough to swallow a person whole and is ringed with crystalline teeth. When hunting, it uses thick vines to ensnare prey and secretes a burning fluid.

Years & Dating Systems

Current year (date):

Year of the Ruddy Undertow 510 RU. The year when the Dragonspine War erupted across the Dragontide region. The "Ruddy Undertow" refers to the bloodshed that stained the Undertow Sea crimson during this brutal conflict.

Months

The 12 months of the Shorling calendar:

Glacespire (January)
Seafoamfurl (February)
Wavespinner (March)
Thawtidelap (April)
Spraysaltrip (May)
Keelwaker (June)
Swellberthed (July)
Harstbrine (August)
Ripharvest (September)
Neapreaper (October)
Galestormer (November)
Cradlebirth (December)

Weeks & Days

7-day week cycle

Ryna (Monday)
Wavyn (Tuesday)
Spyxe (Wednesday)
Bryxe (Thursday)
Ryxe (Friday) A day of study for Shorling's but a day of battle for Dragonkin..
Kaalm (Saturday)
Lune (Sunday)

Timekeeping

Two 12-hour periods: Daytide & Nighttide

On calm days, the Drakken Bells ring out in a steady, melodic succession from the bell tower at the heart of Crystal Shores.

If there are any threats, the bell ringers will sound a discordant, arrhythmic clangor as a warning.

Divided into 4 Drakken Bells each:

Daytide:

Dawnbell - Marks the start of morning

Noonbell - Highest point of the day

Nighttide:

Eveningbell - When night begins to fall

Midnightbell - The deepest part of night

Dragontide's Son

Connie S. Myres